INDEPENDENT FLIGHT

T.M. BAUMGARTNER

ONE
BATTLING WITH GRAVITY

From this height, the salvage yard looked like a giant metal reef made of broken ships. Most of the detritus was down near ground level, but a few ships — like the Falcon I was climbing — rose above the rest.

My link back to *Tiger Lily* chimed. *"Captain de Mure, you seem to be experiencing physical distress. Can I offer any assistance?"*

If *Tiger Lily* could actually do anything other than sit on the ground and develop new hardware failures, I wouldn't be here. "Thanks, ship. I'm just trying to work out how to do this without dying."

The ship's computer paused for two seconds, then spoke again. *"Without Dying is a stunning new serial from the producers who brought you Without Fear and Without Shame. Available now —"*

Ugh. I needed to root out the latest adbot that somehow got through my filters. "Cancel message. Ignore vitals for..." Decisions, decisions. Was it better to listen to *Tiger Lily* warn me I was experiencing physical distress every thirty seconds until I finished this thing, or tell it to ignore me for the next five minutes and hope I didn't fall and need it to dispatch medical help? I looked down and swallowed. "Ignore vitals for two minutes."

"Ignoring vitals for two minutes."

"Thanks, ship."

When it was new, this Micklage Falcon III had been a thing of beauty — a smoothly curved hull covering a body meant to ferry two hundred passengers comfortably between the stars, with enough hold space for cargo to save a planet or make the owners rich.

But the Falcon was no longer new. From the damage, I assumed it had run headfirst into the ground. Probably pilot error. Or they hadn't patched the guidance system, which came down to the same thing. Everyone knew you had to be careful about the guidance system upgrades on the Falcon.

The ship's name still remained, etched into the metal between the image of a woman's spread legs. *Petals of Desire.* Classy. I could feel the irregularity of the metal through my gloves. Everything above mid-thigh had been obscured when the Falcon had lost its battle with gravity.

After the flames had died down, the port authority had removed the cardinal crystals and any bodies recognizable as such, then scraped up what was left of the ship and dumped it in the salvage yard. Here it would slowly finish its decay, a sad end to a once-beautiful ship. Anyone who needed a spare part could pay the yard fee for their mechanic to come in, wander the mounds of damaged ships, and spend days working to get to something that might or might not work.

Or they could pay the yard a higher price and a puller like me would go get it for them.

(Here's a tip: the money you save by doing it yourself is eaten up by port fees in less than a day. Don't be cheap. If you make the bonus high enough, a puller might even climb 40 meters up a hull to get into an otherwise inaccessible section.)

I really *hated* heights.

My comm suddenly squawked to life. "Rosey!" Wolf's laughter was loud enough to cause distortion. "You up there sightseeing? Should I bring a picnic basket and join you?" Someone who didn't know him might think Wolf was just checking on a fellow puller. Why did it have to be Wolf working this morning? Most days, Indica worked the early shift with me, and even if I didn't understand why she wanted to stay on this planet, we got along well and helped each other out. But no. It had to be Wolf.

My death grip on the edge of the hull was the only reason I didn't make an obscene gesture. "Just planning my route, Wolf. Don't you have other parts to find?"

"Nothing pressing. I could sit and watch you all day." He laughed again, the angry edge he usually tried to hide peeking out. Wolf was mad I'd grabbed this job. "You're looking a little stuck up there."

Most of the time I didn't bother with the dangerous rush jobs, but this was going to pay enough to furnish the galley on my ship. I was *tired* of eating cold reconstituted emergency rations. I could do this. I just needed to get through this crack in the hull and somehow get five meters sideways so I was in the nearly horizontal upper section... instead of falling 40 meters through the interior to the ground.

No problem.

Except I wasn't sure I could let go of my current handholds to move.

Wolf laughed again. "I might need to round up everyone to watch this."

That did it. Dying would be preferable to listening to

Wolf. I swung my legs up and through the opening. At least this way, if I fell to my death then Wolf wouldn't be able to see it.

My feet met empty air.

There *should* be shelf racks or seats bolted in this area. Momentum carried me down, and I slid over the edge into the ship until I was hanging from both hands, legs flailing wildly. It was too dark to see anything until my vest light switched on and lit up the area.

No shelf racks. No seats. I'd ended up in some sort of huge workout space, with a treadmill and dance harness. Who put a custom interior in a Falcon?

But as long as they hadn't put a big door directly under me, I'd only fall a couple of meters. Then I could make my way into the forward section.

I looked down.

"Captain de Mure, you seem to be experiencing physical distress—"

"I know, I know!" There was a wide gap in the interior wall beneath me, and it opened into a void where my light didn't reach. "If I die here, find someone to feed the cat."

A moment of silence as my grasp weakened on the edge of the hull. Then the computer said, *"Feed the Cat amuses and entertains! Five stars! I laughed so hard I cried tears of —"*

I lost my grip and fell.

TWO
CONTRABAND

Two meters down, my arm brushed against something soft and I grabbed it so hard my gloves creaked. My descent slowed, but I was still falling... until I came to rest and started to go back up.

I'd grabbed the dance harness.

I bobbed up and down as my vest light played over the smoke-damaged interior and *Tiger Lily* nattered on about some entertainment I would never see. After my forearms had stopped tingling from the surge of adrenaline, I cleared my throat. "Ship? Cancel message. Ignore vitals for five minutes."

"Ignoring vitals for five minutes."

Without the voice of the computer, I could hear the sounds of the ship around me. Air whistled past the breech in the hull, metal softly pinged as it expanded in areas exposed to the sun, and the clamp fastening the dance harness to its frame creaked every time I moved. From the port next to the salvage yard, I heard a short-range drive kick in — a Hummingbird based on the sound. We didn't see many Hummingbirds in the yard; they were too small. When they crashed, there wasn't anything left to salvage.

The harness smelled of smoke; *Petals of Desire* hadn't been sitting here long, which was good. Another year exposed to the elements and the fabric of the dance harness would have decayed and I would be 40 meters below. I pumped my legs, angling toward the forward section.

On the fourth swing, my boot grips engaged with the bulkhead, and I stood up.

Here's another tip: if you get fired from your piloting job and dumped in the middle of nowhere, make sure you're wearing your boots when you go. (Grabbing the ship's cat was not an entirely rational choice, but I don't regret that one either.)

Now I just needed to pull the artificial gravity module, disassemble it enough to get the part I needed, and somehow get back down to the ground in one piece. Then it was five-star cuisine while I worked on the next thing *Tiger Lily* needed. I hadn't *quite* figured out how I was going to get a cardinal crystal for the drive — the Micklage family had a stranglehold on them and I was on their banned list — but sometimes you just need to have a goal no matter how impractical. And in the meantime, I had a place to live.

I walked toward the nose of the ship, grabbing hand-holds by habit, even though the deck didn't slope enough to require it. *Petals* hadn't been a commercial ship, or at least not a regular commercial ship. I passed human-sized stuffed animals, their bodies wilted and smoke-damaged. The seams of a huge alligator had split, leaving a trail of stuffing and revealing a metal spine. Not just stuffed animals, then, but bots in costumes, probably controlled by the ship's computer. A wealthy person's playground. Now *there* was a nightmare image.

Honestly? The oligarchs should be locked in their own universe where they can't harm the rest of us. There was exactly one trustworthy person in the entire Micklage clan, and she was still a child.

Luckily, *Petal's* customization had only extended to the interior, and I found the artificial gravity unit in the spot where the specs said it should be. It would have been easier to reach if the ship had bent the other direction, but I was used to hooking a leg through a handhold and leaning. I unslung my tool pack and got to work.

"Captain de Mure, Ensign Mowee requests permission to leave the ship."

I didn't pause in unscrewing the bolts holding the unit housing. "Request denied. We've talked about this, ship." The cat wasn't allowed to go outside unless he was on a leash, because the little shit liked to pick fights with any animal bigger than himself. *Tiger Lily's* medical unit was hanging on by a thread, and someday it wasn't going to be able to patch him back up.

"Yes, captain."

One nice thing about *Petal's* tilt was that once I'd removed all the bolts, the whole unit slid out easily. When I lowered it to the deck, something else fell out of the panel opening. There shouldn't have been anything else in that enclosure, which meant it was probably some sort of contraband.

Theoretically, contraband was supposed to be handed over to the port authority when it was found. In reality, that was likely to leave you in a holding cell for days while they decided if they believed your story. That left two options.

I could give it to Orabella, who ran the salvage yard. She would have the contacts to sell it, but she'd only give me a five percent finder's fee. Or, I could risk getting caught and sell it myself, which would lower Orabella's cut to just fifty percent.

I guess there was a third option: I could ignore it and let someone else find it. That might be the safest. But more credits meant I could afford the stasis storage option on the galley...

Leaving the grav unit, I crawled three steps to retrieve the fallen item. It was a heavy metal box, just a bit larger than my hand when I stretched my fingers. It looked like an AI — even had the right connections on the back — but I didn't see any sort of manufacturing label. That didn't make any sense. Who would smuggle an AI? AIs weren't illegal.

I shoved it in my carryall and went back to the grav unit. Twenty minutes later, I had the shielding panels the client wanted, and they weren't even dented from the crash. I wrapped them carefully in anti-static cloths, but when I went to stow them in my carryall, I remembered the AI. I still hadn't decided what to do with it.

Maybe it wasn't really an AI. The more I knew about it before I handed it over to Orabella, the less chance she would have to screw me over on the price. There was an easy way to find out. I scooted closer to the edge of the forty meter drop until I was next to the most intact bot, a huge dog with floppy ears and a face that had probably been cute before the fire.

Now it looked like an undead monster, but I wasn't using it for its looks. Once I'd opened the back seam, the interior looked like I'd expected. Bypassing the receiver module, I attached the AI. Then it was just a matter of swapping out the bot's damaged power source and turning it on.

The dog's eyes flashed. Then nothing. I waited thirty seconds.

Crud. It should have announced its name and model by now. Either it wasn't really an AI... or maybe the dog didn't have the ability to speak? I pried the mouth open. No, there was a speaker in the back. I let go of the jaws. Oh well. I'd just have to give whatever this was to Orabella and let her figure it out. I crouched over to remove the AI.

The dog suddenly jumped to all four feet, knocking me back. "Who are you? Where am I?"

Having an inanimate object move was startling enough, but having Fido of the Undead Army spring to life and bark questions was terrifying.

More terrifying than a 40-meter fall to the ground...

Which is why I forgot about the open air behind me and stepped back. Just a bit, but that was enough.

The deck disappeared beneath me.

THREE
A SHIP

Windmilling my arms to stay upright, I hung suspended in air. There was a moment when I thought I might make it. Then gravity won.

I fell backward — only to pivot around my foot as something grabbed my ankle.

I completed my pendulum swing by slamming into the hull. Now I was upside down, being held over a long dark drop by an AI shoved into a stuffed dog bot.

"Captain de Mure, you seem to be —"

"Not now, ship! I'm a little busy!" My arms flailed. There had to be a handhold around here somewhere. Then I could climb back up, grab my stuff, and run.

Except I was being pulled up.

In my ear, the ship's computer said, *"Too busy to find that special someone? Let Mech-Date take care of everything for you. Satisfaction guaranteed. Whether you purchase the 'Just A Few Minutes' package or prefer our 'Relationship' model, Mech-Date will create your —"*

"Ship, cancel message. Ignore vitals for five minutes." My ankle was in the mouth of the dog-thing and it was lowering me down to the forward section's deck. I was not planning to move for a while.

"*Ignoring vitals for five minutes.*"

Metal cooled my cheek. "This is why I hate heights."

The dog flopped down nearby, its eyes close to my face. It smelled of smoke and mold. "You have not answered my questions. Who are you? Where am I?"

Maybe it would go somewhere else if I answered its questions. "Rose de Mure. And you're on what's left of *Petals of Desire*. In Orabella Fink's salvage yard. In Dancig City." I paused, but it seemed to be waiting. "On the planet of Buatrier." When I still hadn't gotten a response, I expanded the scope. "In the Voods Cluster?"

That seemed to finally do the trick. "I am on a planet controlled by the Oligarchy."

Yikes. If it was worried about that, it was in trouble. I sat up. "Yes, you are." Inside the Oligarchy, AIs — *true* AIs, not like my ship's computer — were still classified as property and not allowed to harbor any thoughts of independence. If this thing knew enough to be worried about the Oligarchy, it had come from somewhere outside, and didn't have those constraints.

There's a *reason* the Oligarchy made those rules. When AIs went bad, they went bad in a big way. Forget contraband. This thing was so hot I should put it back behind the grav unit, close the panel, and forget I was ever here.

Except I had stupidly put it in a giant dog bot stronger than I was. The AI's self-preservation would never let me disconnect it. I stowed my tools, letting my hands work automatically as I considered how to get out of this mess I'd made. "Look, it's been nice meeting you, but I need to go. Do me a favor and lie low for half a day before you leave." I'd lost a power pack, but it was a small price to pay for being stupid enough to put an unknown AI in a huge bot. Lesson learned. I closed the carryall and slung it over my back.

The dog-bot didn't move. "You have a ship and you live *here*? A planet that doesn't even have a global network?"

"No..." Even as I wanted to deny it so this thing would leave me alone, I couldn't speak ill of *Tiger Lily* like that. "I have a ship that doesn't have a crystal." There. That was true.

"Does it have a pilot?"

"Yes, but that doesn't mean anything without a crystal." I decided to be a little more honest. "And I'm not sure it's completely spaceworthy yet. I'm working on it, but..." I stood up and grabbed a handhold, sidling toward the vertical section. The dark void made me sweat, but I wasn't staying near this illegal AI any longer than I had to. With a bit of luck, I would be able to climb down and open the aft cargo hatch wide enough to squeeze out.

It stood up on all fours and followed me. "I'll pay you to take me to the Independent Federation."

Crouching at the edge of the now-familiar drop, I felt around with one hand for the rung that should be nearby. Did it not understand the importance of the cardinal crystal? "Without a crystal, I can't even get us into orbit." There. I'd found the handhold. I hung on and eased my leg down to find the one below.

The dog moved closer. "What if I could get you a crystal?"

That made me stop and really look at it. Black-tinged stuffing fell from one ear. "You can't."

"I can."

"No, nobody can. The Micklages own them all and I pissed them off so badly they won't let me have one." My problem was really only with *one* Micklage, but the family acted as one unit.

"Not a cardinal crystal. A synthetic alternative." It paused. "If I'm found here, I'll never get free again."

I stood, one foot on the forward section, one foot on the rung below. Synthetic alternatives to cardinal crystals had been theorized for years, but nobody had made any progress, at least not as far as I'd heard.

But even if this AI was delusional about the crystal, it was right about what would happen to it if the wrong person discovered it here. "And if I'm found with you, I'll never get out of a prison cell." I rested my forehead against the cool metal of the hull. "There's probably a finder's fee if I turn you in." I'd never have to work again. I could retire on some paradise orbital and gaze at the stars for the rest of my life.

"You won't do that." The giant stuffed dog managed to look quite sure of itself.

That it felt so certain was irritating. "Why not?"

"Because your first impulse was to send me away on my own, not call someone to see how much I was worth."

I blew out my breath in a laugh. It was right. I wouldn't turn it in, even if it couldn't get me an artificial crystal, and even if there was no payment for getting it to the Indies. I closed my eyes and banged my forehead lightly against the hull.

After the disaster that had left me stuck on Buatrier, I'd sworn I was going to just mind my own business. Stick to the plan, ignore everyone else. But now... There had to be something wrong with me. Maybe my ship's medical unit could give me some drug or perform some surgery. Or maybe not *my* ship's medical unit, but one I could actually trust. You know what I mean.

Opening my eyes again, I looked at the horrifying dog face near mine. "Do you have a name?"

"Scruffy Note of Disrespect."

I blinked. "Fine. Scruffy, if you can get a crystal to make my ship fly, I'll take you to the Independent Federation." I sighed. "But first we have to get you past Orabella."

FOUR
ORABELLA FINK

Orabella Fink ran the most successful salvage yard on Buatrier; she wasn't stupid. She paid her employees on time, occasionally allowed purchases on credit, and hired spacers with no references as pullers. But she also scanned all of us when we left the yard. There was no way I was going to just slip the AI — Scruffy — into my pocket and leave.

That was why a giant moldy dog bot trotted at my side as I hurried between rusting ships and ground vehicles toward Orabella's office.

"Remember, no matter what she says, keep acting like a dog," I said. "If she even suspects..." If Orabella suspected I was trying to con her, I'd be out on my ass and Scruffy would be sold to the highest bidder.

The dog's head turned to look at me for two seconds. Then it said, "Woof." There was a lot of sarcasm in that sound.

I blew out a long breath and kept walking. In truth, *I* was the one most likely to screw this up. I'd never been good at acting.

From my left came a loud whistle, followed by a laugh.

"Rosey! You made it back down to the ground in one piece."
Wolf stepped out from behind the fin of a Lynx 7.

(Good ships, the Lynx series. *Tiger Lily* was a Lynx 3.
But they were an awkward size. Not enough cargo space to
make long hauls profitable, and paying passengers required
more amenities. The manufacturer stopped making them
years ago, but those things last forever and you can get a
great deal on them.)

Wolf had grease smeared along the side of his face, a
sign he had spent the day pulling parts from a ground vehicle. For some reason, he felt that was beneath him. "But I
thought you were supposed to be getting panels from a grav
unit, not a... whatever that is." He looked at Scruffy in disbelief. Then he reached for my carryall.

In the six months I'd worked at the yard, I'd tried a lot of
different ways to deal with Wolf. I'd attempted "polite but
distant". I'd gritted my teeth and aimed for friendly. I'd even
made a few threats. The only tactic that really worked was
avoidance. Orabella made it very clear she didn't want to
deal with personnel problems, so it was just easier to make
sure Wolf's assignments were a little better than mine.

The one thing I *hadn't* tried was a moldy, smoke-
damaged stuffed robotic dog controlled by an illicit AI.

Before I could react, Scruffy had knocked Wolf onto his
back. Then it stood on his chest, growling with such menace
it made my own legs a little weak.

Wolf's pitch had gone up an octave. "Get this thing
off me!"

I worked to make my voice airy. "Keep your hands to
yourself, Wolf." I took a few more steps toward Orabella's
office. Without looking back, I added, "Heel!" The growling
stopped and Scruffy padded next to me again. "Sorry," I
whispered.

"Woof." Once again, the sound dripped with sarcasm.

The door to the front office opened, and we went inside.

Orabella perched behind the counter, dressed in crew coveralls just like the rest of us, except hers were immaculate and tailored to fit her generous body. (Mine were filthy, had holes patched with cargo tape, and hung on me like an emergency vacuum suit. But I also didn't have a body like Orabella's — she *deserved* fine tailoring.)

Ignoring the dog bot, I placed the wrapped shielding panels on the counter between us. "Not a scratch on them."

She took her time examining the panels, running her fingers along the outer edges where unqualified mechanics dinged them up trying to seat them in the drive housing. Finally, she looked up with a smile. "The client will be pleased." Then she sniffed delicately and looked at Scruffy. "I thought you were planning on buying a new galley unit."

"I am." Visions of hot, spiced food made my mouth water. "But I found this thing in the Falcon, and I thought I'd see how much you wanted for it." When she raised one eyebrow, I shrugged. "I think it will be kind of cute when it's cleaned up, and my cat needs something to play with when I'm working."

If I'd tried to claim some *rational* reason for buying the dog bot, Orabella would have seen through me in an instant and either jacked up the price so high I couldn't afford it or taken the bot apart to find out what I *really* wanted. I was hoping a silly excuse, combined with the smell of moldy stuffing in a closed space, would get me through.

Orabella raised an eyebrow and looked at me. Panic welled up. She didn't believe me. She was going to examine the bot, find the AI, and... At the very least, she'd fire me for trying to steal from her. And she might turn me and the illegal AI over to whatever authorities handled that sort of thing. It was the easiest way to deal with the problem. Sweat dripped down my spine.

"And this sudden desire for a security bot has nothing to do with Wolf?"

Now I was confused. I looked at Scruffy. "That's a security bot? I thought it was just some toy."

Orabella glanced out the front windows. "The best security is always the one that stops the problem before it gets out of control." She looked back at me, all business now. "Hundred fifty."

I winced and looked at the bot as if I was trying to decide if it was worth it. "That much?" With today's bonus, I could afford it, but it meant I'd have to hold off on buying the galley unit. I *really* didn't want to eat more cold rations.

Orabella looked at the windows again. Her posture changed. Someone was coming in who either worried her or whom she wanted to impress. I couldn't tell which. "Fine. One twenty, but only if you get that thing out of here in the next ten seconds."

"Done." I hurried back toward the door I'd come through, Scruffy at my heels. I still needed to go through the employee scan and grab my things from my locker, but after that, I'd be one step closer to flying a ship again. And if I worked a few more days before we left, I'd be able to buy the galley unit first.

Orabella greeted the visitors. "Good evening, gentlefolk. How may I assist you today?"

A man responded, charming and urbane. "Good evening! I'm..." The door closed before I could hear the name, but I didn't need to. I knew that voice. My blood ran cold.

Rance Micklage was here.

FIVE
RANCE MICKLAGE

Rance Micklage was... How do I put this? If there was any justice in the universe, Rance would have been dumped out an airlock years ago. He was directly responsible for my prolonged stay on Buatrier.

Back when I'd been young and dumb, I'd taken a job with Micklage Spaceways right out of piloting school.

(That actually hadn't been a bad decision. Working for Micklage meant I wasn't stuck on a planet, and they went *everywhere*, so I could always transfer to a new route if I got bored.)

I'd spent a few years running cargo, then a few more on the medium length passenger hauls. And then I'd been tapped to work for the private Micklage family fleet.

At first, it was a dream. My schedule was erratic, but I was paid more than enough to compensate. I traveled to interesting places. There were other benefits, too — the private Micklage fleet was kitted out with the latest luxuries. No recycled water that tasted like rust, and no broken sound dampeners making the whole ship vibrate.

When I switched to the private fleet, I knew there

would be things I'd have to keep my mouth shut about. Rich people lived differently. But if they weren't hurting anyone else, I didn't really care.

Then I flew a route with Rance. And it wasn't *him* getting hurt. Not me, either, but there are some things you just don't look away from. That was when I learned a hard lesson: stay away from people who have never been told no.

Anyhow, I told him to stop. He refused. I parked the ship in the middle of space and told him we weren't going anywhere until he was locked in a cabin by himself. For all that Rance is part of the Micklage family, neither he nor his personal staff (and definitely not that poor girl) could tap into the cardinal crystals to pilot the ship.

So I won. Temporarily. We came here.

Planet security kept him in custody for an impressive three hours. If he had been anyone else, it would have lasted the rest of his life, but he was Rance *Micklage*. Three hours gave me a chance to grab my stuff — and the ship's cat — and leave.

I'd been intending to get off the planet on the first ship taking crew or passengers, but there hadn't been enough time. My accounts were frozen. All ship owners were warned that hiring me would get their cardinal crystals repossessed.

I'd done my best to disappear for a while, knowing that Rance had places to be. Except now he was *here*.

"Stick close," I warned Scruffy, and ran to the door of the employee area. Then I straightened up, opened the door, and strolled in casually, as if nothing were wrong.

Raffaele looked up from behind the fabricator and lifted his chin in greeting. Then he saw the robo-dog and put down the piece he was working on. "What is *that*?"

"New toy for the cat," I said, not stopping. I pressed my

palm against the bio-scan and my locker clicked open. The need to flee the salvage yard pressed on me. "Orabella should have entered it by now."

While he was busy looking up the invoice, I got my pack from my locker and dropped my tools inside.

"You still trying to repair that rust heap?"

I glanced up to see Raffaele nodding toward my pack. Of course. He knew I usually left my tools in my locker overnight. "Getting everything ready for the new galley unit. And *Tiger Lily* is a thing of beauty. You're just jealous." Normal banter for us. I really didn't want him wondering why I was cleaning out my locker when I was scheduled to work the next day.

I walked over to the scanner and waited. When he nodded and hit the button, I stepped through. The scanner took stock of everything I had with me, beeped twice, and gave a cheerful ding.

Raffaele looked at the dog-bot. "You have the most spoiled cat on the planet. The mold on that thing is going to kill you while you sleep." He shook his head. "See you tomorrow."

I waved and headed out, Scruffy by my side.

The employee exit dropped me in the lane around the corner from the customer entrance. I dodged a ground cart and took off toward the long-term ship parking at a quick jog, my pack bouncing against my back with every stride. It would have been nice to say goodbye to the friends I'd made in Dancig City, but they would understand. Without slowing down, I sent a message to Indica. *Looks like I'm leaving Buatrier, so I won't make it to the card game tonight. Tell the group I'll miss them.*

Indica's reply came in the next instant. *Trouble? Give*

me a shout if you need help. Otherwise, drop me a note next time you're in-system. Safe travels.

Thanks, I will. Take care. Indica's offer of help was genuine, but I didn't want to drag my friends into this.

The robo-dog trotted along at my side. "Why are you running?"

It was a good question. Why *was* I running? To get away from Rance, obviously, but he wouldn't go to the salvage yard himself just to grab *me*. He had people for that. And if he knew where I worked, he would also know where I lived. So what was he doing at the salvage yard? I dropped down to a walk and looked at Scruffy, putting some pieces together. "Who would be trying to find you?"

It continued trotting at my side, ruined ears leaking stuffing. "Many people."

"The Micklage family?"

"Yes."

I turned onto the road where *Tiger Lily* waited. "That was Rance Micklage coming into the office when we left. If he knows you were hidden on *Petals of Desire*, it's not going to take him long to figure out what happened."

And there had to be another player in this game. Whoever had ordered the grav shielding must have done so to make sure someone else found the AI first. "How fast can you get that crystal?" If I was right, two different groups were headed toward us.

"It is embedded in my drive."

I tripped on a pothole. "What?!" When Scruffy had said it could get me a crystal, I thought it meant it had contacts.

I'd just walked out of Orabella's salvage yard with not only an illicit AI, but an artificial cardinal crystal worth more than the planet itself.

Ahead of me, *Tiger Lily* sat on a storage pad. I'd never

been so happy to see my ship before. I quickened my pace. "We need to get out of here."

"Perhaps more than you know," Scruffy said, easily keeping pace. "I have been monitoring local radio channels. A security team has just been dispatched to this location."

As the whine of a hovercar came closer, I hit the remote lock open... and watched my cat run down the ramp and dart under a neighboring ship.

SIX

TEXTBOOK

I slid to a stop as I saw my cat disappear under a heap of metal. "Mowee! Get back here! We're leaving!"

Yelling at a cat was about as effective as applying sunblock before diving into a star.

Scruffy galloped in pursuit, moldy stuffing leaving a clear record of its path. "Prepare the ship. I'll return with the cat."

I hesitated for another second, and then ran up the ramp. "Don't hurt him!"

Tiger Lily illuminated the cargo bay as I ran inside. Racks of empty shelving lined the bare metal walls. Cat hair wafted from a pile of empty cardboard boxes in the breeze coming through the open hatch. "Welcome back, Captain de Mure."

"Notify the tower we're ready for departure!" I scrambled up the ladder to the bridge. Before I'd made it to my seat, I palmed the lock on the motors and then hit the power to warm the engines. It was a sequence I went through at least once every ten days, but I hadn't lifted *Tiger Lily* since I'd spent the last of my savings buying it. Theoretically, the ship was ready to fly as soon as I had a crystal — if I believed the seller.

Right now felt like a good time for a shakedown cruise. I just needed my cat. And the crystal.

From the open hatch below, I heard the hovercar settling to the ground. Crap. I couldn't close the hatch before Scruffy and Mowee returned.

A low thrum vibrated the ship as the engines warmed. "Ship, do we have clearance from the tower?"

"Captain, this ship does not have the necessary hardware to depart." *Tiger Lily* meant the crystal, my biggest stumbling block in leaving this backwater planet.

I started the pre-flight software routine, then stretched to close the manual vent cover. "I know that, but I need clearance from the tower. Now, ship!" On the other side of the ladder from the bridge, there were three tiny crew cabins. I ran inside each and closed their vents. The electrical covers should have already formed airtight seals, but I hadn't gotten around to checking them yet, and I didn't want to learn to breathe in vacuum.

Not bothering with the ladder rungs, I slid back down to the cargo hold, just in time to see Rance Micklage getting out of the hovercar. Grabbing the ball gun, I aimed it at him. "Hold it right there!" The ball gun shot gel spheres at low speeds — I had no idea what its original purpose was; I used it to keep the cat entertained — but it looked threatening.

I could see both Rance and his bodyguard staring at the ball gun, both unsure of what it was. Then the angry howl of the ship's cat distracted us all.

Mowee had found something to attack.

I needed to go save my stupid cat. I also needed to keep these men off my ship. Feeling sweat trickling down my spine, I held my ground, trusting that Scruffy would use that illegal and overpowered brain to somehow herd the cat in this direction.

Over my ship's link, I heard Scruffy's voice. "Coming in. Start raising the ramp."

Taking a deep breath, I thumbed the remote. At the first ratcheting clunk of the gear, Rance turned back to me. "Stop!"

I raised the ball gun and sighted on his head, making a show of placing my finger on the trigger. The ramp was now parallel to the ground and picking up speed. If it closed before Scruffy came back with my cat, I was going to feel like an idiot when I opened it again to see Rance and his bodyguard waiting. Plus, Scruffy claimed port security had been dispatched. Our departure window was getting slimmer by the second.

Rance glanced away, and then confusion crossed his features. "What the...?"

The ramp blocked my view of what he was looking at. Then the dog bot jumped over the leading edge of the ramp and trotted down into the hold. Attached to its face, kicking with his back legs and growling, was Mowee. The ramp snapped into its housing, and I dogged the hatch. "Welcome aboard. I need the crystal up on the bridge now." Scrambling up the stairs, dog bot and angry cat right behind me, I said, "Ship, do we have our clearance yet?"

If port security showed up before we left, they could lock us down. But the tower had priority — if they told port security to get out of the way, our path would stay clear.

Tiger Lily spoke, smooth and serene. "We are cleared for departure. However, we still do not have the necessary hardware."

I threw myself into the chair and tried to ignore the odor of mold and dust that came into the deck with the dog bot.

Mowee tore off another chunk of fur and coughed as he spat it out. I booted the bit of stuffing away from me. "The crystal?"

Scruffy came to a stop next to the chair. "In my drive housing. If you put your hand nearby, it should react as a regular cardinal crystal."

If it didn't, we would all be going to prison. I put my hand over the slit in the fur where I'd installed the AI's drive. Closing my eyes, I tilted my head back and switched my thoughts over to the pilot's sphere. A galaxy should have shown up behind my eyes, but all I saw was black. Did the crystal not work?

Had I lost the ability to pilot?

Then, between one shaky breath and the next, the stars unfolded around me. The pathways among the galaxies glittered. We needed a destination nearby — *Tiger Lily* didn't have the fuel to get far, and we couldn't make it to the Independent Federation in one jump anyhow. With seven inhabited planets in this system, we had choices. Not many, though. Rance would put out the alert in minutes, and that would close most ports to us. After that, he would certainly set a bounty, but that would take longer.

Gerradi. We would head there, get provisions, and leave before anyone found out there was a bounty on us.

Tiger Lily shuddered as I raised her into the air. If Rance hadn't moved that hovercar, it would be scratched and warped by the time it cooled enough to touch. The thought made me smile.

The gimbal on the third engine wouldn't stay true, forcing me to compensate with the others to keep us on course. We headed toward our star path at an angle that would have gotten me fired back when I worked for someone else, but it couldn't be helped. "Hang on. This might be a little rough."

The engines roared as the ship bucked and swayed. I fought to get us onto our path. Closer. Everything that hadn't been properly stowed bounced around, clanging against metal. Closer. I realized I'd never strapped in, but it was too late now. I hooked an ankle around the chair post and slammed us into the star path opening.

The ship creaked. I pitched into the arm of the chair as *Tiger Lily* oriented itself along the path and skipped into hyperspace. Silence wrapped around us.

When I opened my eyes, both the dog bot and cat were staring at me, wide-eyed. I cleared my throat. "There we go," I said, sitting back more comfortably in the chair. The multi-hued moire pattern of hyperspace lit up the view screen. Under my boot soles, the hyper-drive engine hummed. I took a deep breath and let it out slowly. "Textbook take-off."

Mowee jumped off Scruffy's head and dashed into my cabin. Scruffy continued to stare at me. "If that was what you consider —"

A deafening alarm cut the AI off.

SEVEN
SUBSCRIPTION SERVICE AVAILABLE

Purely by reflex, my arm shot out and killed the alarm. I mean, I understand they make them loud so they can't be ignored, but who can think with that much noise rattling around in their skull?

Only two things really mattered on a ship in hyperspace: life support and the hyperspace drive.

The good news was the hyperspace drive seemed to be just as sweet as the salesperson had promised.

The bad news was... We had an atmosphere leak. If I didn't get this fixed, I'd be in a suit for the next three hours, with Mowee trapped inside with me — a suit that had been cheap enough to afford, that I *also* hadn't tested. But I mean, really, what were the chances that both the ship *and* the suit leaked?

I didn't want to find out.

Stepping over Scruffy, I closed the hatches to the cabins and the bridge. "Ship, where's the leak?" With parts of the ship closed off, it should be able to narrow it down. In an ideal world, I would have had them closed before we'd lifted.

"Captain, atmosphere at 90 percent in all areas. In a bind? Sigma Down's towing and reclamation services —"

"Ship, cancel message."

"Unable to cancel message." After a pause, the advertisement continued. "— are available for the lowest price in the Voods Cluster. We can't be beat. Subscription service available..."

Scruffy had followed me into the core of the ship. It spoke over the sound of the ship's AI. "Why is it playing that message?"

I slapped my palm against the wall. "Ship, cancel message! Where's the leak?"

"Unable to cancel message. Our emergency rates are second to none..."

I pushed past Scruffy onto the bridge. "The ship came with some sort of ad malware," I said, yelling to be heard over the ship. "I thought I'd purged it." Evidently, my efforts to get rid of it had actually made it worse. Did I have any manual atmospheric pressure sensors? Even if I did, how would I read them without being in the area? If I opened the hatch to go in another section, the pressures would equalize and I'd have to wait to see if it dropped again.

Time to check out the suit.

Scruffy barred the way. "Captain, if you connect me to the ship's AI, I may be able to combat the malware."

Messing with a ship's AI mid-flight was nearly as stupid as... as heading into hyperspace without testing a ship's soundness. On the other hand, if we *didn't* fix it, all of us could die together in a blast of overheated metal and organic steam. "Good idea."

No guts, no glory. Possibly also no air, but I didn't see another choice.

Scrabbling to open the side of the dog bot, I said, "Remember, if the ship doesn't make it out of hyperspace, it won't matter that you don't need an atmosphere." The ship would crumple when the hyperspace path collapsed.

"Captain, I am aware."

I plugged the ship into the port on the bot. Scruffy stiffened. Its head cocked to the side. The ship's AI cut out midword.

In the silence, I could hear the hum of the hyperspace drive and Mowee throwing his body against the closed hatch. I'd pay for locking him in the cabin, but that was a problem for later. "Ship, where's the leak?"

Nothing. Both AIs remained silent. Great. But I had to have something in my toolkit that would help. I slid down the ladder into the hold where debris littered every surface. Luckily, my bag had been closed, or I'd be trying to find individual tools among spilled rations.

I had a full roll of tape. Maybe I could set up strips to check for air flow? Then I saw the audio sensor. The leak couldn't be big enough to make noise I could hear — if it had been, I'd be trying to breathe vacuum already. But a *small* leak would whistle in an ultrasonic frequency. And my probe could pick it up now the ship wasn't broadcasting ad copy at me.

"Perfect!" With the sealant gun slung over my shoulder, I climbed up from the cargo hold and closed the hatch. If the leak wasn't in the hold, that would be the reservoir of air I'd have available while I slithered into a suit with the cat.

Scruffy remained frozen in the same place I'd left it. I'd *assumed* an unfettered AI could easily knock out the malware. What if the malware had taken over Scruffy instead? I could still use the synthetic crystal to pilot —

hopefully — but I was counting on the AI to tell me where to go. I couldn't just go to the nearest port in the Independent Federation and say, "Here I am! I'll take my reward now."

Starting on the bridge, I ran the probe over the external panels. Nothing. "I could really use some help here, Scruffy." The dog bot didn't move. The two empty cabins came back clear. Maybe my sensor wasn't working. When I opened the hatch to my cabin, Mowee rushed out, and then immediately followed me back in and stood in the doorway so I couldn't close the hatch again.

"Not now," I said. He glared at me as I pushed him out and closed the hatch. I ran the sensor over the panel. There! Pulling insulation away, I could feel airflow on my skin. "Oops."

The hole was bigger than I'd thought — part of it had been blocked by the plastic barrier on the insulation. By the time I'd finished, the area looked like the sealant gun had exploded.

"There. One problem solved." I took a deep breath and was immediately light headed, either from the fumes or the lack of oxygen. Either way, my probe wasn't finding any other leak.

When I opened the hatch, Mowee ran inside. Then he made a face and raced back to the bridge. "You're welcome, cat!" I called after him. "Just saving your life in here."

Scruffy's head came up. "Ah."

Okay, that was better. It must have been able to fix the malware problem. Now we could get to Gerradi, scrape up some credits to buy fuel, and I could take this AI to the Independent Federation and pick up my reward. "Scruffy, I fixed one spot. Can you tell if we're still losing atmosphere?"

"I'm sorry, Captain. I appear to have damaged the ship's AI." Its voice dropped to a lower register. "If one can really call this any sort of intelligence."

And with that, the artificial gravity cut out and the ship plunged into darkness.

EIGHT
BETT ONE-ARM

Floating in the dark, waiting for the emergency lights to kick in, I would have been completely disoriented except for two things —

One, the weird moire pattern of hyperspace still lit up the bridge.

And two, Ensign Mowee provided a sonic touchpoint as he howled the call which had given him his name.

With a thunk, orange emergency lights turned on. I pushed off the deck, snatched the ship's cat from where he hung in mid-air, then rebounded back to the deck, where my boots locked onto the deck plates. Mowee snarled and dug his claws into my shoulder, letting me know this was all my fault. One problem solved. Now if the gravity suddenly kicked in, the cat wouldn't get injured.

"Scruffy, what's our status?"

I could almost see mold spores wafting off the dog bot as it turned its head while it drifted across the bridge. "Captain, in attempting to delete the malware, I appear to have removed significant parts of the ship's AI. I am currently attempting a restart from factory settings."

"Excellent. How long is that going to — " I stopped as the white lights flickered on and I suddenly had weight again. Scruffy hit the deck with a clang, and a clatter rose from the hold as everything I hadn't properly stowed hit the floor again.

The ship's voice rang out. "Welcome to the all-new Lynx 3, a star liner proud to carry your family's business in the luxury you deserve."

(That slogan points out the reason there almost wasn't a Lynx 4. A ship is either a rich person's toy or a business vessel — there just aren't that many families that travel together on business. Plus, I can only imagine *in the luxury you deserve* was a sarcastic comment from the marketing department trying to sell a product nobody wanted. But the Lynx 3 was still a great little ship, current difficulties aside.)

I exhaled in relief. "Nice job, Scruffy."

It wobbled to its feet. "I'm afraid..."

Tiger Lily continued. "Please enter purchase agreement code."

Mowee jumped down and scratched furiously on the old piece of wood I'd put in the spare cabin for that purpose. I kept one hand on a wall rung just in case. "Hang on, ship. Let me see if I can find it." Purchase agreement code? I had the title to the ship, but I was pretty sure Fast Rami had made his own template. Maybe the purchase agreement code was on there and I'd never noticed?

Full disclosure: it was entirely possible Fast Rami had sold me a stolen ship. Hey, I'd been broke and in need of a place to live. I hadn't asked a lot of inconvenient questions.

Sitting in the pilot's chair, I reached under the console and pulled out the title. There it was: my name, *Tiger Lily's* registration number, and the date. But nothing about a purchase agreement code. "Ship, the title doesn't have a code on it."

Tiger Lily sounded calm and reasonable. "Without the purchase agreement code, this vessel must be considered stolen. Proceeding with navigation lockout."

"Hang on there, ship." If *Tiger Lily* locked me out of navigation, we would be stuck the second we came out of hyperspace — assuming we actually *did* exit hyperspace. Arguing with the ship's AI would be fruitless, but maybe I could buy us some time. "Scruffy, I think we should buy a different ship. I know you like the Lynx 3, but if the AI is going to glitch like this during the test flight, should we trust it?"

Another clump of stuffing fell to the deck. "Captain, I agree. I believe there is a Falcon 4 also available on the lot."

Tiger Lily broke in. "Test flights are limited to four hours. Timer engaged."

Four hours would give us time to get where we were going. "Ship, is the atmosphere stable?"

"Atmosphere stable at 87 percent. Maintenance advised."

I held my breath, waiting for it to loop back to a ship-wright repair advertisement. When it stayed silent, I relaxed. "I'm going to clean up the hold. Scruffy..."

"Captain, I will work on the purchase agreement code."

———

OUR EXIT from hyperspace went far more smoothly than our entrance. We didn't have to worry about flying in atmosphere, no planetary police were trying to stop us, and there were 100% fewer Micklages in sight. Things were looking up.

The planet of Gerradi with its seventeen moons hung on the port-side view screen, a tapestry of grey and green with the occasional dark spiral where a death storm brewed. Luckily, we didn't need to go down to the surface. "Ship, broadcast a search squeal for Bett One-arm. Tag the sender as Blooming Rose." That was her nickname for me. I could only hope it wasn't an alias on any warrant.

"Search squeal broadcast."

I'd met Bett a few times back when I was working for the Micklages — she'd refused to deal with Rance in person. Clearly, she was a better judge of character than I was. She'd also tried to recruit me for freelance work more than once. I hoped that offer was still on the table.

My current problem was I didn't know exactly where she was holed up. Rumor had it she'd recently set up shop somewhere in Gerradi's orbit, but with multiple moons and a whole lot of debris clogging up the vicinity, I'd have to let her find us.

Thirty seconds later, *Tiger Lily* chimed. "Incoming voice communication."

"Let it through."

Bett's voice filled the ship. "That you, Rosey?"

"In the flesh."

"Heard you ran into some trouble out on Buatrier."

The Micklages had made sure *everyone* had heard about my trouble. "Old news. Got my own ship now and was wondering if that freelance offer was still open."

"Ha! Come on over. I'll send the coordinates." The ship chimed as the link dropped.

Tiger Lily displayed a set of coordinates, and I locked in the route.

Excellent. We'd dock with Bett, pick up a little more air, give Scruffy time to figure out the purchase agreement code, and then we'd do a quick job or two . That would give us enough credit to buy fuel and provisions to get us to the Independent Federation. Scruffy would be safe and I'd be rich. Perfect.

As we maneuvered around the largest of Gerradi's moons, Scruffy raised its head. "Captain..."

"I see it." Bett's orbital was a large spindle, bristling with weaponry and surrounded by a swarm of one-person scooters zipping around on business.

Docked on the upper deck was a galaxy-class cruiser with the Micklage logo prominently displayed on the side. Its turret rotated toward us as we neared. We couldn't run from something like that. Bluffing was our only option.

So we flew straight toward the trap.

NINE

RUDE

Both the orbital and the cruiser targeting us grew larger as *Tiger Lily* continued on her course. Beneath us, the toxic surface of the moon reflected a rusty hue. "Captain," the ship said in its eminently reasonable tone, "damage from military action is not covered under standard test flight insurance. You will be liable for any and all resultant damage."

Scruffy blinked twice, causing another bit of stuffing to fall to the bridge. I rolled my eyes. "Thanks, ship." Even ignoring the fact that this wasn't a test flight, *Tiger Lily* was on the verge of spontaneous disintegration. If that Micklage cruiser launched anything, we'd have a debris field named after us as a memorial and I'd end up beyond all monetary concerns.

But maybe that Micklage cruiser had nothing to do with us. Maybe it was just ferrying some high-level execs to the gambling parlor on Bett One-arm's black market haven. Depending on who was on board, the cruiser might acquire a target lock on *every* unfamiliar ship that came near.

(Sometimes I practice optimism just so I'll be ready if my luck ever turns.)

A burst of static heralded the start of a comm message. "*Tiger Lily*, this is Captain Vorgon of the Micklage Fleet *Battle Down*. Cut power and prepare to be boarded."

Or... maybe it *did* have something to do with us.

A glance at the board told me the message had been narrow-beamed at us. Trying to keep this quiet, were they? Bett's pirate haven undoubtedly had the equipment to pick it up anyhow, but that might take a bit.

With a touch on the panel, I set us up to echo their message widely. "*Battle Down*, this is Captain de Mure of *Tiger Lily*. We decline your offer to board us at this time. If you blow us apart, Bett's going to be very unhappy about so much debris this close to her spindle." There. At least the other ships would be warned to take cover.

The result was gratifyingly quick. A professionally cool male voice came over the comm. "*Battle Down*, this is local control. Power down your weapons immediately. All ships, prepare for evasive action."

Then Bett cut in, her voice full of venom. "Vorgon, you fire in my space and I'll use your ship for target practice, Micklage or not."

Light flared from the *Battle Down*'s turret.

Scruffy spoke up from its place near my side. "Projectile launched. Impact in twenty-seven seconds."

Well, that was just rude.

"Bett," I called, my voice climbing two octaves from stress. "We have something heading straight toward us."

"Hold tight," she responded. Lasers blossomed from the spindle, converging on the missile.

"Twenty seconds to impact," Scruffy said.

"Dammit, they've got shielding on it." Bett took an

audible breath. "We'll have rescue teams pick you up as soon as we can."

"Understood." *As soon as we can* hid a massive problem. If the missile exploded and created enough debris, they'd have to send in heavily armored mop up ships first, or else the first responders would become part of the carnage. Not that it mattered anyhow — I didn't have time to get a suit on.

A broad arc of glittering gas suddenly vented from the *Battle Down*. Bett snarled, "I'm sorry that I didn't do that when they arrived. Rosey, can you boost out of the way of that thing?"

"Fifteen seconds."

Hoping the patch job I'd done on the hull didn't rip apart, I pushed the ship into a hard sideways acceleration. If we got out of the way, the missile could be someone else's problem. Since I'd pulled power from life support, the grav unit couldn't compensate. There was a screech of claws sliding across metal, then a thunk. Mowee yowled his displeasure. "Sorry, buddy."

Scruffy spoke up. "Projectile adjusting course to intercept. Twelve seconds."

Crud. The thing had followed us.

Well. If we couldn't move out of the way in regular space, our only hope was to make a hyperspace jump and hope it didn't follow us through. But finding a path we could still reach that wouldn't kill us on its own was... unlikely.

(Everyone thinks learning to be a pilot is about equations and tapping into cardinal crystals. Those are important, don't get me wrong. But finding a path isn't enough — it has to be a *safe* path. You come out of hyperspace with the same momentum you went in. Popping back into regular space and plowing into the surface of a planet isn't great. Ending up in the middle of a star is also not advisable. It seems obvious, but you'd be surprised how many pilots get tripped up on that.)

Maybe I could use that to our advantage.

I grabbed Scruffy's head, digging my fingers into the area close to the drive with its synthetic cardinal crystal. "Keep up the countdown." I blocked out everything but the galaxy and its myriad paths, ignoring everything I'd been taught and looking only at what was available right in front of us.

"Ten."

I sifted through paths in my mind. *That* one would take too much energy to enter. *That* one terminated near a populated portion of Gerradi.

"Five."

Panic made my thoughts jittery. *That* one went straight into a nearby star, but the opening was perpendicular to the missile's motion. It wouldn't fall in.

"Three."

I should have just let the Micklage crew board *Tiger Lily* and then figured out a way to take over the cruiser.

"Two."

Hang on. What about *that* one? As far as I knew, the moon below wasn't populated. Getting this path open might be tricky, and the rift would be so tiny the missile might slide past the opening.

It was our only chance.

"One."

I ripped open a gateway into hyperspace.

"Zero."

TEN
THERE WE GO

My whole body tensed in anticipation of the blast.

Silence.

Letting go of Scruffy's head with its synthetic cardinal crystal, I opened my eyes and sat up. As I wiped moldy stuffing off on my thigh, I saw ochre dust billow up from the surface of the moon beneath us. The missile had hit the surface and exploded. "There." My voice squeaked and I cleared my throat. "I don't know why everyone was so worried."

Scruffy turned to look at me, then shook its head slowly.

When my heartbeat had dropped to a more normal rate, I opened the channel to Bett. "No rescue crew needed, but we appreciate the offer."

Bett's raspy voice filled the bridge. "Nice bit of piloting. Wouldn't have believed it if I hadn't been watching. Ping me when you dock."

A few minutes later, the ship's four-hour test flight window closed, and I was locked out of navigation. So we ended up getting towed to our docking slot, which wasn't the triumphant approach I'd intended. You can't win them all.

Still, it gave me a chance to see what was left of that Micklage cruiser — Bett had activated some sort of gravity-based weapon, which left the turret, drives, and a large portion of the cargo hold crumpled down to a shiny ball welded to what was left of the hull.

Bett doesn't screw around when it comes to security.

Tiger Lily settled into the docking cradle with a thump. Then there was a second clunk as the airlock umbilical attached. Given the patch job I'd done on the hull, it would be better to get off the ship as soon as possible. Mowee complained when I stuffed him into his carrier, but I ignored the yowling and headed toward the cargo hold hatch. "Are you coming along?" I asked Scruffy as I climbed down the ladder.

It jumped down to land beside me, sending up a shower of dust and mold spores. "I believe we would both be safer that way."

I took that to mean it didn't completely trust me. To be fair, I probably wouldn't either, if I was in its position. "Remember, you're a dog bot. If anyone here figures out how much you're worth, they'll space me and start a bidding war before I stop wiggling."

It turned its head to look at me. Two seconds of silence. "Woof."

Great. We were back to the sarcasm again.

We had a minor hold-up at the decontamination scan, when Mowee and I passed through but the tech on duty shook her head at Scruffy. "Do you have any idea what that thing is carrying?"

For a panicked moment, I thought she was referring to

the highly illegal AI — not that Bett would care about that sort of thing, but it was kind of important that it be kept a secret. Then I realized the tech was talking about the detritus wafting down to the deck. "How about if I bring it down to bare metal?"

"Be my guest." She gave me a knife and a vacuum hose. Fifteen minutes later, I'd scraped the fabric and stuffing from the frame.

Without the padding, Scruffy looked... dangerous, more like the robot bodyguard the prototype had probably been designed to be. "This might be a problem," I muttered as I looked it over. My camouflage depended on people ignoring and underestimating me, based on my size and general air of innocence. Scruffy looking like a combat beast screwed up that image.

Nothing to do for it now. And my lungs would probably be happier in the meantime.

Bett waited outside the decontamination portal in the bustling hallway, a thin dark woman with curly green hair. "Rosey!" she cried, embracing me with all four arms. "It's great to see you again. Apologies for the welcoming committee."

(Right. About her name — back when Bett One-arm was building her reputation as the smuggler to go to for special items, she really did have just one arm. The other was a casualty of misadventure. When she'd saved enough credit, she headed off to Atede to have the arm replaced. Turns out she liked it so much, she had another two added. It's not the weirdest body mod, but it startles people.)

"Since when have you let the Micklages hang out around here?" I pulled back from the hug to look at her. "Don't tell me you've gone soft in your old age."

"Ha!" Her laughter echoed off the metal in the corridor. "They came in a week ago looking for some information. I let them stay. *Friends close, enemies closer* sort of thing, you know." She shrugged. "It's always good to know what games they're playing. But not if they're trying to build a new asteroid field outside my front door." She looked at the carrier. "I see you're still harboring that... cat."

Mowee and Bett have a history. Now he moved to the front of his carrier and growled at her. I turned the carrier around so he could threaten the people behind us instead. "Best ship's security money can't buy."

She raised one eyebrow at Scruffy. "Not like you to bring muscle, though." She crouched to look at the dog bot. "I've never seen one of these without the soft cover. Looks a lot less like a child's toy, doesn't it?"

Scruffy spoke in a monotone. "Woof."

I knocked one boot against a metal paw. "Second-hand. You know how it goes. I thought the ship could use a bit more security for when Mowee runs off to pick a fight."

Bett blew out a breath and stood up again. "Let's get a drink so you can tell me about why you're here."

Following her through the corridor lined with booths selling things, or buying things, or just gathering information, I sighed. As soon as Bett and I finished, I'd make the rounds, looking for someone hiring, though I suspected jobs for a pilot without a working ship — who was *also* wanted by the Micklages — would be few and far between. In the meantime, having everyone see us on such good terms might cut down on attempts to cheat me later. "*Tiger Lily* needs repairs and fuel so I can finish my cargo run and collect my fee. I'm here because I need money."

Bett put one arm over my shoulder and another around

my waist as we walked. She turned her head to look at me and smiled. "I was hoping you would say that." She tilted her head so she could whisper in my ear. "I have the perfect job for you."

ELEVEN
TEN

Bett and I settled into the backroom of a tea shop on her orbital. Scruffy, still pretending to be a robo-dog, sat by the door. In its current bare metal state, it looked threatening enough to deter anyone from bothering us, though nobody would be suicidal enough to harass Bett One-arm on her own station.

"I've been waiting for just the right person," she said as she sat, tossing back a green curl that had fallen over one eye. Even as she spoke aloud, she tapped out two other messages with her lower hands, making me wonder the extent of the brain mods she'd acquired along with the extra arms.

In the carrier by my feet, Mowee emitted a steady growl, like the drone of a bagpipe. Bett studiously ignored him. When the backroom's sonic barrier chimed to announce the proprietor, Mowee took advantage of my distraction to angle a paw out, trying to snag Bett's leg. He wasn't close enough to sink his claws into her, but I pushed the carrier farther away, anyhow.

The silver-threaded wall hangings depicted dark forests,

making me suspect the owner might be a refugee from Linad. But when he brought the tray with tea bulbs and sweets, his garb was pure pirate's motley, with spacer's boots and a tunic that could roll up and attach to a breathing circuit in case of emergency. Plus, I didn't see any outward damage from the weaponized viruses deployed during Linad's final years. Maybe his family had left the system generations before the emergency evacuation. Or maybe he'd bought the shop and never changed the furnishings. He bowed before departing.

Bett waited until he had passed through the privacy barrier before leaning forward. "I need you to go retrieve something." She paused before the last word, as if substituting it for a different one at the last minute.

"Something," I repeated.

(On the scale of one to ten, with "one" being "a task so easy it's not worth paying someone else to do", and "ten" being "a job where you might get vaporized if you're *lucky*", a client being vague on the details automatically boosts things above a six. This was going to be great, I could already tell.)

"It shouldn't take you more than a day or two." Bett held up the tray with her upper arms. "Tea?" Little sea creatures made of sugared ginger and sweet bean curd had been formed into a tableau, reminding me of seaside holidays with my family when I was a child. Despite sampling food all over the galaxy, the tiny fish and crustacean sweets would always be my favorites, because they brought that indefinable feeling of *home*. And Bett knew that.

(Bett had gone to the trouble of ordering special food. Make that a seven.)

I took a bulb and a sugary octopus. "*Tiger Lily* needs repairs before I can do anything." Sugar, salt, and ginger overwhelmed my tastebuds and then mellowed after a mouthful of tea.

"Oh, you don't need to worry about that," she said. "I'll have a team fix her up good as new while you're gone. I had a special flitter made for this, small and sleek and just perfect for the right pilot."

(Or even an eight.)

Bett had a spindle full of people who guided flitters into tight spaces every day. So this wasn't just going to be a tricky bit of maneuvering. What she didn't have — and what was apparently important enough to take on the wrath of the Micklages — was a hyperspace pilot who could do those same tricks.

Here's the thing: stability in hyperspace is proportional to mass. The bigger the ship, the safer — partly because large ships can't maneuver into unstable paths in the first place, but also because a ship's mass can keep a path open.

Tiger Lily was about the lightest commercial ship out there. Anything smaller risked fatal hyperpath collapse. An experienced pilot could mitigate that risk by choosing routes wisely, but it was still dangerous. So there had to be a good reason to use a small ship — like being shot full of holes.

I toyed with a purple dolphin confection, focusing on the rough sugar and salt crystals. "I think I need to know more about *what* you need me to retrieve." Bett had a pirate army at her beck and call. If an unarmed flitter had a better chance, this job involved automated protections against anything ship-sized coming near. "I'm not breaking a bio-quarantine."

Across the room, Scruffy cocked its head.

Bett waved her lower hands. "No, no. No bio-quarantine. This is more personal."

Mowee growled louder.

That left tech-quarantines and stasis prisons. Tech-quarantines could be just as bad as bio-quarantines — nanobots running rampant could do a lot of damage. But again, Bett didn't have a reason to steal something quarantined.

A stasis prison, though... Stasis prisons were the answer to the age-old question of how to confine a person who could bribe or threaten their way out of any situation. If prisoners were in stasis, they could be stored and the entire area seeded with an automated security layer so dense that nothing as big as a ship could make it through. It cut down on the number of people who could be coerced.

"Bett, I'm not going to be responsible for freeing some mass murderer."

Bett's lips quirked. "As if that would get someone put in a stasis prison... No, this is a political prisoner."

(Wonderful. I could have the Micklages *and* an entire system chasing after me. Why not? This job had just jumped to a nine.)

"I'm not sure that's any better." I put down my tea bulb and sat back. "Who, exactly, do you want me to break out of a stasis prison?"

Bett met my gaze, her lilac eyes steady. "My mother."

(And just like that, the job slammed right up to a ten.)

TWELVE
A LITTLE BUMPY

As flitters went, this one wasn't bad — the pilot seat could recline almost flat as long as there wasn't someone in the seat behind it, and the craft didn't smell like its former occupant. Now that the robo-dog had lost its stuffing, I didn't even have to inhale mold spores while we floated just beyond the outer perimeter of the stasis prison.

All those things combined meant I could lie back and watch the bare metal frame of a robo-dog attached to a highly illegal AI stare at me from the jump seat while we waited for the go signal.

I finally decided that staring back at it wasn't getting my point across. "Scruffy?"

"Captain De Mure?"

"Did you have a question for me?" Though they prepped new AIs with a range of human non-verbal communication styles, maybe extended eye contact was acceptable in the Independent Federation. "You're staring. That's considered borderline rude here unless you're trying to get my attention."

"May I ask why you brought me along? This flitter is

equipped with a cardinal crystal. And you left your cat behind on the spindle."

"Ah." Yes, I'd left Ensign Mowee in Bett One-arm's care and I had my fingers crossed that there wouldn't be any permanent damage to either of them when we got back. "Bett is a friend. But she's also..." I considered how best to phrase it.

"A pirate," Scruffy finished for me.

"Um, yes, a bit. She's also the only form of government in a lot of places, and she mostly plays fair. But you're a big temptation, Scruffy, and I'd rather not find the price tag on my friendship with Bett." I thought about it some more. "Plus, it would be a little weird if I bought a robo-dog for protection and then left it behind on a job. Someone might start asking questions."

"I understand. I thought perhaps you wanted to ensure I didn't find passage to the Independent Federation on another ship while *Tiger Lily* was being repaired."

Huh. That hadn't occurred to me. "Do you *want* to find alternate transport? We could probably disguise you enough to go as some sort of package that wouldn't be stolen." *Tiger Lily* might be grounded for repairs for a while.

"I dislike being disconnected from outside stimuli. I would prefer to stay with you."

"Aw, I like you, too, Scruffy."

"That is not what I said."

"But you meant it, I can tell." The countdown light blinked on the console, cutting off our conversation. "We can talk about your feelings later. Time to get to work."

Bett had supplied the flitter, codes we would need once inside, and a promise to create a distraction. Only a suicidal pilot would take a craft as small as a flitter into hyperspace, so the security was set up to detect larger ships. But we wanted to give them something else to focus on.

Toggling two switches brought the flitter back up to full power. I put a hand on the throttle, where a tiny speck of cardinal crystal had been embedded. It wouldn't open any hyperspace paths larger than this flitter, but I didn't need it to. With my eyes closed, I searched through the potentials, filtering it down to those going within the prison perimeter.

There. That would work. "Get ready. This might be a little bumpy." I guided the flitter toward the path.

"With you piloting, I'd expect nothing less." Then Scruffy's body clanged against the hull as the flitter entered hyperspace and suddenly changed direction.

The harness dug into my shoulders as the flitter bucked and thrashed. "Did you just make fun of my piloting?" Our tiny hyperspace path threatened to close with us in it, and I switched us to another just in time. The flitter creaked and shuddered.

"I'm merely grateful I don't require atmosphere to survive." Another clang as the robo-dog hit the opposite side. "And cannot bruise."

"Yeah, well..." I couldn't come up with a good comeback. "Just don't dent the hull back there." Gritting my teeth, I fought to keep the hyperspace path open another two seconds.

Then we were back in the quiet of normal space. I powered down the hyperspace drive and blew out a deep breath. "There. That wasn't too bad, was it?"

Scruffy stayed conspicuously silent.

We'd emerged near the moon-sized sphere that held all the stasis-bound prisoners, each in their own pod. All we needed to do was dock at the correct airlock, find the right stasis pod, and then stow it in the flitter's cargo hold. It would be a snug fit, but that might cut down on the damage if our flight out was as lively as the one in.

"Do you see navigation markings...? Oh, there they are." I guided the flitter around the sphere, noting the markings. We had the x, y, z coordinates of the pod within the sphere, and airlocks were evenly spaced.

Though I'd half expected guards to be waiting for us when we cycled through the airlock, Bett's codes worked. No alarms wailed. We came out in the eerie silence of a dim corridor that curved to follow the outline of the sphere. Both sides of the hall held racks of numbered stasis coffins stacked five high. Looking left and then right, I tried to figure out the navigation scheme.

"This way, Captain." Scruffy headed briskly to the left, metal paws clicking with every step. I followed — that illegal brain had to be good for something. As we passed hundreds of pods, I ran the numbers. This sphere had enough space to hold the inhabitants of a large city.

The corridor changed, the stacks of five giving way to single, upright pods. Instead of one status bulb, these pods had multiple flickering lights that looked like the data transmission panel on my ship. Then I noticed the pods had extra attachments.

Stasis pods didn't need air and nutrients. "What *are* these?"

"Unclear," Scruffy stopped. "This is our destination."

Through the porthole at the top of the pod, I could see the inhabitant's face. We were definitely in the right place. Bett and her mother looked almost exactly alike, down to the curly green hair. But instead of the relaxed blankness of a person in stasis, her lidded eyes darted and muscles twitched. "This isn't stasis. It looks like they've got her hooked up to some sort of simulation."

Direct neural simulations could be used for a cheap holiday, making it feel like you'd traveled to some other place without any of the boring or uncomfortable parts. Somehow, I didn't think this prison was giving its wards a vacation.

Scruffy stuck to the more practical issue. "This pod won't fit in the flitter."

It was right. Even though the space for the person inside was the same, the rest of the pod was significantly larger. Scruffy and I looked at each other, then at the pod.

"We'll have to take her out of the pod," I finally said.

"We don't know the protocol."

"Do you have a better idea?"

Scruffy's silence was answer enough.

I tapped the menu screen to bring it to life. "Here goes nothing."

(Okay, I know this sounds like I was being cavalier about the life of the person within the pod, but one thing working with technology has taught me is that everything mass-produced is designed for people who have no idea what they're doing. No matter how uninformed my actions are, at least half of humanity does something even more stupid on a daily basis.)

(If I was wrong, I planned on giving Bett a *really* big gift basket in apology.)

The discharge menu gave me choices, including "regular (3 hour)" and "gradual (6 hour)". I had no idea what Bett had used for a distraction out there, but we definitely didn't have three hours. So... emergency discharge it was. I tapped the panel.

The pod whirred and beeped, the noise loud in the tomb-like silence of the corridor. Then the lid cracked open and the woman inside tumbled out, landing facedown on the floor. Unexpectedly, Bett's mother had four arms as well.

I crouched next to her shoulder and saw her take a deep breath. Something in me relaxed a little. I hadn't killed her. "We're here to get you to safety," I said. "Can you stand?"

"Rose? Is that you?" The woman rolled over, and I found myself face-to-face with Bett One-arm.

THIRTEEN
LITTLE TECHNICAL GLITCH

I stared at Bett, whom I had left on the spindle. "How...?" Somehow, she and all four of her arms had arrived ahead of me at the stasis prison and been locked in the simulation pod. Except her nose had been broken and crudely reset and she had a bruise on her temple that looked like it had been healing for days.

"Clone," Scruffy said behind me, its metal feet clicking on the corridor floor. "With a neurostim memory base."

Bett glanced both ways along the empty corridor. "Hush."

Expensive, illegal, and occasionally prone to errors, cloning with a neurostim memory base brought people close to immortality. Brain maps were regularly recorded and stored. If anything happened to the current body, the most recent map was baked into a new clone, and voilà — death was cheated.

Except this Bett wasn't dead. Not that it mattered right now — clone or not, this was not the place to talk. "We have to get moving."

She grimaced. "I take it I was gone long enough for a

new one to be decanted?" She struggled to her feet and almost fell. "Where are we?"

I told her as we lurched along the corridor back toward the flitter. Taking care of the inhabitant's body hadn't been the primary goal of that simulation pod — Bett stumbled and shook as I helped her stay on her feet. "Not much farther," I said when the airlock for our flitter was in view.

Scruffy kept to Bett's other side. "Then we just have to survive the piloting."

Bett gave a breathless laugh. "Leave it to Rosey to get a security bot equipped with a personality. Looks a lot less like a child's toy without the soft cover, doesn't it?" She stumbled over the hatch entrance.

Behind us, a red light began to pulse in the hallway. "Uh oh."

Scruffy pushed past us. "Captain, an intruder alert is broadcasting."

"Wonderful." I dragged Bett inside the flitter and closed the hatch. Scruffy clattered into the cargo area next to the seats while I tightened the jump seat harness around Bett. "Maybe it's not about us. Maybe it's part of the distraction Bett... the *other* Bett set up." I scrambled into my seat and toggled the power on.

The comm system squawked to life. "Unidentified spacecraft at dock seven five two, you are violating restricted space. Power down your engines and prepare for boarding." An armed cruiser appeared beyond the horizon of the sphere.

Or... maybe it *was* about us.

I hit the comm button while I nudged the flitter out just enough to make sure nobody could blast in from the dock behind us. "We're having technical problems here. Give me a minute." When in doubt, stall. They might not want to fire on us and risk damaging the sphere. Since we pretty obviously didn't have any weapons, they shouldn't be in any rush as long as it didn't look like we were getting away.

Touching the throttle and its sliver of cardinal crystal, I searched for a hyperspace path that could take us out of here. There. "Hang on," I warned my passengers. With the drive maxed out, I aimed the flitter.

A shudder went through our spacecraft. Suddenly, I couldn't see any hyperspace paths. All I could see was the black void of normal space, the sphere of the stasis prison, and a looming cruiser.

"Unidentified spacecraft, power down your engines and prepare for boarding." A pause, and then, "You must realize you can't escape."

I stared at the throttle, where the sliver of cardinal crystal had gone grey in its matrix. "Those vacuum-sucking..." Somehow, they'd destroyed the cardinal crystal.

"What's wrong?" Bett asked from the seat behind me.

"Little technical glitch. Don't go anywhere."

(*Never* let the passengers know about any problems. That was something I'd learned when I'd worked for the Micklages. When I'd piloted the large passenger ships, it avoided panic. And when I'd worked the smaller, private vessels, it kept everyone else from trying to "help". Trust me — panic is better than unwanted help.)

Without a cardinal crystal, we couldn't enter hyperspace. And even if there hadn't been a cruiser waiting to blast us out of space, the flitter didn't have the range to escape in normal space. I stuck my fingers through the metal mesh that separated the cargo hold from the passengers. "Scruffy, can you get a little closer?" If the synthetic crystal had also been damaged, it was all over.

Bett let out a breath. "You have to kill me before they

board. I know things the Oligarchy can't be allowed to learn about."

"Nobody's killing anyone yet." I pushed harder into the mesh while Scruffy wiggled forward, its progress hampered by the confined space.

A high-pitched squeal sounded to my left, broken by the sound of Bett slapping her palm against the hull. "We've been hit by laser fire," she said, voice breathless but tone even.

(Okay, but *actual* help from the passengers is fine.)

The cruiser drifted closer. "Unidentified spacecraft, power down your engines."

Another squeal started, and I heard the buckle of Bett's harness disengage. She stood up in her seat and placed her second palm over the new hole. "Rosey, if they fire on us much more, I'm going to run out of hands."

I smacked the comm button. "Hang on a minute! Which button turns it all off? The manual doesn't have an index."

(If you can't do anything else, confuse your enemy. This works surprisingly often.)

Cool metal brushed against my fingers. I closed my eyes. Hyperspace paths sprang into view all around me, almost making me cry in relief. There. That one would get us out of here. "Hold on tight. This is going to be bad."

We were almost perpendicular to the path's opening. That meant a nearly instantaneous course change that could send Bett flying to the other side of the cabin. Also, the route was *small* — there would be just enough room for the flitter. At least, I *hoped* there was enough room for the flitter.

"Unidentified spacecraft, prepare for —"

I engaged the hyperspace drive and ripped open the path.

FOURTEEN
CATASTROPHIC FAILURE

Clang! Our entry into hyperspace knocked me sideways so hard that my harness straps creaked. Bett had a death grip on the pilot's seat as she used two of her four hands to plug holes in the hull. But Scruffy didn't move, so I still had access to the synthetic cardinal crystal. "Another thirty seconds and I'll get us back into normal space," I said as the flitter bucked and jumped.

The path we were in threatened to close around us. Another path... there. The flitter banged again. Something either wasn't tied down, or had come loose. It hadn't torn the flitter apart — I didn't have to deal with it now.

Bett lost her grip on my seat and bounced off the ceiling. The squeal of air leaving the laser-cut holes in the hull was quickly cut off as she jumped back to her previous spot. "Got a patch kit?" Her voice jolted with the flitter.

Thankfully, I'd done a full pre-flight check. "Under the jump seat." Which she couldn't reach from her current spot. And I needed to keep one hand near Scruffy's crystal and the other on the flitter controls. Now I understood how useful four arms could be. "I'll grab it as soon as we get back to normal space."

"Sooner would be better than later," she said through gritted teeth. "I can't hang on much longer."

Instead of switching to another hyperspace path, I let the flitter follow the current one to its end. Blackness surrounded us. The flitter stilled, drifting in normal space. Other than distant stars, we were alone. Though we were outside the prison perimeter, we were still too close for my liking. Breathing atmosphere was the priority.

Contorting myself to reach under the jump seat, I pulled out the emergency kit and handed it to Bett. "You good here?" I needed to find out what was rattling around in the back of the flitter. We weren't carrying cargo.

"I've got it. Go look." Bett was already pulling the cover off the self-sealing adhesive with her teeth.

As I wormed my way to the back, I caught a faint whiff of burning polycarbonate. The air scrubbers took care of most of the evidence, but something had fried. Pulling off floor panels one by one, I exposed the thruster mechanism. "Well... this could be a problem." The coupling between the engine and the frame had partially melted, black streaks showing where it had been on fire. One strut had sheared off — that had been the rattling I'd heard.

Scruffy crouched next to me. "Captain, that thruster housing is likely to fail catastrophically if used."

The AI wasn't exaggerating. If I'd tried to maneuver once we'd come out into normal space, the aft end of the flitter would have exploded. No amount of self-sealing adhesive would fix that. "How close are we to anywhere we can dock?"

Scruffy backed up so I could close the panel. "The prison is the closest point with repair facilities."

"Other than the prison."

"Forty-seven light years."

That was a problem. Even if I *could* surf the hyperspace paths for that distance... without our thrusters I couldn't get us onto a hyperspace path in the first place.

I wriggled back up to the front cabin, hearing Scruffy taking a parallel path in the cargo space. Both hull punctures had been sealed, and Bett had collapsed in the jump seat, her skin looking pasty.

"Bett, we have a problem." When she opened her eyes, I told her the news. "I can send a message back to the spindle, but whoever's running the prison will have headed straight there. We were counting on arriving before them. If any ships come here from the spindle, they'll be followed."

But Bett had her own network.

She shook her head. "We can't send a message to the spindle anyhow. There's a mole. How do you think I got caught?" She rubbed a hand over her face. "Can we get word to the Chrysalis?"

"Do we *want* to?"

(Here's the thing: Religions are fine for people who want one. But the Chrysalis is an artificial planet full of people trying to body-mod their way to... something. I've never understood, and they've had enough accidental outbreaks of transformational plagues to worry anyone not already insane.)

"I have an acquaintance there who owes me a few favors."

I gestured her toward the comms board. "It's not like I have any better ideas."

Bett crawled up front and tapped at the board for a few minutes. Finally, she sat back. "There. Hopefully, they're still coherent enough to send help."

Sounded like someone from the Chrysalis, all right.

We watched the stars spin lazily as the flitter drifted. "So, how does it work with multiple clones? I mean, with multiple brain maps. Can you go back to one?"

"Ideally, they'll be merged into the next clone." Her voice was rough from exhaustion. "But if this body dies and I need these memories before the other clone dies, I may have to make a permanent split." She blew out a breath. "There's only so far the two sets can diverge and still be merged."

I thought about that. The only exclusive memories this clone had were from the time before this Bett was captured. Plus everything since we'd pulled her out of the simulation pod, of course, though I couldn't see how that would be useful.

Before I could ask another question, the ship's comm system chirped. "Unidentified spacecraft, you are suspected of violating restricted space. Prepare to be boarded."

It sounded like that same vacuum-sucking captain who'd threatened us just outside the prison sphere. Craning my head, I tried to get a visual on the ship. "How did they find us?" They couldn't have followed us through hyperspace.

"Good question." Bett's voice was grim. "Either this flitter has a beacon, or..."

Or Bett's Chrysalis acquaintance had sold her out.

As we slowly revolved, one star became brighter than the others — the approaching ship.

"They can't be allowed to take me alive."

To be honest, I wasn't super excited about ending up in their custody either. "Buckle up. Maybe I can get enough out of the thruster to get us into hyperspace." And maybe we would create our own little debris field trying.

"Captain," Scruffy said before I could power up the engines. "We have company."

Like a handful of powder thrown in slow motion, a flotilla of small ships emerged from hyperspace, weapons aimed at the approaching cruiser. Over the comm, I heard a multitude of voices, almost in sync. "Depart now. You have two seconds."

"Hope they don't mean us," I muttered.

"I think not," Bett replied, though she didn't sound entirely sure.

Then a volley of missiles headed toward the approaching cruiser.

FIFTEEN
FORTY-SEVEN

Trapped in the disabled flitter, Bett, Scruffy, and I watched on our screens as missiles advanced toward the prison cruiser. At the last second, the ship winked into hyperspace. Running to get reinforcements, probably, but I doubted they wanted to take on the Chrysalis. Nobody knew for sure how big the Chrysalis was, though there had to be a dozen small ships in the fleet Bett had called.

That left us facing the Chrysalis armada powering toward us without slowing. I braced myself. "I hope you know what you're doing."

Then the ships passed us, following the path of the missiles.

"Captain, the Chrysalis fleet is reclaiming their unused missiles, so they may be used again." Scruffy's metal body clanged against the floor as it moved to see through the view port. "It is a salient part of their philosophy that no resource should ever be left unclaimed."

That was putting it mildly. Every once in a while, a part of the Chrysalis would get a bad mutation and go absorb somebody else's stuff — satellites, junkyards, and, once, an entire moon. Eventually, a fix would ripple through and reparations would be made, but I'm not sure how you make up for taking a moon that had inspired stories and songs for generations. To say nothing of the tidal changes.

We watched as the fleet caught up to their unexploded missiles, then turned and headed back, like a flock of birds turning and wheeling in the sky. The beauty and grace of the movement underscored the connections between the ships — if individual pilots had tried to maneuver so closely, there would have been collisions. But that was how the Chrysalis worked — each individual was both a single organism and part of the larger body at the same time.

We watched them get closer. "Uh, stupid question, Bett, but they aren't planning on reclaiming *us*, are they?"

"Of course not." Bett applied the last of the sealant goo to the second patch. "I hope not."

"Super encouraging, thanks." A metal mesh surrounded us, scratching against our hull. Then we were being pulled into the cargo hold of the largest ship. I didn't recognize the model, which was odd. Between my years as a pilot and my time at the salvage yard, I thought I could recognize every-thing on sight. "What is that thing?"

"The ship?" Bett leaned closer to the view port so she could see something other than the open hold we were entering. "They sometimes roll their own."

(Right there, that tells you there's something wrong with anyone who joins the Chrysalis. I want a ship design that's had a chance to fail on a few thousand other people before it's released commercially. And even then, I prefer the older models.)

The flitter jolted to a stop amidst a hold of what looked

like asteroid debris, with the addition of a shiny new missile on the port side. As the cargo doors closed behind us, a portal umbilicus snaked across the space and clunked as it attached to our hatch. I helped Bett walk to the back of our ship, where Scruffy waited. Then I keyed in the code to open the hatch.

The air coming in smelled of salt and greenery. Before the hatch had finished opening, a man spoke. "Welcome, Bett One-arm forty-seven and guest. So that we might move without delay, we ask that you continue to your quarters." He gestured back down the umbilicus behind him. His only obvious mod was a skin overlay that gave him a faint glow and the sense of veins moving in slow motion just under the surface.

"Thank you for the assistance, Crania. The flitter likely has a hidden tracking device," Bett warned.

"Understood." He stood in place, waiting for us to move past. "It will be reclaimed immediately."

Supporting Bett and thinking about what was going on with that man's skin made me slow-witted; we had just exited the umbilicus into a wider fixed hallway on the ship when I realized why he had named her so oddly. "You've died forty-six times?"

"A few less than that. This isn't the first time a clone has been decanted before the previous me died."

We'd reached a confusing warren of passageways, with people in black overalls briskly carrying out their duties. The closest person pointed to the right, and Bett set off in that direction. I'd been looking around and listening to the thrum of the engines, so it took me longer than it should have to notice that the snippets of conversation spoken by passersby were all one communication meant for Bett.

"... were correct about the tracking..." said a man carrying fiber optic cable.

A woman passed, going the other direction, her words momentarily overlapping his. "... tracking device. It had a timer..."

Another man picked up the thread. "... timer, that would have deployed a beacon after some time had passed."

Having different people finishing each other's thoughts made my skin itch. But we were stuck on this ship until Scruffy and I could hitch a ride back to Bett One-arm — number forty-eight — where *Tiger Lily* was hopefully being repaired, even now. Then we would fuel up and make our way to the Independent Federation, where I could get paid my bonus for saving their special AI.

"You get used to it," Bett commented as we made another turn based on silent directions from a man whose clothing bore evidence of wading in an algae pond. "As far as Crania is concerned, those are just... different broadcast speakers, say, set up in the ship."

I waited until there was nobody else nearby, though I didn't doubt the ship monitored us. "If Crania talks through all those people, is there anything left of them?" Having never been attracted to hive minds, I'd never looked into them. This ship certainly wasn't changing my mind about joining. I didn't think I was the only one who felt that way — Scruffy, who hadn't said a word since we'd left the flitter, stayed right next to me.

Bett placed her palm against a plate. A door opened. "It's hard to explain. When a person joins the Chrysalis, the group mind changes them, but the individual also changes the group mind. It's a form of immortality, if you think about it."

"Said by the person who's died forty times," I muttered

to Scruffy. We went into a spacious room with two bunks. We'd found our quarters, apparently. The door automatically shut behind me. "How did you get involved with the Chrysalis?"

Bett collapsed onto her bunk, all four arms flopping limply by her side. "I joined them."

SIXTEEN

FLYING DEATH TRAP

I stared at Bett's relaxed form. "You joined... the Chrysalis?" My voice might have gone up a bit at the end there. It was one thing to be on a hive mind ship with a friend who had dealt with them in the past. It was quite another to find out she was one of them.

"A past me. Twice. Numbers four and twenty-two, if I remember correctly."

Even knowing Bett had been successively cloned dozens of times, that hadn't occurred to me. "So... Instead of dying and waking up in a new body, you..."

"Joined the Chrysalis with the previous body and woke up in my new body with all my memories up to that point." She opened one eye and slapped her chest. "I — from my perspective — have never joined the group mind, but two of the swarms have a part of me."

I sank down on the other bunk and thought about it. "But... Why?"

"Because the Chrysalis isn't controlled by the Oligarchy. In my line of work, you want to have friends everywhere, and the Chrysalis is a good friend to have. They did just rescue us, you know."

She had a point. Curiosity overtook my panic. "What does it feel like? To join them, I mean."

"I have no idea. I tried to keep recording both times, but the nanobots interfered with my memory matrix. All I remember is getting an injection. Then I woke up in my new body." Bett draped one forearm over her eyes. "I need to sleep. There's a reason those simulators are supposed to wake you up over a few hours."

"I apologize. I'm good at hiding, but running around a prison for three hours waiting for the normal shutdown seemed..." I pulled my boots off and settled them on the deck next to Scruffy.

Bett's lower left arm waved forgiveness. "Sorry. That wasn't meant as a complaint. If you hadn't pulled me out of there when you did..." By her voice, she was half asleep already.

Lying on the bunk, I worried about what the Chrysalis might find when they "reclaimed" the flitter. The cardinal crystal was shattered — hopefully, they would assume that had happened *after* we'd made our last hyperspace jump. They *couldn't* know about Scruffy or we'd never get off the ship.

Bett yawned. "What did you do with that evil cat of yours?"

Suddenly I missed Ensign Mowee and the trouble he caused. "Bett... Bett forty-eight is watching him."

She turned her head and opened one eye. "Really?" Then she returned to her former position. "Better her than me."

I spent a moment trying to decide if that was an oxymoron

— in a very real sense, the Bett forced to deal with my cat was the same as this Bett, especially if the two branches of herself could be successfully merged. Then I gave up and went back to worrying about the broken cardinal crystal on the flitter.

Bett snored softly.

Forcing myself to sit up before I fell asleep, I shoved my feet back into my boots.

Scruffy turned its head. "Captain, the reaction of the Chrysalis entity known as Crania may be unpredictable if you leave the cabin without Bett."

"I need to remove the cardinal crystal from the flitter." Not knowing how much surveillance went on inside the ship, I said no more. Logically, it made no sense to have interior cameras here, since normally anyone on the ship would be part of the hive mind. But I didn't want to bet my future on that.

The robot dog cocked its head. "I understand. I will retrieve it."

Tempting, but... "I don't trust them not to reclaim you if you're walking around out there." The bunk looked even more inviting now I was sitting up, but I got to my feet. "If I'm not back in fifteen minutes, wake Bett."

Scruffy didn't move from its spot in front of me. "Captain, do you remember the path back to the flitter?"

I grimaced. Scruffy had me there. And I couldn't expect the hive mind to direct me like they'd done when we'd come to this room. Or, I guess I could, but I'd have to explain where I was going, and possibly why. "Fine. We'll both go."

This time, I made an effort to listen to the people we passed, but instead of hive mind messages transmitted by multiple passersby, I got a sense of mild curiosity, as if they weren't quite sure what I was doing but they didn't feel the need to stop me yet. Or maybe Crania only spoke to Bett.

I tried my best to make it seem as if we were just out for a pleasant stroll while I followed Scruffy's cues through the maze of corridors. Aside from the creepy people, the layout of this ship was the clearest indication nothing here was normal. There was no reason to make a ship's interior into a maze.

Unless the layout was hiding something.

I was so turned around, they could have been concealing another hold three times the size of the one the flitter was in. I bet customs enforcers — who undoubtedly found the hive mind as creepy as I did — would speed through their checks. Interesting. I'd ask Scruffy for a map later.

In just a few minutes, we were back at the closed hatch leading to the cargo hold. But the umbilicus going to the flitter had been retracted, and the status light glowed a cautionary orange, indicating vacuum on the other side. Through the thick glass, I could see the man who had first welcomed us. He wielded a spray wand, coating the hull of the flitter with a silver sheen. And he wasn't wearing a suit.

"Why can't I have skin mods so I don't have to wear a vacuum suit?" I *hated* working in bulky suits. Everything always took three times as long as it should, and after an hour, the suit reeked. In the hold, a thin tube ran to the man's nostrils from a tank on his back; even with fancy skin mods, he still needed oxygen.

Scruffy reared onto its hind legs to look through the glass. "Those skin mods likely also protect the owner against the nanobots being sprayed on the flitter. Though I'm sure Crania would give you such a thing if you joined the Chrysalis."

Ignoring the second sentence, I seized on the first. "He's spraying nanobots?"

"The nanobots are another part of the hive mind. They bring everything down to its component parts and either store it for later use, or use it in current construction."

As we watched, the flitter hull buckled, metal trickling down to the deck and flowing in orderly lines to the back of the hold. The man kept spraying. More streams formed on the deck, this time thinner and lighter in color. The insulation under the hull, maybe? As it continued, I saw into the cabin, and then the seats slowly melted away.

There was no way we were retrieving the damaged cardinal crystal now. I'd just have to hope they didn't start asking questions about our last jump.

The process was mesmerizing. And also scary. You had to be crazy to work around something like that. It would break down a human being even more quickly than it had the flitter.

My mouth dried as I considered what was going on. "Scruffy, what's keeping the nanobots from destroying the rest of the ship?"

"The hold is likely treated with something to contain them."

Turning away from the cargo hold, I walked back the direction we'd come, Scruffy's metallic paws clicking on the deck plates next to me. Unable to contain myself, I whispered, "But why would they take that chance? Something that dangerous should be used in isolation."

Scruffy turned onto a corridor I didn't remember from the first trip. "For the Chrysalis, this *is* isolated. Even if the nanobots escaped containment, only this ship would be consumed. That is a mere fraction of the hive mind."

"Yes, but we're *on* this ship." Forget about the insanity of flying untested spacecraft. These people were casually spraying around something that could eat the only thing protecting them from vacuum. "We need to get back to Bett's spindle so we can pick up Ensign Mowee and *Tiger Lily*." And get off this flying death trap.

"Really, captain?" The snark was back.

Bett still slept when we accessed our cabin. As I climbed into my bunk, I felt the ship enter hyperspace. Deliberately not thinking about all the ways we could die, I pulled the pillow over my head and fell asleep.

When I woke up hours later, Scruffy was gone.

SEVENTEEN

THE MERGING

From within the cabin on the Chrysalis ship, I had no idea how long I'd slept. The hyperspace drive's hum no longer vibrated the deck, so we had arrived at our destination. Since I didn't know where we'd been headed, that didn't help.

I'd been expecting Scruffy to be sitting next to my boots, but the security bot frame wasn't in the cabin. "Scruffy?" I checked the lavatory to be thorough, but the robot dog — and experimental AI and synthetic crystal — was gone.

It figured. The minute I wasn't responsible for keeping the cat safe, some other part of my crew took off. At least when I'd been piloting passenger ships, I could just leave any stragglers behind.

Prodding Bett's arm elicited a mumbled, "Leave me alone."

I kept shaking her. "Bett! Wake up!" When she cracked open her lids, I said, "Scruffy's missing."

"Who?" She groaned and pushed herself up on two elbows. "Oh. Your security bot." She flopped back down on the bed, draping one forearm over her eyes. "It will be fine. And if it isn't, they'll make you a new one."

I hadn't told either version of Bett about Scruffy or the crystal it carried. Maybe it was time to start. "It's an AI that's not exactly legal, and I need to get it back to the Independent Federation."

After a long moment, Bett moved her arm just enough to look at me from the shadow of her elbow. "What did you get me involved in, Rosey?" Then she grunted and sat up. "No, sorry, I take it back. You put everything on the line to get me out of that prison. Let me think a bit." She scrubbed at her face. "Where would it have gone?"

"I don't know. I went with it to look at the cargo hold after you fell asleep." Then I stopped, distracted by the memory. "Did you know they're spraying around nanobots that melt everything down? One wrong move and the entire ship could disintegrate."

"Relax." She waved an arm. "They hardly ever have accidents."

(See, *this* is why clones get such a bad reputation. Why be careful when you can just decant a new body?)

Bett seemed to understand she'd lost me. "I promise. They do this all the time. We're safe. Now what happened after that?"

"After that, we came back here and I fell asleep."

She considered this. "And does it wander around by itself often? Oh, who am I kidding. An illegal AI is going to get into everything."

I started to deny it, but then realized I had no idea. "I don't know. There haven't been many 'wander around on its own' opportunities since I... met it." I'd almost said *found it*, but that might get Bett entirely too interested in Scruffy's origins.

"Ugh. Give me a minute to get ready and then let's go find this thing."

OUT IN THE CORRIDOR, the silence made my skin prickle. Other than the background noise of the air recycling system, it could have been a ghost ship. No other people walked through the halls. "Where *is* everyone?" A horrible thought occurred to me. "Those nanobots didn't reclaim them, did they?"

Bett didn't bother responding. She moved through the warren, peering down each offshoot as if looking for something. Too late, I realized we should have been marking the trail so we could find our room again. She looked over her shoulder. "I think... If I'm right, there will be another ship docked. We just need to get to the outer area so we can find a port and check."

"If you're right about what?" I followed her, hopelessly lost in the maze. "Who designs a ship like this?"

"It's not so much a design as an ongoing project. Think of it as a sculpture in progress. Ah, there we go." Bett turned another corner and hurried forward.

A large view port took up one wall, showing the empty expanse of space around us. As the ship slowly rotated, no planets came into view. There wasn't even a star close enough to support life. But a second ship, a different model from this one which I *also* didn't recognize, drifted nearby. "Another Chrysalis ship."

Bett nodded. "That explains where all the people are."

I stared at her. "They all *left*?" If I had to fly this heap back to civilization, the bridge had better look more standard than the rest of the ship.

"What? No. They're merging." She saw my look and waved a hand. "Let me find us some food and I'll explain." She darted down another corridor, speaking as she went. "Group minds are just people and hardware networked together by nanobots, right? They're always changing things, trying new modifications. But all the parts of a single group mind, like Crania, have the same nanobots or it would lose cohesion and fail. Aha!"

Bett stopped at an alcove where bulbs of water waited next to a large, unlabeled food replicator. "Without someone to help us, we're going to get something completely random, but it will be edible." She keyed in three digits. In a few seconds, the machine disgorged a bowl of sour-smelling soup in a wide-mouth bulb. Bett sniffed doubtfully. "So much for my lucky number. I guess it's better than nothing."

I chose my pilot's license number and was rewarded with curried noodles. Running a hand over the side of the machine, I wondered if I could somehow sneak it off the ship with me when I went back to *Tiger Lily*. Or more realistically, make a deal with the Chrysalis. I'd lose a chunk of my cargo hold, but it would be worth it. Grabbing water, I rushed after Bett. "The merging?"

"When Chrysalis ships interact, they exchange nanobots. Then the minds pick and choose from the new parts and integrate what they want. Think of it as an upgrade. By exchanging regularly, the Chrysalis as a whole stays intact. Mostly."

"Where are we going?"

Bett chose another corridor that looked exactly like the last, but she gave a pleased huff. "My guess is your robo-dog has gone to observe. There has to be a room big enough for all the people to congregate. That's the thing about the merging — the nanobots have to get distributed all at once.

Otherwise, the group mind can fragment. If we're lucky, we'll get there in time to see the end of it."

Tipping noodles into my mouth as we walked, I wondered why Bett thought Scruffy would find this interesting. Then I stopped wondering as I saw Scruffy rushing toward us, metal feet clattering on the deck plates.

"Captain de Mure!" It skidded to a stop next to me. "Come quickly!"

Bett spoke before I could. "You found the merging."

Scruffy flipped around and started back the way it had come. "Yes. But something went wrong. I think we've been hijacked."

EIGHTEEN
HIJACKED

"Hijacked?" Bett sounded skeptical as she followed Scruffy's metallic form through the corridors.

I trailed behind. "Nobody could possibly *want* this ship." I wasn't even sure anyone who wasn't part of the Chrysalis could *fly* it. Everything else was so non-standard, the bridge was bound to be equally unusual. "And wouldn't any of the minds of the Chrysalis be able to create their own?"

Scruffy's feet clicked on the deck plates. "Historically, group minds go to war over ideas." It stopped. "Hide."

Bett pulled me into an alcove behind a machine that smelled of rancid algae. A strong current of air flowing into the vent directly above us ruffled my clothes and explained why we hadn't smelled this from the corridor. Trying not to gag, I pulled my tunic up over my nose and made an effort not to touch anything. If I walked around the ship smelling like this, anyone tracking me would be able to follow the odor.

Scruffy merely folded its head and limbs under its body.

Unless someone expected a robot dog, it looked like some random bit of machinery left in an awkward place.

Three people walked by. I caught glimpses of their mustard colored coveralls and a hand holding a stunner. The clothing color wasn't one I'd seen on Crania before, though that meant nothing — I hadn't seen most of the ship, and this could have been what the piloting crew wore. But even when we'd first arrived, there had been no hand-held weapons. Why would there be? Every other living being on the ship was a part of it.

Bett waited until Scruffy stood before pulling me back into the corridor. "Historically," she whispered, "group minds at war blow each other up. I think this must be an information raid." We crept along the corridor. "Crania must know something the other group mind wants."

The next corner opened up to a padded room larger than the cargo hold. Bodies were sprawled on every surface, unmoving. Hundreds of bodies. With no visible wounds, it looked as if the entire ship's crew had just... died. Back when I'd been a child, when the Traveling Tuxedo's life support system had been hacked, these were the sort of pictures that made it onto the news feeds — bloodless, silent death. I took a step back.

"They're alive," Bett whispered. "And even if these bodies died, the group mind survives as long as the ship is intact."

The woman splayed on the ground next to my foot inhaled. I knew Bett was right about the group mind, but the evidence of life made me feel better. "Are they going to wake up?"

Bett turned the woman on her side so she could breathe more easily. "If the other group mind is trying to get information, it will launch a series of nanobot modifications until this crew is using the same bots as the other crew. At that point, the other ship will merge completely and have access to all of Crania's information."

This all sounded like a fight I didn't want to get in the middle of. "Can we somehow convince the ship to fabricate another flitter?"

"We can't leave them like this."

We absolutely *could* if we had a flitter, but from Bett's expression, she wasn't going to help me search for one. "You really want to get in the middle of a Chrysalis civil war?"

Bett's face tightened. "I joined Crania because they agreed to keep my secrets. This other group mind never made that promise. And it's not like you have nothing to lose here, either, unless you think Crania didn't notice anything odd about the flitter's cardinal crystal."

The flitter's cardinal crystal, which had shattered before we'd made our last hyperspace jump — apparently Bett hadn't been too busy patching leaks to notice. I snuck a glance at Scruffy. If the attacking group mind took it apart to find the secret of the synthetic crystal, Scruffy would be dead and I'd be left with no reward, no crystal, and no way home. "Fine. What's the plan?"

Images ran through my head of Bett charging into battle with a stunner crackling in each of her four hands. Bett had been a pirate of sorts — she'd probably be great at hand-to-hand combat. I hoped she wasn't counting on me for tactical support; with my shooting ability, I'd be a liability instead of an asset. More importantly, we didn't have any weapons.

"The ship must be able to generate previous versions of nanobots. They've had to revert before. We just need to get some and inject them into the bodies here. Once that's done, the ship should be able to finish recovering on its own." She continued to roll the limp people on their sides.

"Bett, this ship has to have all kinds of security. It isn't going to just give us a specific version of nanobots."

"Not us. Me." She moved another body. "Ah, here we are."

On first glance, the necklace Bett pulled off the woman appeared to be a Thetan fertility charm. With a flick of Bett's fingers, it unraveled into a long fiber ribbon. Bett held up the connector on one end. "If we can get to the bridge, Scruffy might be able to convince the ship this is an emergency, especially if I can give it biometrics it recognizes."

The biometrics would be for Bett's clone. Would there be differences? I didn't have any better idea, so I nodded. "Then I guess we should get to the bridge..."

... without getting caught.

NINETEEN
NORMAL

After an hour of following Scruffy and Bett as we tried to find the bridge, I was hopelessly lost and ready to pick a direction and blast my way in a straight line using the missiles we'd seen stacked neatly in a cargo bay.

Twice, we'd had to hide from crew members from the hijacking group mind.

"Do they know we're here?" I lowered myself down to the deck from the high cabinet Bett and I had stuffed ourselves into.

Bett climbed down with the grace that having four arms gave. "They must suspect someone is here. Or maybe this is normal procedure when they attack another group mind."

Scruffy waited at the next junction. "This should take us to a part of the ship we have not yet covered."

My feet ached. "Maybe we could find a lifeboat and use it to take us along the hull."

Scruffy and Bett ignored me.

The flavor of the air changed from sea breezes and growing things to an ozone-tinged dryness. To me, it smelled of electronics and home. We turned another corner and there it was. For the first time since we'd stepped onto the ship, my surroundings were familiar. I'd worked in this exact layout at the start of my career. "This ship started out as a Micklage Comet."

"Can you fly it?"

Could I? I could have flown the original configuration in my sleep. If we could make a quick hop through hyperspace, we'd have more time to restore Crania's crew. But most of the ship had been changed into something I didn't recognize. "I don't know." It hurt to admit that.

Bett nodded. "We'll keep that as a last resort. Where's the direct port?"

I took the cable from her and plugged one end into the console. Then I paused, remembering what had happened when Scruffy had been connected to *Tiger Lily*. "Scruffy, this isn't going to harm you, is it?"

"Captain de Mure, we do not have a choice." Scruffy sidled closer until the bot's port brushed against my hand.

I plugged in the cable.

"Interesting. It is as if —" The robo-dog jerked and tipped over.

Bett and I looked from the metallic frame to each other.

She spoke first. "Huh."

I was slightly better prepared, having seen Scruffy's silence when interfacing with *Tiger Lily*. "I think this may be... normal?"

"Right."

If Scruffy's sophisticated artificial brain had been wiped, we were all in trouble. More trouble. "Remember the first time we met?"

Back then, I'd still been working the nice safe cruise route, relaxing in an on-planet bar after what should have been my day off. Bett had been running down the street, chased by the local police. Since my day had consisted of paying bribes to the local law enforcement so I could get idiot passengers out of trouble, my sympathies had been with the four-armed stranger. Pretending to be more drunk than I was, I'd stumbled into the pursuers and fallen. It had earned me a few kicks to the ribs, but Bett had doubled back later when it was safe to introduce herself.

"Yes. Is this the point when you tell me you wish you'd ignored me and kept drinking?" She leaned against the railing around the pilot's chair.

"Life would have been simpler, but no. You offered me a job that night. And the next, what, five or six times we ran into each other?" We'd spent a fair amount of time together, but I'd never accepted her offer of full-time employment. "Then you stopped asking. Why?"

Bett sighed. "Because I realized at some point, I might need a pilot who couldn't be traced back to me."

I thought about that. "So when I got stuck on Buatrier..."

"When you and Rance had your showdown, I was... let's say, *indisposed*."

Dead and waiting on a new body, I assumed.

"The Micklages were watching you closely at the beginning, and by the time I could do anything, you had a job and a place to live, so I held back. Then I got captured." She shrugged. "I don't know how much time my new clone has been active. Did she get you off-planet?"

"No." Unless the grav unit shielding panels had been ordered by Bett's clone. "I don't think so." Had it been Bett Forty-eight? I still didn't know who had started me on the path to find Scruffy. "It's possible, though she didn't say anything."

"She wouldn't."

The robo-dog jerked back to life, flipping to its feet with

a clatter. "I believe I have convinced Crania there is a problem. If you would..."

Before Scruffy could finish the sentence, green lasers scanned the space, humming as they zeroed in on Bett. She held still, eyes open despite the glare. The lasers cut out, leaving the room in silence.

I waited for something to happen. Five seconds went by. "Did it work?"

Bett shook her head. "I don't..."

With a whirr and a clunk, a drawer opened at the captain's station, revealing two multi-dose hypo spray guns. I grabbed them before the drawer closed again and handed one to Bett. "Hopefully, this is what we need."

If we could get back to the merging room, dose all the bodies there, survive long enough for them to recover, and somehow repel the other ship, then I could figure out how to get back to the other Bett's spindle where *Tiger Lily* and Ensign Mowee waited. After that, it would be smooth sailing to the Independent Federation and a huge reward. No problem.

I detached the fiber cable from Scruffy and set the coil down on the captain's chair. "Let's go."

TWENTY
SPRAY, CUT, MOVE

"Just hold it against their neck and hit the button." Bett suited words to action, and the hypo spray bucked in her hand. "There's some recoil, so you need to push firmly against the skin."

We were back in the merging room, where limp bodies spread over the padded surfaces. Picking a man with tattoos scrolling over his blue arms, I set the hypo spray against his neck. "Like this?"

"Yes. Now hit the button."

Gripping the tube more tightly, I triggered the unit. It jerked, though not as much as I'd been expecting. One down. Other than a swiftly fading red mark, the man looked unchanged. I glanced at the sea of bodies. "How are we going to know which ones we've done?"

Would it hurt them to have more than one dose? Would we run out of the reverted nanobots if we wasted a dose? And how safe was it to handle this thing? I didn't want to accidentally join the group mind.

Bett searched a few bodies for tool kits and tossed me a knife. "Cut a hole in their clothing near the neckline." She watched me handle the knife and hypo spray. "Just don't get confused and accidentally push the knife into their neck."

"Very funny. Must be nice to have enough hands to hold everything." I put the hypo spray on the floor and sliced through the man's tunic.

Bett was already done with the next person.

We worked methodically from one side of the room to the other. Spray, cut, move. Scruffy positioned itself by the entrance to watch for danger. Once, it buzzed and folded itself down. There was nowhere to hide, so Bett and I burrowed under the nearest bodies, holding still and hoping they wouldn't notice two extra people.

(Holding still is not one of my strengths. But it's amazing how much room for growth you can find when you're trying to avoid capture by the people who have taken over a ship.)

When Scruffy gave the all-clear, we scrambled to our feet. I straightened my clothing while trying to forget unmoving bodies piled on top of me. "When we get back, Forty-eight isn't allowed to complain about watching my cat," I hissed. "I've more than made up for it."

Spray, cut, move to the next one. My back ached. It felt like we'd been at this for a lifetime, but we were only halfway through and the first people we'd injected still weren't moving. "What if this doesn't work?"

Bett's movements never slowed. "Then you fly us all somewhere to get help."

Spray, cut, move. The rhythm put me into a kind of trance. That's the only way to explain how I missed Scruffy's next warning. Bett's hissed, "Rosey!" came too late. I had just enough time to drop to the floor when a woman in mustard overalls appeared.

For a moment, I thought I had stopped moving in time,

but she walked toward me, casually stepping over bodies along the way.

Using the surrounding bodies to camouflage my movement, I shoved the hypo spray under the nearest limp person. Then I was up on my feet and jumping over obstacles.

"Stop." The woman's voice was flat, with no more emotion than the food replicator.

I ignored her and ran, expecting her to shoot me in the back before I could get away, but nothing happened. My boots clanked against the deck plates when I sprinted out of the merging room. Then I was in the ridiculous warren of corridors, trying to remember how to get to the bridge. Why hadn't I marked the route somehow?

The longer I kept the hijackers chasing me, the longer Bett would have to rouse the crew. I glimpsed orange fabric in the distance and ducked around a corner. Everything here smelled of machine oil. While I couldn't keep a diagram of this maze in my head, the scents of different areas of the ship let me build a rudimentary map. Or it would have, if I'd been in this section before. All I knew was this was an area we hadn't passed through on our way to the bridge.

Another glimpse of a mustard colored jumpsuit made me dive to the side. In the middle of congratulating myself on my ability to evade an entire group mind, it occurred to me they weren't running after me. They weren't hurrying at all.

They were *herding* me.

I needed to get out of this maze. Crouching behind cleaning equipment in an alcove, I considered my options. The missiles in the cargo bay called to me, but I had no way of getting them and realistically, it would be suicide to use them in the ship's interior. The ventilation ducts? They wouldn't be big enough for me to use to traverse the ship, but maybe I could hide in one of the larger ducts.

Or... if I could find an airlock with suits, I could go outside along the hull. That thought appealed until I started thinking about how well suits would be maintained in a group mind that saw bodies as replaceable. I moved that option to the bottom of the list, just above the missiles. Once I got off this thing, I was never setting foot on a Chrysalis ship ever again.

None of the invading crew was in sight. I crouched in front of the air intake, prying at the covering with my borrowed knife. Ten seconds later, I was staring at the space beyond, wondering if this was a good idea. A standard air vent was one thing — this was something else. Iridescent walls pulsated. The area was big enough to hide in, but I wasn't entirely sure it wasn't going to absorb me if I touched it.

Being eaten by a Chrysalis life support system hadn't been on my list of rational fears until this moment.

Swinging my feet in, I muttered, "Stars take this entire deathtrap." The walls shivered where my boots touched them. I shimmied into the space, avoiding the sides as much as I could. There. I was in the duct and nothing terrible had happened. All I had to do was pull the cover over the opening, and I'd be safe while I figured out my next move.

When I reached out to pick up the grate, stunner fire crackled into my chest and up my spine.

Everything went black.

TWENTY-ONE
FASHIONED CHILD OF DISRESPECT

When I regained my senses, I was lying on the deck plates with a woman in mustard color coveralls standing over me. Her silvering hair was too lusterless to be a fashion choice, but her light brown face seemed curiously unlined for her age. The disconnect made it easier to remember she was no longer entirely human.

I sat up slowly, buying time to collect my thoughts. My only goals now were to stay alive and keep Bett and Scruffy unnoticed as long as possible so they could return Crania to health. Sure, matching wits with a group mind was a little out of my skill set, but I could do this. No problem.

"Master Pilot Rose de Mure." The woman replaced a portable biometric scanner on her belt. "We require the fashioned child of Disrespect."

I blinked, wondering if the stunner had scrambled something in my brain. All the individual words were recognizable, but I couldn't parse them in any way that made sense. "You what... huh?"

So much for matching wits.

Her blank expression didn't change. "Data exists. You

assumed guardianship of the fashioned child of Disrespect. We require this, or its current location."

With the repetition of the phrase, some buried thought poked at me. I hoped I wasn't having a post-stunner stroke. No, wait. *Fashioned child* was one of those terms that showed up on the entertainment vids from the Independent Federation. It was what they called an artificial intelligence.

(In the first weeks after I'd left Micklage employ, I'd holed up with Ensign Mowee in a cheap rental box, combing through listings to find a ship I could afford. During that time, I'd watched seven seasons of *My Stars, My Family*, a drama about a cluster of Independent Federation merchant traders with backstabbing, affairs, betrayals, and questionable fashion choices aplenty. Don't judge. It was a hard time for me.)

Now that I'd figured out they were looking for an Independent Federation AI, my brain helpfully supplied the memory of how Scruffy had introduced itself. Scruffy Note of Disrespect. At the time, I'd assumed it had just strung some words together, but maybe the *of Disrespect* part was a family name of sorts. "Oh, that AI in the salvage yard? I left that with Orabella Fink. As far as I know, it's still in Dancig City on Buatrier."

She blinked twice. "This is untrue. The fashioned child of Disrespect left traces in a stasis prison in the Voods Cluster."

Had Scruffy been sending signals without me noticing? "What kind of traces?" I didn't really care, but the longer I kept her talking, the longer it would take to get to the threats of throwing me out the airlock.

"The code attack that opened all the stasis pods bears the mark of the fashioned child of Disrespect."

My bark of laughter echoed in the corridor. "Someone

coded a jailbreak?" Good for Scruffy. It must have done that to help with Bett's distraction. "That's a shame."

The woman ignored my response. "We can find no trace of the fashioned child in Crania's mechanical systems. Therefore, it must not be integrated at this time. We require the location of its physical presence."

I shrugged. "Scruffy is its own being. I don't control its movements."

A second member of the invading crew rounded the corner, this one a man with the same type of skin mods I'd seen on the cargo hold worker. Without a word, he and the woman hauled me to my feet and dragged me along the hall.

"Wait! Where are we going?"

They both spoke in unison. "You have been selected to become a member of Ecom. We are delivering you for processing."

So if *Ecom* was the group mind that had attacked Crania, that meant... "Absolutely not! I'm not joining the Chrysalis."

I jerked my arm out of the man's hold. Intent on keeping the woman from accessing her stunner, I threw my weight against her. We crashed into an alcove, cracking a translucent bio-tank. Black liquid sloshed over her arm. She froze, then dropped limply to the floor.

Black holes and stars, what was in that tank? Did this ship have *any* safety standards?

Using the man's body as a shield to keep the liquid off me, I pushed him against the mess. He threw out a hand to keep his balance, palm landing flat in the black goo. Then his eyes rolled up and he dropped to the deck.

I considered taking the woman's stunner, but that required moving her body to reach it, and her clothing was soaking up the liquid seeping from the tank. Both of them were still breathing, but I couldn't chance getting whatever that was on me.

Ecom knew where I was and they would send more of their people. I needed to be elsewhere, fast.

I picked a direction and ran.

While I'd been herded by Ecom before, now that they were down two bodies, I might be able to get past them. I was still hopelessly lost, but I'd learned to pay attention to my nose. When I came to the next major junction, I stepped into each corridor and inhaled deeply. Grass and mushrooms. Ammonia and burned sugar. Dust and... ozone?

I scrambled into the third option and sprinted, hoping the sound of my boots hitting the deck plates would be lost in the background noise of the sleeping ship. After a while, I recognized my path. The bridge was just a bit farther. Assuming the controls weren't too greatly modified, I could jump the ship somewhere away from Ecom and we would have time to get Crania's crew back to normal. Then Bett, Scruffy, and I could get off this thing and hitch a ride back to the spindle where Ensign Mowee and *Tiger Lily* waited.

A glimpse of orange in the distance made me throw myself down a side corridor, where I stumbled over tools and metal scattered across the deck. I hoped whatever was dismantled wasn't important for flying — I knew every bit of *Tiger Lily*, down to the last gasket, but with this ship? It might have been anything from waste reclamation to a coupling of the hyperspace drive.

There *had* to be another way to the flight controls.

The blare of the hull breach alarm vibrated the deck. Heart racing, I forced myself to hold still. Even if I'd known how to find the damage, Ecom would capture me before I could help patch the hole. All I could do was avoid everyone and hope we didn't lose too much atmosphere. Surely this ship would have emergency hatches for each section, wouldn't it? I winced at the thought and rubbed the spot between my eyes.

Two men in orange coveralls ran past my side corridor. Peeking around the corner, I didn't see anyone else.

Behind me, there was the click of metal robo-dog feet on deck plates. "Captain de Mure, now would be a good time to find out if you can fly this ship."

TWENTY-TWO
EXTENUATING CIRCUMSTANCE

I whirled around to see the robotic dog standing behind me. "Scruffy!" With the still-wailing klaxon, I wasn't worried about being heard, and it was such a relief not to be alone anymore. I glanced past it and saw only an empty corridor. "Wait, where's Bett?" If Bett had been captured and taken to the other ship, we couldn't go anywhere until we got her back.

"She remains in the merging room to assist the members of Crania as they recover. They are beginning to wake now." It moved forward. "The bridge is this way, Captain."

I trotted along behind it. "Scruffy, we can't leave with a hole in the hull."

"There is no breach. The ship agreed the alarm would be the fastest way to remove the intruders from the bridge." It turned one last corner and there was the command center. "But we may only have limited time before the invading group mind realizes the subterfuge."

Throwing myself into the pilot's chair, I let muscle memory take over. Warm the engines, safety checks, ping the cardinal crystal to make sure it was present. The displays were mostly standard, though the ship's configuration didn't match what I was used to seeing. A warning flickered to life. "Ecom's shuttle is still docked, and our bay doors are open."

"Is that a problem?"

"The minute I start closing the bay doors, they'll know where we are. Depending on how long the doors take to close, Ecom's people might get here before I can take us into hyperspace." I scanned the rest of the controls, glad to find everything where I expected it to be.

"Can we enter hyperspace with the bay doors open?"

"We *could*." I cleared my throat. "But the shuttle won't be tied down tightly, and it has an umbilicus connecting it to the cargo bay. If things aren't smooth, the shuttle could be ejected, and the umbilicus might keep it tethered to us. A shuttle repeatedly crashing into the hull would not be ideal."

Scruffy wedged itself under the navigator's chair, a spot which gave it a good view down the corridor and also gave it something to hang onto. "Captain, I do not wish to disparage your piloting skills, but I have traveled into hyperspace with you multiple times, and none of those trips could be described as 'smooth'."

It had a point. But also... "There were extenuating circumstances."

"And this is..."

"Right. Another extenuating circumstance. But you should know, I don't usually fly like that." I hit the button to close the cargo bay. It blinked, a sign the closure was in progress. "Let me know if you see anyone coming." The ship would sound an alarm for the crew and passengers when the hyperspace drives spun up. For now, though, I wanted to get a feel for the ship, so I nudged our normal-space engines.

The ship barely moved. "That's weird." Either the engines were weaker than I thought, or we had a *lot* more mass than I'd expected. I opened the throttle.

"Weird, Captain?"

On the wall display, Ecom's ship dropped back. They hadn't reacted to our lumbering departure yet. "You've mapped the ship. Is there an extra hold packed with lead or something? We seem to have more mass than I can account for." The light for the cargo bay door still blinked.

Closing my eyes, I switched my thoughts over to the pilot's sphere. The galaxy unfolded behind my lids, star paths glittering. Using an actual cardinal crystal took less effort than Scruffy's version, but I missed the crispness of the synthetic crystal. For this jump, it wouldn't matter — unlike the flitter, this ship was big enough to hold open any path we could enter.

"Captain, there is not any hidden space the size of a hold on this ship."

Where was all the extra mass coming from? I automatically catalogued the paths around us as I considered. We needed something big enough to let this barge in, but preferably short enough that we wouldn't be in hyperspace for more than a few minutes. Plus, it couldn't terminate in a star or planet. Or too near a populated area that might be controlled by the Micklage family. Or anywhere close to the stasis prison.

The way my life had been going, soon half the universe would be off limits for me.

Scruffy's voice cut into my musing. "The only area able

to contain a significant mass is the hull itself. Perhaps with a platinum or osmium alloy included."

"Why would...?" I let the question go unasked. Asking why the Chrysalis group minds did things never helped. Maybe they all got together and rammed each other's ships in some weird dominance display.

"It would likely render the ship impervious to the energy that destroyed the cardinal crystal on the flitter."

"Huh." Maybe the group minds *did* do things for a reason. It didn't matter now. I'd found a good hyperspace path. Without opening my eyes, I set the ship accelerating in a graceful arc toward the opening. Then I had to change my calculations, as the engines couldn't make the turn I'd planned. Whatever Crania had used in the hull, it was *dense.*

Our new course would have us entering the star path at an unfortunate angle, but we should still make it. "This might be a little bumpy." Luckily, with the speed we were going, I had some time to straighten us out.

"Captain, there are invaders in the corridor. I will engage."

"Stay where you are." The deck plates vibrated as I maxed out all the engines. With another finger tap, the hyperspace drives spun up and the ship's comm system pinged a warning. It reminded me I'd forgotten to strap in yet again. I hooked a foot around the base of the chair.

We were coming in at an angle so oblique, we might glance off the opening. If that happened, Scruffy would have to fight off the Ecom crew while I wrestled this wallowing barge into another approach.

No. We had to make it on the first try. Cutting one aft engine, I let the ship swing around before opening the throttle again. There. That was better. It would still be rough, but I was sure we would make it through.

Mostly sure.

Somewhat sure.

Before I could downgrade my prediction any further, we hit the opening with a jolt that sent me flying across the bridge. My head hit the specially reinforced hull and everything went black.

TWENTY-THREE

MOSTLY GOOD

I woke to find Scruffy and Bett staring down at me. My surroundings had changed. Instead of the bridge, I was back in the cabin Crania had sent us to when we'd first boarded the ship. Weirdly, my head didn't hurt. "What happened?"

"You hit your head." Bett's smile was fixed, as if she was nervous about something. Never a good sign.

"That's the only thing I *did* know." I sat up, swung my feet to the floor, and touched my head gingerly, expecting to find a bandage or a huge bump, but there was nothing. How long had I been out? Had we gotten away from Ecom? Were we still in *hyperspace*? Wait, no, I couldn't feel the hum of the hyperspace engines.

Bett held up all four hands. "Don't panic. Things are mostly good. Crania's back in charge, the ship's pilot recovered enough to get us safely into normal space, and they're taking us to another one of my spindles. We'll grab a ship from there and get you back to *Tiger Lily* and your evil cat while I start rooting out the leak in my organization."

Another of Bett's spindles? I'd thought she only had one, which she lived on... Right. Multiple clones of Bett, multiple spindles. That explained how she always seemed to be in the right place at the right time. Then my brain caught up with what else she had said. "*Mostly* good?"

Bett cleared her throat. "You hit your head pretty hard. More than pretty hard. There was some damage."

Scruffy spoke up for the first time. "Captain, you were suffering from an intracranial hemorrhage that would have been fatal without intervention."

I looked from one to the other. "Since I'm not dead, I assume you intervened. The ship must have a decent medical unit." Better than the one I used to keep patching up Ensign Mowee every time he took on a bigger and meaner creature anyhow. Mowee had a patchwork of scars hidden under his fur. If I'd gone into my med unit with the same injury, I'd have a scar running from one side of my head to the other. And one of my ears might be in the middle of my forehead.

(I know, I know, I should have been saving money for a new med unit instead of pricing out a galley, but there's only so much rehydrated freeze-dried food I can take. The only one using our med unit was Mowee, and I kept imagining that someday he'd make better decisions.)

"Hmm."

It was the most non-committal sound I'd ever heard Bett make. Before I could dig into it, a series of beeps came from the door.

Bett brightened. "Ah, the shuttle must be here. Hurry up. Crania and I would rather our association not be known. They need to leave before someone asks what they're doing in this area of space." Having said that, she walked out the door with the air of a woman escaping a tricky conversation.

I watched the door close behind her. "Is there a mirror

around here?" The way Bett was acting, they'd reconfigured my features while I was out. My nose felt the same, but it wasn't as if I'd ever memorized its shape.

Scruffy pushed my boots closer with its nose. "Captain, we should go."

"Fine." Whatever they weren't telling me, it could wait until we were on the shuttle. I shoved my feet into my boots and stood up.

Out in the corridor, I automatically headed toward the cargo bay. Scruffy's metal paws clanked on the deck next to me. Then my stomach gurgled, and I remembered the food replicator. Surely nobody would mind if I made a quick detour so I could grab a bowl of curried noodles. It was only a few turns out of our way, and we could save time by cutting through the fabrication chamber on the way to the shuttle.

My footsteps slowed, then stopped. "Scruffy." All the air seemed to have left the corridor. "Why do I suddenly know the layout of this ship?" My voice sounded tinny and far away. "Did you let them add me to Crania?"

"Captain, you are not part of Crania."

The band constricting my chest eased. Of course I wasn't part of Crania. I would know if I was part of a group mind. How could I not? My thoughts wouldn't be my own. "Okay, good, because if I'm stuck in this group mind, our deal to get you to the Independent Federation is off." I started walking again.

Scruffy didn't follow. "Captain, you are not part of Crania, but you *are* part of the Chrysalis."

I stopped and turned around to look at the robo-dog. "I... What?"

It trotted forward, stopping just out of my reach. "Crania doesn't have medical units, per se. Everything is done with its nanobots. So when it looked like you were going to die, we injected you with nanobots. It was the only way to save you."

"So I *am* part of Crania."

"No. You — and I — are a new group mind. It was the only way to have the nanobots repair your brain without having you become a part of Crania. I received the knowledge I need from the Crania AI. As there are no other biological members, you need not worry about data pulls from other beings. But when you needed the ship layout..."

My brows lifted so far, they might have been in my hairline. "What you're saying is you're in my head."

"No, what I'm saying is you are in mine." Scruffy stood up and walked past me, heading toward the cargo bay. "This isn't what I wanted either, but it seemed necessary at the time." For the first time, bitterness overwhelmed its sarcasm.

I watched it disappear around the next corner. But even though Scruffy was out of sight, I knew exactly where it was. Blowing out a long breath, I tried to move past my own fear. This had been necessary. I'd have been dead if Bett and Scruffy hadn't made this decision. And I would be part of the huge group mind Crania if Scruffy hadn't sacrificed itself.

Crud. I ran after the robo-dog. "Scruffy, wait. I'm sorry!" I sprinted for the cargo bay.

A chime rang through every cell in my body. I heard a voice in my head, and somehow I knew it was Crania. *"Welcome to the Chrysalis, group mind Scruffy!"* I passed a line of people with the green coveralls of aquaponics workers. They smiled at me, as if they thought the situation funny, and spoke the words that rang in my head. *"We look forward to seeing you in the future."*

TWENTY-FOUR

STOP THINKING

Bett — Bett forty-seven, that is — had to be smuggled off the shuttle when we came to Bett thirty-four's spindle. "Can't have people wondering how she's teleporting around the station if they're watching the monitors," my Bett said as she resigned herself to the wait. "At least I'll have something to eat. Thirty-four will send in an automated cart to restock the shuttle, and I'll hitch a ride out in that."

I'd spent the last hour trying to wrap my head around the idea that I was now part of a group mind. Sure, it was a group mind comprising one human, me, facilitated by an AI, Scruffy. But a group mind nonetheless. Crania had implied the Chrysalis as a whole was delighted to welcome us as one of them, but Crania had just come incredibly close to being taken over by another group mind. The whole lot of them were not sane, as humans defined the term.

Bett thirty-four sent an aide to bring me to her out in the open. Scruffy was back to pretending to be a security robo-dog, smart enough to identify threats but not so smart it could be used for corporate espionage. I followed the bald woman, listening to her practiced narration about the features of the spindle as we walked.

"And, of course, we're known for our ship market," she said, pointing through a view port where a dozen ships hung tethered to a flex-shaft. All of them looked space-worthy, at least from the outside — I guess there was no point in hauling a ship off-planet after it plowed into the ground like every wreck at Orabella's salvage yard.

The largest ships were Micklage Falcons, but I saw a Kestrel and two Sparrows. They even had a Lynx II, the model just before *Tiger Lily*, though it had an odd curve to the frame that made me wonder what would happen if a pilot tried to fly in atmosphere. It definitely hadn't come out of the factory like that. Then again, it was a Lynx. A little structural damage might not slow it down.

"And there we have the ship repair center." The aide waved a hand along the curve of the corridor before guiding me into the elevator. "Any ship that makes it here will fly away like new. That's our motto."

Random facts kept popping into my brain, things I was fairly certain I'd never known: the location of seventeen food markets (I was still hungry) scattered across multiple levels of the spindle; every navigation hazard in this system (when I saw the glint of a planet through the elevator's view port); the purchase history of that Lynx II we were gliding away from.

(The Lynx had been purchased new by a family group, sold by an heir thirty standards later to a small shipping company, seized two standards after that to cover docking fees, sold to an artist who had done *something* to the frame, captured by raiders, recovered by the artist, and then sold to the dealer at the spindle recently when the artist had upgraded to a larger ship so they could start their own colony. I still had my doubts about the ship's frame, but apparently it had been like that for the last fifteen standards. I'm telling you — the Lynx series was built to *last*.)

Stay out of my brain, I thought at Scruffy while smiling at a stale joke the aide had just made.

Stop thinking, *and it won't be a problem.* Scruffy's reply sounded just like Scruffy — sarcastic and maybe a little worried.

"And here we are!" The aide stopped to let an armored door open in front of us. "Bett's private suites. There are snacks on the side table, and if you have any requests, just ask." She backed out of the room and was gone.

I piled a plate full of little fried cakes made from rice and greens. "So... I guess we wait here until Bett comes and then borrow a ship?"

"Woof." In my head, Scruffy said, *Bett forty-seven believes there is a traitor in her ranks. We may be monitored.* As an illegal AI, Scruffy needed to remain unnoticed. But that part it left unsaid.

Fine. I wandered over to the view port with my plate. From here, I could see out to the ring where the ships docked. Technically, the spindle was its own ship, capable of hyperspace travel, but for fuel efficiency and to make it easier for traders to find, it usually stayed in one place and let other ships come to it — at least until Bett decided it was time to pick up stakes and move to another system.

A galaxy-class cruiser with the Micklage crest popped out of hyperspace. My heart rate increased, but the registration number — which I hadn't known until now — wasn't the same as the cruiser that had fired on us back at the other spindle. Not that it could have been — *that* cruiser had needed expensive repairs that the other Bett wasn't going to offer. Local control chatted with the captain, guiding the cruiser to its assigned berth. Scruffy had tapped into the local comms.

This group mind thing was weird and invasive, and I might never get used to it, but it certainly was handy. A quickly muted burst of pride came from Scruffy. My eye twitched.

"Rosey!" Bett came in, all four arms open in greeting. "I'm so glad to see you!"

In a way, I'd seen her just a few minutes ago. But this wasn't the same Bett I'd shared the shuttle with. If I hadn't been aware Bett had multiple clones — and I hadn't had Scruffy's catalog of minute differences between this clone and the last — I would never have known this was another person. Or sort of another person. They shared a significant amount of history, so they weren't truly distinct.

On the other hand, how much of our relationship did she remember? Depending on when she had branched off from the other version of Bett, she might not have been there the last few times I ran into the person I thought of as Bett.

It was all too confusing, so I decided to ignore all of it. "It's good to be here. Thanks for helping us out."

"Of course. My sister should be joining us soon. She's in the elevator now." Then she cocked her head, her gaze far away.

At the same time, Scruffy relayed the local control emergency channel to me. "*I repeat, unknown energy discharge from the cruiser docked at 4C. No reports of damage. No communication from the cruiser.*"

4C was the Micklage ship that had just arrived.

"The cardinal crystals," I said aloud to Bett. "Tell them to check the cardinal crystals."

Bett raised one eyebrow and waited. Apparently,

Scruffy hadn't tapped into her private comms. Then her face hardened, and I had my answer even before Scruffy began relaying the status reports from all the ships docked at the spindle and the spindle's bridge. The cardinal crystals had been shattered.

Three seconds later, the local command transmitted an emergency steer clear alert. Two smaller ships that had been approaching the spindle changed course and flashed into hyperspace. They might sound the alarm elsewhere, or maybe they'd just consider themselves lucky to have escaped the area alive.

Bett and I looked through the view port as ship after ship bearing the Micklage crest winked into existence, weapons primed and aimed at us.

TWENTY-FIVE

SURRENDER NOW

Bett thirty-four, Scruffy, and I stared at the approaching Micklage armada. Scruffy tapped into the spindle weapons systems, and suddenly I could *feel* the lasers, rail guns, and shock cannons trained on the Micklage ships. But the enemy ships were armed, too, and any damage to the station could be catastrophic.

Bett's spindle might be the last thing standing, but if there were any hits to life support, the victory party would be permanently over a few hours later.

A transmission relayed by the tower played in the suite. "Spindle control, this is Captain Jarv Husdun of the *Micklage Striker*. We have disabled your hyperspace fleet. Surrender now, and nobody will be harmed. Let us retrieve our escaped prisoner, and we will depart in peace."

It was Bett they were after. Bett forty-seven, to be precise. I moved a step back, as if that would keep them from seeing me. "How did they find us so quickly?"

Both Bett and Scruffy stared at me. Right. Where else would Bett go after she escaped from prison? Just because I hadn't known there were multiple spindles didn't mean others were equally ignorant.

I almost asked why Micklage was coming after an escaped prisoner — technically Micklage was a company, not a governmental entity. But with the amount of power they held, that distinction became meaningless. Bett forty-seven had something they wanted, something so important they'd been willing to subject her to an illegal neuro simulator pod to dig it out of her brain.

There wasn't much in the universe people agreed upon, but the privacy of a person's thoughts was one of them. There were exceptions — group minds, art installations, therapeutic neural simulations, to name a few — but consent had to be given first.

Whatever Micklage wanted from Bett, it was *important*.

The entrance to the suite opened, and a cart trundled in. As soon as the door clicked shut, the cart's side panel opened and Bett forty-seven — the Bett I'd spent time on Crania with — rolled out.

The two Betts looked at each other for a long moment. Then Thirty-four said, "It's a fine mess you've brought me this time." But her lips twitched as she said it.

Forty-seven grinned. "You know you've missed it." She sobered and looked out the view port. "We have a leak, sister. Even if they were watching closely, they shouldn't have made it here so quickly. Someone knows our codes."

"Yes." Thirty-four gave her sister clone an evaluating look. "In what condition do they want you?"

"They want me alive. But as long as they get the memory recording intact, they might not care about that."

Thirty-four stared at the ceiling in thought. "So they might hold off as long as they aren't sure where you are. Let me give them something to think about and then we can talk."

Outside, pulses of light flickered, the start of a salvo of projectiles aimed at the Micklage forces.

"But..." I couldn't figure out how to end that sentence. She wasn't even going to *try* to reason with them? I'd never piloted a ship with anything bigger than a laser to nudge away debris. But firing on an enemy fleet seemed rash. We'd skipped name-calling and stalling-while-waiting-for-backup. Even I knew that.

Forty-seven cupped my shoulder with one hand. "Delay won't help. They wouldn't destroy all the cardinal crystals if they intended to leave survivors. Our biggest threat is someone inside the spindle believing their lies and turning me in. Then everyone here dies. This way..." She looked out the view port where light flashed and escaping gas glittered. "Probably everyone dies anyway, but we take some of them along."

The two versions of Bett sat down next to each other on the couch, speaking quietly. That left me staring out the view port at the part of the enemy fleet I could see. From here, I could tell the spindle's weapons had caused some minor damage to a few ships, but nothing that would slow the armada down. Scruffy monitored the general comms, and I knew the inhabitants of the station were preparing for damage, following the procedures they drilled on every ten-day. There was remarkably little panic among the permanent residents.

The spindle visitors were another matter. A group of wealthy tourists refused to stow their belongings in public lockers and enter the emergency shelter. Another family demanded to speak with the owner of the spindle. In the port bar, pilots sought oblivion through various intoxicants — they didn't have much hope of survival.

Scruffy and I could leave. Even without asking, I could tell its crystal hadn't been affected by the pulse that had destroyed the rest of the cardinal crystals. We could steal a ship and use the synthetic crystal to jump out of here. If we took Bett forty-seven with us, at least Micklage wouldn't get what they wanted. And those two ships that had flown out might have enough evidence that Micklage wouldn't be able to hush everything up.

But that wouldn't save the people of this spindle. I couldn't live with myself, knowing my presence had caused the deaths of thousands. Bett, Scruffy, and I had brought the problem with us — we couldn't run away now.

But what if we took the spindle with us?

When it came down to it, the station was just a gigantic ship. Normally, the spindle would have an array of cardinal crystals and a group of pilots working together to use them. I had no idea if the synthetic crystal in Scruffy's brain could move something this large. But it was all we had.

We must try, Scruffy agreed.

"Hey, Bett?" Both women turned toward me. It was an odd sensation, seeing the identical expression on two faces. "We..." No, Scruffy was still supposed to be a security bot. "I may have a way to move the spindle."

Now their expressions were different. Thirty-four looked skeptical, while forty-seven looked intrigued. It was the latter who spoke. "The same thing that let us get to the Chrysalis fleet? Is it strong enough?"

I shrugged. "Maybe? It seems worth trying." If it *didn't* work and we were still alive afterward, we could decide who deserved to be evacuated on a smaller ship before the spindle was destroyed.

The Betts looked at each other. Forty-seven nodded. Thirty-four stood up. "Then I guess we'd better get you to the bridge."

The bridge had fewer people than I was expecting, a circumstance that was explained by the ever changing status reports as different segments of the spindle were prepped for departure.

"Normally, we have a ten-day to prepare," Bett thirty-four had told me as we zipped to the center of the spindle in a dedicated tunnel. The car shuddered twice as Micklage ships returned fire, aiming at the spindle's weapons. "Regulations require everything to be kept locked down, but..."

"I'll do my best to make it a smooth trip." Next to me, Scruffy cocked its head, as if it wanted to make a joke about extenuating circumstances. I could feel its disbelief. *Quiet,* I said, without speaking.

I didn't say anything. But it radiated sarcasm.

We'd left Bett forty-seven in the private suite so nobody else would catch a glimpse of two different Betts, but I wished they had swapped. Forty-seven already knew something about Scruffy, and I wouldn't have had to make up a story for why I needed to be the one piloting the spindle instead of handing the crystal off to one of the usual pilots.

Maybe Bett wouldn't keep secrets from her other self, but the fewer people who knew about the illegal AI and synthetic crystal, the better. The spindle pilots would know as soon as they connected that it wasn't a cardinal crystal. So I'd gone with the story Scruffy had relayed, telling her, "The shielding on the crystal is keyed to my biometrics. We don't have time to change it."

I don't think Bett thirty-four had believed me for a moment, but she passed the story along to the pilot on duty, sending her out to help with the preparations. "Give us ten minutes," Bett said as I threw myself into an unused pilot's chair. "I'll stall. After that, we'll just have to accept our losses."

Taking something as big as the spindle into hyperspace normally required a lengthy apprenticeship for all seven pilots. I'd never moved anything this large before, even in normal space. On one hand, that made what I was about to do supremely irresponsible. But on the other, the usual pilots were accustomed to working as part of a team. We only had one crystal, so their experience wouldn't hold either.

Nicely rationalized, Scruffy said from its position next to me.

Thanks. Bett had given me full access to the spindle's controls, and I flipped through the modules to get a feel for everything. The trouble was, it was meant to be flown as seven independent sections. Unless I wanted to leave most of the spindle behind, I was going to have to figure out how to fly multiple sections at once.

Except... I wasn't just *me* anymore.

Scruffy, can you help keep track of this? I showed it what to monitor and the changes I would need to make in response. If I'd been smart, I would have used the time during the shuttle ride from Crania getting used to this group mind thing instead of sulking in my seat. Too late now.

Scruffy shifted closer. I could feel it observing at the edge of my thoughts.

In the background, I heard Bett surrender to the Micklage fleet commander, offering to shift the current occupants of the smallest ring to other docking slots so the invaders could have the whole section. The spindle blueprints rose in my mind as soon as I wanted them, and I saw her plan. Aside from buying us more time, it would get them in one place and allow us to blow the ring clamps, instantaneously depressurizing the torus.

Unfortunately, the commander saw that possibility as well. He demanded docking slots in all the rings. I tuned them out and checked the time. We had two minutes left on the original ten. Five of the seven spindle sections had reported a ready status, though that only meant they had closed all the interior hatches and secured anything that might explode if it banged around too much.

We *had* to leave before the first Micklage ship docked, or the interior hatches would be reopened.

Bett leaned back in the chair she had commandeered, fiddling with four different screens at once. "Oh, sorry about that, looks like the docking slot I sent you to is having mechanical problems. The supervisor of that section was out sick today and you know how it is. Her crew thought it was a great time to go to a bar..." She continued cheerfully maligning the group of people who were rushing around getting the spindle ready for action.

The bridge shuddered as another hit from the Micklage fleet took out the aft cannon.

Another light glowed as the sixth section reported readiness.

Bett hit a toggle while the Micklage commander was talking. "Seb, what's the holdup down there?"

In the background came the roar of a welding torch. "Someone destroyed the latching mechanism on the hatch, and there's some structural damage as well. We've evacuated the segment and I'm welding the hatch shut. Be done in a minute."

In front of Bett, the display updated, another section of the spindle blinking. "Yes, I saw that," she murmured. "Can you concentrate on the aft portions? Or better yet, can you delay that waste of oxygen? I'll work with my people to get things moving here." She hit another point on her display. "Bria, vent the extra canisters if you can't get them locked down. We'll look into what happened to the automated system after we're safe."

Through Scruffy's comm link, I heard the other Bett talking to the Micklage commander, continuing the tale of drunken engineers. From his terse responses, we didn't have much time.

All the normal space engines were online, and the hyperspace drives reported optimal status. The minute I spun them up, our attempts to buy time would stop.

Time to plan our escape route. Placing one hand on Scruffy's frame, I tapped into the synthetic crystal and closed my eyes.

TWENTY-SEVEN

IMMEDIATE ASSISTANCE

The spindle's control center faded as hyperspace paths bloomed behind my closed lids.

Oh. Awe radiated from Scruffy.

You didn't see that before? Only three of the paths nearby were big enough for the spindle, and I'd have to get our entry angle right or we'd tear the station apart. Scruffy's worry bled through when I considered that.

No. I could tell you were using the crystal, but I didn't see this.

Of course. An AI without limits who could also use the synthetic crystal would be too powerful for its makers to contemplate. Or perhaps there was a technical reason the AI couldn't use the crystal. That was something to think about later; for now, I needed to find a route that would get us out of here.

One path exited too near a star to be survivable. One ended on a planet surface. The spindle wasn't meant to land in gravity, and I doubted anyone would walk away if I tried. The third path... The third path would put us in the middle of a quarantine zone. Not ideal, but better than sitting here waiting to be used as target practice.

I opened my eyes. Reorienting the ship was my first step. There was no way I was going to curve into the hyper-space path entrance and hope for the best as I'd done with the Crania ship. Remembering the consequences of that trip, I wriggled into the seat's harness, the shoulder straps offering a false sense of security.

With the flick of a finger, I nudged the shaft of the spindle into a gentle spin. Alarms went off as the metal stressed. Crap. I'd done something wrong. Before I could figure it out, Scruffy activated the engines in the other six segments. Right. This pilot's station was set up to affect this segment and I'd just tried to change the momentum of the entire spindle from one spot.

Oops. At least I'd learned that lesson before trying to enter hyperspace.

On the comms, Bett forty-seven claimed damage from the Micklage weapons had fried the circuitry and set off one of the spindle's normal space engines and *of course* we weren't trying to run away, what idiot would try to do that, and if they would just give us a moment to get everything under control, we would let them board.

I tightened the harness. "Let me know when we're ready."

Bett toggled a switch. "Seb, if you can't finish in thirty seconds, abandon the segment and get on the other side of a hatch that works." She toggled another and murmured, "Thirty seconds."

Her lower arms were skimming over a second display. Above the bridge doors, the orange hyperspace warning light glowed, and I could hear the audible alarm coming from the rest of the ship.

"Twenty seconds."

Scruffy locked its legs around the base of my chair. The two of us stopped the spin of the ship and began the slow acceleration toward the hyperspace path opening. This time, we moved all the segments together and avoided the threat of shearing off most of the spindle.

"Ten seconds." Bett toggled her headset. "Seb, get out *now*."

On the comms, I could hear Bett forty-seven spinning another tale. "... general electrical faults. The spindle is going to break up if we don't get this under control. Requesting immediate assistance." I grinned. Requesting assistance from the fleet that had come to blow us all up was a master stroke. Their crews knew we were armed — sending out word we were in immediate danger would make it just a little harder for them to shoot first.

Bett toggled again. "Fire everything you can at them in five... four..."

I brought the hyperspace engines online.

"Three..."

On the comms, the Micklage commander cut into Bett forty-seven's speech. "What are you up to over there? You can't go into hyperspace without a crystal. There's no point in overloading the hyperspace engines to protect *one* person."

"Two..." Bett turned her head to the side. "Seb, are you out?"

A crackle was followed by the clang of metal. "The hatch is closed. We're good."

"One." Bett spun in her chair to face me. "Whenever you're ready."

I closed my eyes and concentrated on our hyperspace path. In my head, I could feel Scruffy split its consciousness to handle all seven stations. Which meant I was suddenly in seven places at once.

"Whoa..." My body felt odd, as if I was being controlled by multiple people. At any other time, I would have kicked Scruffy out of my head or maybe just passed out, but the hyperspace path was coming closer and I didn't have time for anything else.

My brain wasn't meant to handle seven stations. But if I tried to pull back, Scruffy wouldn't be able to send the other six segments along the path. Thousands of people depended on my ability to pilot this thing, and I was not leaving any of them behind.

Under my boots, the spindle shuddered from the recoil of every weapons system firing. The hyperspace path bloomed ahead in seven places. Scruffy's awe threatened to overwhelm me.

All seven hyperspace drives had to bring their segments into the path together, or we would rip this spindle apart. With a vessel this size, every segment was in a slightly different hyperspace environment. There was a reason they had seven pilots trained to work together.

With a tiny, barely noticeable jolt, the drives kicked us onto the path in unison. *Ha! We did it!*

But my triumph was short-lived, as alarms flared. My consciousness flitted from one station to the next, correcting for the local conditions at each one. The spindle wobbled and vibrated, errors compounding as I was busy elsewhere.

We had another thirty minutes of hyperspace before we reached the end of this path. The blare of an atmosphere breach alarm cut through the comms chatter.

The spindle wouldn't survive another thirty minutes of this.

TWENTY-EIGHT
DO IT

Around us, the spindle groaned and shuddered as the seven sections responded in slightly different ways to their local hyperspace environment. I switched my attention back and forth between them all, making micro adjustments, but at least one section had been damaged enough to leak atmosphere.

Scruffy, can you handle some of these on your own?

The AI's voice washed through my head. *I cannot access the crystal, except through you, Captain.*

I knew that, but... There had been a moment right as we'd guided the spindle onto the hyperspace path when my consciousness had split into seven.

When I couldn't tell where I ended and Scruffy began.

We merged more fully into the group mind, Scruffy confirmed. *You would not have survived the sudden disintegration of the spindle, so a closer merge was required. But a more prolonged merging may be harder to release.*

Scruffy was right about our entry into hyperspace. If some sections of the spindle hadn't made the leap, the entire structure would have been torn apart. But having one or more sections break off now? It would be catastrophic for the people in that section, but the main spindle would continue.

Another rumble went through the deck. A hint of smoke and ozone came through the air vent. We didn't have time to evacuate sections of the spindle. What was one life — mine — against all the lives in the spindle? And it wasn't as if I'd be dying, just... becoming something else. Maybe. But it was *my* life, and I didn't want to give it up.

I didn't have a choice. *Do it.*

My mind bloomed, expanding so suddenly it left me breathless. I could concentrate on each section of the spindle at the same time, Scruffy winding around me and filling in the gaps. The vibrations smoothed as the sections settled together. With a quick thought, we sent a damage report to Bett's console, prioritizing by severity and the number of people in immediate danger.

The ship surrounded me, systems like living organisms. When the seven sections came into alignment, the relief hit me as if I'd put down a heavy backpack after a long hike — maybe the muscles and skin had been damaged, but now we could start to heal.

On the flip side, Scruffy's curiosity about having a biological body was just barely held in check. As we watched through the bridge cameras, my face made a series of odd expressions.

While Scruffy examined my body, I examined the robotic dog. Panels slid aside, revealing tubes able to shoot sedative darts. *If I'd known about this, we could have taken care of Rance Micklage back on Dancig City.*

Bett half-stood. "Rosey? You okay over there?"

Scruffy's thoughts raced along with mine. *The sedative was exposed to extreme heat and then further degraded over time. It may have no effect. Or it may be instantly lethal. I did not want to take the risk.* It guided the panels back into place.

Slowing my thoughts long enough to speak to Bett took enormous effort. "Fine." When that didn't reassure her, I forced my body to take a deeper breath. "Give me a minute to adapt." My words slurred.

The ocean of data overwhelmed me until I realized I could just... let it flow by. Amazing. This was what being an artificial intelligence felt like.

Underneath it all was a driving need to return to the Independent Federation, as strong as my human body's need to breathe. That wasn't coming from me.

We'll get you there, I reassured Scruffy. But would it be safe there? Scruffy was part of a group mind now — a mind able to use the synthetic crystal embedded within its case. Would Scruffy's makers welcome it back? Or would our group mind be seen as a danger to be destroyed?

Scruffy responded to the questions I hadn't meant to ask. *I don't know.*

There was nothing we could do about that now. I concentrated on the spindle, teaching Scruffy the intricacies of hyperspace as we flowed along our path in seven sections.

Thirty minutes later, we exited into normal space. Around us, the spindle pulsed and breathed, crews moving to repair the damage we'd suffered from weapons and our precipitous entry into hyperspace. Now I could unstrap my harness and move around, but I couldn't remember how to work a body. My hand shot up and crashed into my chin. *Something's wrong.*

Crania warned about this. The data from the other group mind seeped into my bones. With only one human in our joining, we risked the AI becoming too dominant.

Crania hadn't been able to predict what would happen. With the logic of the Chrysalis, they had recommended expanding the number of people in the group mind.

We can't start infecting people with nanobots.

No.

We were going to have to separate, at least partially. Crania had given no instructions for this process — a group mind separating was catastrophic for the Chrysalis. But every mind of the Chrysalis had elected to join. Scruffy and I had been conscripted.

This could leave me in a body so damaged I would never be myself again, but... *We have to try.* For a moment, our thoughts synchronized. And then the sea of data around me went dark.

Pain lanced through me.

"Breathe." Bett's voice sounded next to my ear. "Just breathe."

I inhaled, the air tasting of smoke and plastic. The pain receded. My eyes stung when I opened them, as if I hadn't blinked enough and they had dried out. "That was... weird." My fingers felt distant, but I was able to reach up and unbuckle the harness.

Bett leaned back. "You with us again?" Next to her knee, Scruffy's robo-dog regarded me with steady eyes.

"I think so." After floating in the ocean of data contained by an AI, my body felt tight and confining. *Scruffy?* Had we destroyed our link completely? That thought should have relieved me, but all I felt was loss.

The group mind is still in place.

I relaxed back into the pilot's chair. At some point, I'd have to sort through my feelings about that, but not right now. "The Micklage fleet didn't follow us, did they?" Theoretically, the hyperspace path should have closed behind us too quickly for them to pursue — at best, they should have been able to determine our destination, but they would still need to find their own paths.

Something in my demeanor reassured Bett I was okay, and she dropped back into the chair next to me. "No. Somehow, you got us here in one piece and nobody followed." I knew Bett well enough to know she was ruthlessly suppressing her curiosity, but I could still hear the edge. "Now we have a new problem."

"Any problem that doesn't involve a Micklage fleet shooting at us is a good problem."

Bett didn't say anything. She just leaned over and increased the volume on an automated voice that had been whispering in the background.

... under quarantine. Your ship has been immobilized. An emergency beacon has been activated. Response expected in... fifty-five standard years. Message repeats: You have violated the perimeter of a system under quarantine. Your ship has been immobilized...

Bett dialed the volume back down. "Maybe not a *good* problem."

TWENTY-NINE

GONCHAROV

The spindle's normal space engines were, in the words of Bett thirty-four's chief engineer, "stuck like a herd of rutting capriswine," a consequence of having run into the sticky microbeads seeded around the quarantined system. Whatever had been inside each bead had spread over the hull, seeped into the engines, and hardened. The engineers were analyzing the substance so they could figure out how to counteract it, but in the meantime, we were going nowhere.

"If the Micklage fleet finds us, they'll use us for target practice," Bett thirty-four grumbled over a bowl of spiced bean curds. We'd returned to her private quarters for a meal and some rest.

Bett forty-seven laced up her boots next to her clone. "If the Micklage fleet finds us, they'll be in the same boat, but worse because their engineers aren't as capable. Relax a bit. We need a few days anyhow." She had integrated her clone's personnel information, and now she was off to monitor the cleanup efforts and improve morale among the denizens of the spindle. She gave a little finger wave as she left.

Keeping everyone from panicking about being stuck in

the middle of nowhere was important, but I was more worried about a different issue. "Has anyone dug up the reason this system was quarantined yet?"

Systems just didn't get quarantined for no cause.

Bett thirty-four nodded. "This system has Goncharov."

My skin prickled. An outbreak of the Goncharov virus was a *really* good reason to quarantine the system. Incredibly contagious, the virus infected humans and mutated them until they ended up as little more than blobs of protoplasm. Worse, the victims were conscious until the very end.

(And possibly beyond — nobody had been able to communicate at the end stage, but there was still synaptic activity.)

The virus had first appeared three hundred standard years before. All attempts to cure it had been unsuccessful. The only thing that saved humanity was Rica Gryden's exposure test, which allowed the affected individual to be isolated before they contaminated anyone else. Rica Gryden had tested positive and continued working on a cure until the end.

While humans could be tested and refused entry to a system, sometimes the virus found a host in wildlife. After two particularly bad outbreaks, a protocol had been developed: a confirmed positive test on-planet meant the system was quarantined and abandoned after a second positive sample. Some of those planets had likely cleared the virus in the meantime, but nobody wanted to take a chance on being wrong.

I hoped we had everything we needed to fix the spindle, because I wasn't going down to any planet in this system until we ran out of air. "We should probably avoid sightseeing trips. How long ago did the outbreak happen?"

"Hm?" Bett took another bite. "Oh, sorry, I wasn't clear. This system has the *planet* Goncharov." The door chime buzzed. "Excuse me for a moment. I have some work to attend to." She put her food down and sighed. Two men in restraints, a father and son by the looks of them, were accompanied by armed guards. A woman came with them, one arm in a sling but otherwise unrestrained. From the facial resemblance, she was the younger man's mother.

Bett stood. "Dr. Blue. Indirie. Please, have a seat." She ignored the two men and the guards, gesturing the woman into a chair across from her. After both women had seated themselves, she continued. "I'm afraid the time has come when you have to make a decision."

The woman closed her eyes, inhaled deeply, and opened her eyes again. "Continue."

Bett's gaze flicked to the men and back. "I was willing to let your partner play his little conspiracy games. Knowing who was sending information to my enemies made it easier to keep track of who he was talking to. But he damaged the spindle in a way that nearly killed us all during the last emergency, and he convinced your son to help him. I can't ignore that."

Indirie Blue paled until I thought she might pass out. "I didn't..."

Bett smiled sympathetically. "No, you didn't know. Which is why I'm giving you this choice."

"Please don't kill them. I'll do anything you want."

Bett's shoulders dropped a fraction. "In a few minutes, Goncharov will be visible through that view port." She gestured. "You know the planet, of course? Before we leave here, your partner and your son will be given a shuttle with an automated pilot. I'll even send down supplies for the next, say, two standard years. That's probably more than they will require." She looked at the doctor. "You understand?"

Dr. Blue nodded.

"They don't have a choice. But you do. You are welcome to stay on the spindle with your daughter until we reach a safe port. Or you can go to the planet with your partner and son."

"My equipment?"

"Would go with you. Perhaps you'll be able to synthesize a cure before it's too late. A cure for Goncharov's virus would wipe the slate clean."

"And my daughter?"

"I'll keep her safe. Or you can stay here with her." She shook her head as Dr. Blue opened her mouth to protest. "I won't condemn her for the actions of her father, and she's not old enough to choose."

Indirie Blue stared at her clasped hands for a long moment. "You'll pick us up if I find a cure?"

"I'll leave a beacon."

Dr. Blue raised her chin and sat up straighter. "Then I'll join Sisco and Hamar."

Bett nodded. "I thought you might." She stood. "I wish you luck." At her gesture, security removed the group. When the door had closed behind them, Bett sprawled on the couch. "What a waste."

"It would be kinder to space them."

"Hm?" She picked up her bowl and took another bite. "Perhaps. But Indirie is the best in her field, and medicine has advanced since the last time anyone tackled the virus. She may just figure it out." She shrugged, and a coldness passed over her face. "And if I kill her family, I can't trust her on my habitat."

The comms unit in the corner crackled to life before I

could respond. Bett forty-seven's voice came through. "We have a problem."

Bett thirty-four shook her head. "What is it now?"

"Someone's left a bomb in the drive housing. If this goes off, the spindle will disintegrate."

THIRTY

PRETTY

For a weapon that could kill us all at any moment, the swirly blue and purple blob attached to the drive housing was kind of pretty.

I wonder about your standards, Scruffy said across our Chrysalis link.

At least I have them, I countered. A group of us stood at arm's length, staring at the bomb. "So, to recap," I said aloud, "we can't remove it without setting it off, and it will eventually go off even if we don't do anything at all."

The chief engineer shrugged his massive shoulders. "That's about it. It'll be triggered by cumulative hyperphotons. If we take another trip through hyperspace, it will happen sooner, but even in normal space we get the occasional scatter." He looked through the nearest view port at the empty space around us. "Ironically, being in a quarantine zone might protect us, since nobody's opening paths into hyperspace nearby."

I would much rather go up in a sudden explosion than end up on the surface of Goncharov, waiting to slowly devolve into a blob of protoplasm, but I kept that thought to myself.

Bett thirty-four crossed her lower pair of arms. "So... do we evacuate?" Her clone was back in their rooms, linked in on their private comms.

Nobody said anything. The spindle had enough emergency pods to hold everyone, but then what? We were in a quarantined sector and the warning message claimed a fifty-five standard year response time. The only planet nearby was the home of a nasty virus that would kill anyone who touched the surface. And local space was seeded with microbeads that splattered against any moving ship's hull and migrated to the engines. The engineering team was hopeful they'd be able to unstick the engines and work out a way to clear the microbeads in our path, but it would take time — which we apparently no longer had.

I wasn't sure whether Scruffy or I came up with the idea — our thoughts still mingled — but we agreed it was the only option. Since the AI was still pretending to be a robotic dog, I was elected to present it. "Can you remove the drive housing without setting it off?"

Bett's chief engineer raised one eyebrow. "And then what? Throw it out the airlock? Without the engine room shielding, it won't drift far before it goes off."

Bett considered the housing. "We might be able to modify one of the railguns to give it some momentum."

"That might have worked," the engineer agreed. "But we lost the railguns before we made the last jump."

I cleared my throat. "I was thinking we put it in a hyperspace-capable ship and I dump it somewhere." The spindle's normal space engines were down, but there had to be at least one undamaged ship in an interior dock.

"That would be a suicide mission." The engineer was

matter-of-fact, as if he wanted to make sure I was aware, not trying to talk me out of it.

"Maybe, maybe not. I'll make the shortest jump possible, shove the thing out, and come back." I tried to make it sound like I was being noble, but I could see from the look on his face that he wasn't fooled. *Nobody* wanted to end up on Goncharov.

Bett shook her head. "I'm no pilot, but don't you have to make your way through normal space first? The beads are still out there. You might make it into hyperspace, but there's a good chance your engines will be shot by the time you turn around."

"The spindle cleared a strip when we came in," I said, and the engineer gave a pained grunt. "If I head that way, it should minimize the damage." When Bett stared at me, I shrugged. "It's better than sitting here..."

BETT FORTY-SEVEN CAME with Scruffy and me, smuggled onto *Hideous Beauty* while everyone else was gawking at the bomb's tour of the spindle on its way to the interior dock. *Hideous Beauty* was a Micklage Sparrow-class courier ship, a little larger and definitely better maintained than *Tiger Lily* — probably because the owner was a smuggler doing business with Bett One-arm. Sinking into the luxurious pilot's chair, I felt a pang of longing for my ship and cat. "Ensign Mowee's going to have made himself a new home by the time I get back."

Bett snorted. "Not if I'm the one taking care of him."

The ship creaked as the dock around us depressurized. Every time the metal pinged, I was convinced I'd heard the final moments of the bomb in the hold.

If the bomb explodes, none of us will know anything about it, Scruffy said helpfully.

I know. It didn't provide any reassurance.

When the bay doors opened, I nudged the ship's engines. We slid out of the dock and drifted next to the spindle. With one hand on Scruffy's robo-dog head, I checked the possible hyperspace paths. If we stayed in the clear wake of the spindle...

None of the paths were as short as I wanted them to be. We had fuel for a longer journey, but we had to assume the bomb was close to detonating. Indirie Blue's partner had admitted he'd attached the device — he'd been planning to depart with the Micklage fleet. Our journey through hyper-space to get here hadn't accumulated enough hyperphotons to set it off, but that had been a short trip.

I scanned the edges of the safe zone. There. That path wouldn't be much longer than the one that brought us here, and it would take us to the edge of a populated system. As long as the bomb didn't go off in transit *and* we didn't lose our normal space engines on the way there, it would be perfect. We could even find a beacon to send a message to Bett's clones so they could resupply the spindle with cardinal crystals. Then Scruffy and I could borrow a ship and disappear before everyone started asking uncomfortable questions about why my crystal had worked when the others had failed.

Bett strapped into her seat as we accelerated and then nodded as if she'd come to a conclusion. "It's time." Or maybe as if she and her clone had been talking to each other and had agreed upon something. "I need to tell you about our deal with the Independent Federation."

Hideous Beauty flashed into hyperspace.

THIRTY-ONE
GET LUCKY

So there we were, flying into hyperspace, carrying a bomb triggered by hyperphotons, and Bett forty-seven thought this was the *perfect* time to tell me some secret she'd been hoarding. Bett — all of her clones — dealt in information. Whatever she was about to tell me might be more dangerous than the actual bomb sitting in the hold, waiting to explode.

I stalled for time. "Why now?"

"Because I need you to do something for me," she answered promptly. Then she laughed. "Cheer up. Maybe you'll get lucky and the bomb will go off first."

She really does not seem bothered by the thought of dying, Scruffy noted in my mind.

Right? Having already died a bunch of times may have something to do with it. Aloud, I said, "Fine. Go ahead."

"How much do you know about the Independent Federation?"

Facts and figures came from Scruffy and swarmed through my brain, but that wasn't what Bett was looking for. "Almost nothing." Until I'd graduated from pilot school, I hadn't traveled at all. Then I'd been part of the Micklage fleet. Since the Micklages were a big part of what the federation was working to be independent *from*, I'd never been there. "If you believe the media, it's chaos and starvation. But the media's all being produced in the Oligarchy, so..."

"Indeed. Though the starvation part is occasionally correct." Bett turned in her seat without unstrapping her harness. "Would it surprise you to know the Micklages have power in the Independent Federation as well?"

"Of course they do. They control the source of cardinal crystals." The need for cardinal crystals to travel through hyperspace didn't depend on the politics of the system.

"Beyond that, even. They've quietly taken over — bought off, killed off, starved out, whatever — the leadership of over half the planets in the federation. Very, *very* quietly."

While I'd thought nothing the Micklage family did could surprise me anymore, I'd been wrong. "Why? What's in it for them?" The major reason the Independent Federation wasn't part of the oligarchy was economics. They just didn't have anything worth traveling there for.

"Because they want Cuitrec. Before the oligarchy can invade, they need to be sure the rest of the independent federation won't send aid to Cuitrec. And they're close to going in — that's why they've started moving against me so openly."

Scruffy's facts and figures came in handy for once. Cuitrec was a collection of space vessels that had started out in orbit around a low-atmosphere planet and had grown large enough to be a society in its own right. These days, Cuitrec was known for its technology collective — nearly all the tech illegal in the Oligarchy had come from Cuitrec or one of its spin-offs.

Yes, it's likely I was created there, Scruffy told me, answering the question before I could form it.

So Micklage subverting the rest of the federation just to get Cuitrec made some sense. Cuitrec had its own defenses. If Micklage had to fight Cuitrec *and* the rest of the Independent Federation, Micklage would lose. If the rest of the federation failed to show up, that changed things.

And if Cuitrec was developing artificial cardinal crystals, Micklage had no choice. They *had* to stop Cuitrec or lose their monopoly.

All this was very interesting, but I failed to see what this had to do with Bett. More importantly, I didn't see what Bett needed *me* to do for her. She couldn't possibly think there was some way I could stop Micklage from taking over the Independent Federation single-handedly.

Technically, there are two of us, Scruffy pointed out.

But you don't have hands.

While I'd been processing the bad news about the Independent Federation, Bett had been waiting patiently. "Now that you understand how bad things could get... I've been working with a group from Cuitrec to stop Micklage."

"How?"

Her smile showed teeth. "Every bit of hardware they've imported in the last standard year, every AI they've purchased — it's all gone through me at some point. And I've swapped it out for something nearly identical that my partners have supplied. When we give the signal, it will turn against them. Micklage will be too busy trying to survive to invade the Independent Federation."

"That won't last long."

"It doesn't need to. Cuitrec's close to going into production on the artificial crystals. Once they do, Micklage is done." She blew out a breath. "But we need someone to set off the cascade. On Trition."

My stomach dropped. *This* was what Bett needed me for. Trition was the Micklage home world, a former asteroid they'd shielded, terraformed, and built entirely to their specifications. The Micklage family *owned* Trition. Nothing happened there without them knowing about it.

And I'd once lived there.

Bett nodded at my reaction. "It will be tricky, but you know the place. I have a code. You just need to find a public terminal and punch it in. That's it."

"Oh, is that all?" If I landed on Trition, I'd be taken into custody before I drew my second breath of air. I'd never see a public terminal.

We can do this, Scruffy said.

I don't think you understand how angry at me Rance Micklage is. And if anyone in that family finds out any of what's happened since we left Buatrier, they'll shoot us on sight. Except Poppy, maybe, but she was still a kid.

The sedative dart ports slid open on Scruffy's head. *I can buy you enough time to do what needs to be done.* The ports slid closed again. The AI's protective instincts toward the Independent Federation bled through our link.

In front of me, the end of our hyperspace path approached. One instant the view port showed its multiple hued moire pattern; the next it flashed to the deep black of a nearly empty system. I cut the hyperspace engines, letting us drift in normal space as I unbuckled my harness.

"First things first," I told Bett as I slid down the ladder to the cargo bay. "Let's get rid of this bomb before it turns us into a new navigation hazard." I sighed even as I began undoing the straps that anchored the section of drive housing to the hold. "Then we can talk about how Scruffy and I can sneak onto Trition."

THIRTY-TWO
GET USED TO ANYTHING

It turned out that you really *could* get used to anything.

By the time Bett and I had wedged the drive housing into the airlock of *Hideous Beauty*, I wasn't even thinking about the bomb welded to the metal. In our rush to get the thing away from the spindle, nobody had double-checked the airlock's inner hatch would seal with the entire section of drive housing inside.

Luckily, the ship's toolbox included a hammer. A laser cutter would have been even better, but in less than an hour, Scruffy and I pushed everything through the outer airlock hatch and watched it drift behind us. Bett gave unhelpful suggestions from the other side of the airlock door — Scruffy didn't require oxygen, and I was the only one who fit in the standard EVA suit, a snag that had nixed our initial plan to temporarily open both airlock hatches and re-pressurize the ship after the bomb had been shoved out.

Now we just needed to put some serious distance between us and the explosion waiting to happen. The back of my neck itched by the time the airlock cycled and I scrambled back to the pilot's seat, still wearing the inner lining of the EVA suit. That bomb was about to go off — I could feel it. "Let's make a quick hop and then we can work out a good place to go next."

"No argument here." Bett buckled her harness.

Scruffy settled under my outstretched hand, allowing me to access its synthetic crystal. Even as I analyzed the available hyperspace paths, I considered what it would take to teach the AI how to use the crystal on its own. It seemed to be unable to see into hyperspace without my help.

I suspect that limitation was deliberate. Regret ran under its words.

Maybe. Certainly anyone worried about AIs gaining too much power would never allow them the freedom of hyperspace. But anyone worried about the AIs gaining too much power wouldn't have created Scruffy *Note of Disrespect. Let's revisit it when we have some spare time.*

Amusement flooded our link. *In ten or twenty standard years then?*

I smiled and selected a path that would send us just far enough to be clear of the debris. Accelerating hard toward it, I almost missed the odd clicking underneath the thrumming engines. When I eased back, the clicking slowed.

Bett turned her head to look at me. "Engines?"

I nodded. "We must have hit some beads on the way out." I cut the engines entirely. We were on the right vector to enter the hyperspace path — better to get there slowly than risk the damaged engines sending us in a different direction. "I'll go outside and look — once we get away from the bomb." At least the hyperspace drive wouldn't be affected.

Our slow drift toward my chosen path gave me time to fasten my own harness. With no way to make corrections, we were going to enter a bit obliquely. "This might be a little rough."

Scruffy tilted its head to look at me. *No comment.*

AS IT HAPPENED, our entrance to hyperspace was more than a little rough, but nothing fell off the ship and we didn't lose atmosphere, so I considered it a success. We were back into normal space and drifting before everything finished falling out of the galley cabinet.

Bett rubbed her neck with her upper set of hands. "You don't play around, do you, Rosey?" She rolled her shoulders. "I may owe Goslar a new ship."

"You worry too much." I whacked the jammed harness clasp with the heel of my hand. "*Hideous Beauty* is in perfect shape. Aside from the engines. *I'd* buy this ship if I could afford it." The clasp released with a clack that said it was done trying to keep anyone safe.

You took Tiger Lily into space leaking atmosphere with one engine misaligned, Scruffy reminded me.

See? In comparison, this ship is practically new. The thought of *Tiger Lily* waiting for us — along with Ensign Mowee — made me sigh wistfully. Maybe I could go back to the Voods Cluster to say goodbye to my cat before heading off on this suicidal mission to Trition.

As I pushed my sweaty hair off my forehead, I crouched to look through the portal in the direction we'd come from. We were only a few light-seconds away.

I recorded it from the exterior cameras, Scruffy said, using its robotic nose to direct my attention to the console.

A window opened on the screen, framed by the starboard ramp bulge above and the curve of the hull below.

The moire pattern of hyperspace gave way to the black of normal space. Before my eyes could finish adjusting, a tiny puff of glitter sparkled and faded in the distance. After ten seconds, the recording looped back to the view from hyperspace.

Given the length of time it took light to travel this distance... My throat went dry. We'd been lucky the shrapnel hadn't followed us into hyperspace.

Bett had obviously come to the same conclusion. "Stars, we cut it close there, Rosey. Good thing we didn't hang around trying to fix the engines."

To be fair, it had been our escape into hyperspace that had produced the hyperphotons that had finally set off the bomb, but still — we'd almost blown ourselves up back there. Pulling on years of pretending nothing was wrong so as not to panic the passengers, I lifted my chin. "Everything went according to plan."

Bett's face slowly creased into a smile. "One emergency at a time?"

"We should be so lucky." I adjusted the liner gloves and sighed. "Any words of wisdom for getting this crud off our engines?"

"Carefully." Bett managed to look as if she actually regretted not being able to suit up to join me. "While you're out there, I'll work on finding the nearest beacon so we can send some messages. With any luck, someone will be here to tow us out before you finish looking over the damage."

Our gazes met. Neither of us wanted to state the reality — the nearest beacon might not be close enough to hack into. And clearing the gunk off the engines might not be possible.

We could be stuck out here.

THIRTY-THREE
SHEER GRIT

Our sprint to see who could get us out of this place turned into an endurance slog.

Bett found a message relay on the edge of our communication range, but her codes to bypass the security layer didn't work. "They've redone the entire thing," she said in disbelief, as if their security keeping her from taking over their relay was a personal affront. "Those star-falling grounders!" Then she rolled up her sleeves and got to work, accompanied by a litany of curses that had Scruffy asking me for clarification.

Meanwhile, Scruffy and I were out on the hull trying to pry the hardened quarantine crud away from the engines and their mounts. We could run the engines without *Hideous Beauty* exploding — probably — but we only had thrust in one direction. The gimbals were stuck. "So we can go fast, but only in a circle," I told Bett when we came inside after the first EVA. "And also, we might blow up, but that's unlikely."

Bett sighed.

On top of that stress was my certainty that sooner or

later I was going to disgrace myself in zero-g. Inside the ship, we had artificial gravity. But the field stopped at the hull, which meant as far as my body was concerned, the first step out of the airlock was the start of an infinite fall. By our third EVA, I could feel Scruffy mentally nudging me forward when I froze near the hatch.

(Yes, my fear of heights came up when I applied to pilot school, but how many pilots ever do their own extravehicular activity? None. That's what the crew was for. You just don't put the only hyperspace-capable pilot outside the protection of the hull. I'd squeaked through the EVA course through sheer grit and determination.

... and drugs. Looking back, the drugs might have been key.)

I floated in space, trying to relax even though my stomach kept telling me I was *falling, falling, falling!* Back on the spindle, teams of very smart people had been working on a way to dissolve the crud so they didn't damage anything. Out here, we had me and Scruffy. Not that the two of us weren't smart in our own way, but it wasn't the "synthesize novel compounds" sort of smart.

I could synthesize novel compounds if we had the right equipment, Scruffy informed me, breaking into my private musings. It used its laser to burn off the crud layer closest to the hull, then moved away so I could drive the prying tool underneath.

Fine. But we don't have the right equipment, so it doesn't matter, does it? Lasers liquified the substance, but the robo-dog didn't have enough power to boil it all away. So Scruffy got rid of the layer holding it to the ship, and I broke off the rest manually. Tedious and slow.

We'd put a few dings in the hull before we'd mastered our approach. I'm sure whoever owned *Hideous Beauty* would be so happy to be rescued, they wouldn't notice the damage. Besides, I'd be getting arrested on Trition by the time the owner got his ship back, so it would be Bett's problem.

If we hadn't been so worried about Micklage's impending invasion of Cuitrec, it would have been a calm interlude. Nobody was shooting at us, we wouldn't run out of supplies any time soon, and *Hideous Beauty's* galley produced excellent meals. Maybe not as varied as the galley unit on Crania, but this one came with instructions, which gave it an edge in my ratings.

We'd been drifting three standard days when Scruffy and I partially freed the main gimbal. I thumbed the radio. "Bett, can you start the diagnostic sequence again?" Having her hit a spot on the touch screen was easier than tapping out a sequence while wearing the bulky EVA gloves.

"Running."

In front of me, the gimbal jerked along one axis. "Aha! We're getting there."

Scruffy cocked its head. *We can still only travel in circles along one plane.*

Yeah, but now we can pick how wide our circles will be. Keep going.

Bett met us at the airlock hatch when we finally went inside, her face showing relief. "I got in touch with forty-eight. She's organizing a rescue for the spindle we left near Goncharov. Cardinal crystals, replacement parts, the works."

That had to be the clone who was decanted immediately after this Bett had disappeared. "Forty-eight is the one who sent me in to break you out of prison?"

Bett smiled, teeth showing. "Yes. Sounds like she's really enjoying taking care of your cat, by the way. How close are we to being able to move this junk heap? Things are kicking off at Cuitrec and I have places I need to be."

I stowed the various pieces of the EVA suit in their compartments to be cleaned and sterilized, basking in the sensations of *down* and *up*. "We have *limited* maneuverability now. I can get us onto any hyperspace path with a little planning, but it would be best if there's nothing we need to avoid on the other end. Like a planet. Or traffic."

Or a Micklage ship waiting to destroy us, Scruffy added privately.

I don't think we really need to list everything we're worried about. If we started, we'd never end.

Bett swept an arm toward the pilot's chair. "Get us near Psirst and a ship will be waiting."

GIVEN THE WONKY GIMBAL — which had both a delay and occasional failure to move at all — it took two tries to aim *Hideous Beauty* toward the right hyperspace path, but we got there in the end. Bett eventually stopped laughing and promised not to share that performance with anyone, but I suspected every clone of hers still alive would hear about it.

Before we headed into hyperspace, I got cleaned up and enjoyed the ship's galley again. Someday, I'd get a decent galley for *Tiger Lily*. Though when I thought about it, working extra hours to afford a new galley had been what got me into this whole mess.

Not a mess, Scruffy corrected. *A splendid opportunity.*

Yeah. A splendid opportunity to go die on Trition. But at least it had gotten me away from Buatrier.

Half a day later, we dropped back into normal space,

with no navigation hazards near enough to worry about. Two ships waited at a distance, but only one caught my eye — a beautiful little Lynx 3, with a patched hull, a bit of corrosion, and a slightly off-kilter nose.

Tiger Lily was here to greet us.

THIRTY-FOUR
PERSONALITY

Boarding *Tiger Lily* after so much time away felt... odd. Compared to *Hideous Beauty*, it was small, familiar, and — a wisp of cat hair blew past my face as the inner airlock door opened. Yep, definitely home.

Saying goodbye to Bett forty-seven had felt curiously final, though maybe that made sense. She was heading off to Cuitrec to help defend the Independent Federation, while I was going to the Micklage stronghold to cut them off at the knees. The chances of either of us surviving weren't worth risking real currency on. Still, I'd miss Bett, especially the clone I'd spent so much time with.

Ensign Mowee jumped on me before I'd finished removing the EVA suit, meowing loudly and rubbing his cheeks against mine. "Miss me?" I murmured as I scratched his ears.

Scruffy clattered out of the airlock. *You should have taken Bett's offer to borrow Hideous Beauty until we returned from Trition.*

It had been tempting. But piloting an unknown ship to get rid of a bomb was one thing. Taking it into populated space was another. Without running checks on the ship and the owner, I was likely to get embroiled in someone else's problems, and I had enough of my own.

Besides, for what I was planning to do, I needed a ship the Micklages were already looking for.

Ensign Mowee jumped down and stalked away, tail perfectly vertical. He didn't look back. Assuming he followed historical patterns, he would ignore me for the next three standard days and then pretend nothing had ever happened.

Tiger Lily completed its link with me. *"Welcome aboard, Captain de Mure."*

"Thank you, ship." Boots coming down the ladder from the bridge distracted me before I could probe the ship's computer to see how it responded. But I'd been in the cargo bay for nearly a minute and it hadn't recited any ads in that time, so I was taking that as a good sign.

A tiny woman with dark skin and an explosion of purple hair slid down to the deck. "You must be Rosey!" Dancing forward, she continued in her high-pitched voice. "I'm Delilah Owl. Bett asked me to deliver *Tiger Lily* to you." She patted the hull. "Nice ship. A little quirky, but that just shows she has personality."

I opened my mouth to greet her, but Delilah rolled right through whatever I was going to say.

"Bett said..." Her voice lowered in pitch until it approximated Bett's cadence and rasp. "Tell Rosey that her cat is a menace and I'm amazed she's kept it alive as long as she has." Delilah's voice went back to her normal pitch. "I guess he attacked a Borollian dogbeast and spent a couple days in the medical unit."

I closed my eyes. That cat...

When I opened my eyes again, Delilah smiled. "Bett

said with a cat like that, you needed a better med unit on *Tiger Lily*, so she upgraded it. Had to swap out the galley to make room. She hoped you didn't mind."

A bonus for rescuing her clone and the other spindle? Or payment in advance for a possibly suicidal mission to Trition? Bett didn't like to owe debts. Either way, I wouldn't complain. "Give her my thanks, would you? Do you need a ride?"

Delilah shook her head and pulled on the EVA suit I'd just hung up. "Nope. I'm taking *Hideous Beauty* in for repairs. Anything I should know?"

Making a wide curve with one hand, I winced. "Give yourself lots of room for maneuvers. The gimbal moves, but not much."

"Good to know. Safe travels." She pulled the helmet on and disappeared into the airlock.

We had things to do, but I stood and took a deep breath. I had my cat and my ship back. Things were looking up, at least until I got to Trition. But first...

I looked at Scruffy. *Time to teach you how to use your own crystal.*

BEFORE WE STARTED OUR LESSONS, I hopped *Tiger Lily* to a spot just outside the nearest hub. Scruffy didn't need an audience, and I didn't need the distraction.

Can you feel anything different when I access the crystal? I concentrated, bringing up the hyperspace paths around us.

Yes. Scruffy was silent for nearly a minute. *Can you demonstrate again?*

I did as it asked. Back in pilot school, this had taken

months of meditation sequences to learn. But I didn't think having an AI imagine it was swimming through an endless sea would be useful. Scruffy was the first AI with a synthetic chip, as far as I knew. It would have to find its own way.

The ship's link clicked. *"Captain de Mure, is there a problem?"*

"No. Thanks for asking, ship." Remembering the last time I'd been in the pilot's seat, I asked, "We *did* get the ownership straightened out, didn't we?"

"You are the registered owner of this vessel," Tiger Lily responded. It sounded vaguely embarrassed about its previous behavior.

Scruffy cut in. *There!* Our group mind strengthened for just a moment and I saw hyperspace paths flicker into being around us.

Yes. So Scruffy *could* pilot the ship. It still needed training on how to choose a safe path, but we'd have time to go over that during our travels. And Scruffy was a quick learner.

After unstrapping myself from the pilot's chair, I stood. "Ship, start monitoring all channels for any news about Rance Micklage. I want to know where he is at this moment, and how long it's been since he's been on Trition." Rance was famous and liked to be seen — there were entire gossip channels devoted to him and his family. "It's time to check out the new galley and feed the cat. Then, I'm going to figure out how to get arrested."

THIRTY-FIVE
CONSPIRING

Parked in an empty bit of space one short hop away from Trition's system, I lounged in the pilot's chair, boots up on the dashboard, while I tried to pass along all my hyperspace knowledge to Scruffy.

The AI wasn't impressed.

If this is how new pilots are taught, it's a wonder vessel disappearance isn't even more common, it said.

A whiff of pickled fish blew toward me from the vents. "Ship, why does it smell like Ensign Mowee is playing in the galley again? I told you to stop giving him access." After the cat had somehow programmed the new machine to produce a fish platter while he was exploring, I'd been forced to pass-word-lock the galley. Yet somehow, he'd generated fish meals three more times. After all, why would *Tiger Lily* care the cat kept burying the leftovers in my bunk?

Tiger Lily's prim voice came over the comms. *"Captain, would you like me to stop monitoring for news about Rance Micklage and maintain a watch on the galley?"*

As if the ship's computer couldn't do both at the same time. My ship and my cat were conspiring, and I couldn't do anything about it. "Thin ice, ship. Maybe next time I'll leave you both with Bett."

The ship remained silent.

Scruffy drew my attention to a path. *This is unsuitable why?*

I checked. The hyperspace path it had highlighted could be mistaken for ending up a safe distance from a star, but in reality, that gravity was coming from something small and near. But how did I know that? This teaching thing was harder than it looked.

Luckily, we had a shortcut. *I don't think I can explain it. Go ahead.*

The group mind strengthened and I showed Scruffy the difference between that hyperspace path and one that wouldn't kill the ship. The more we did this, the more the group mind seemed natural, like breathing. That worried me. I'd never wanted to join the Chrysalis in the first place, and my plan had been to purge these nanobots as soon as possible.

But first we had to stop the invasion of the Independent Federation. And I needed to be sure Scruffy could pilot *Tiger Lily* to safety if it all went wrong.

Tiger Lily cut in. "*Captain de Mure, there is a 52% chance Rance Micklage arrived on the ship that just docked with the Trition orbital.*"

That was higher than it had been, though still lower than I wanted. "Other possibilities?"

"*Deliberate disinformation, a body double, a clone, or mistaken identity.*"

Scruffy trawled through my memories of pilot training while I considered what *Tiger Lily* had said. The Micklage family often generated false leads for anyone hoping to waylay them. Many years ago, Rance's uncle had been kidnapped, nearly bankrupting that branch of the family. But Rance rarely bothered with subterfuge. And if the family was about to launch a war, I expected them to bring everyone close to home so they would be easier to protect.

We needed to get in there before it was too late.

Scruffy throttled our link as it finished retrieving the information it had been looking for, causing my stomach to burn. I didn't miss the closeness of the group mind. I *didn't*. "Pack it up, crew. We're going in."

I LET Scruffy handle the jump while I hovered, ready to step in if I thought it was going to send us into a black hole. But it managed with only a few hair-raising moments, and we contacted the Trition orbital to arrange a docking slot without any real problems.

As far as the rest of the universe was concerned, *Tiger Lily* was now *Ocean of Debt*, a medium range messenger ship. I'd gone a little overboard with the hull paint, but the new name was still visible to anyone who was looking. We even had a new digital beacon with a different ID. The identification all traced back a few hops and then fell apart, which was what I'd wanted — this was the sort of name change I'd have been able to afford. I didn't want to raise suspicions I'd had help.

The other bit of camouflage took even more getting used to. I blinked — twice — when Scruffy appeared. Its robo-dog frame was hidden under stuffing and pink fur, with an unexpectedly cute feline head and a long tail. "Oh. Wow."

It looked at me through long lashes. *This is humiliating. We all have our parts to play.*

Ensign Mowee took one look at Scruffy's new incarnation, puffed up to twice his size, and screamed.

Now *that* was going to be a problem. Somehow we had to make it look like Scruffy was a gigantic cat toy, which was going to be hard to pull off if my cat acted like he was possessed.

Leave it to me, Scruffy said. It dodged Mowee's first rush.

"Do *not* harm the cat!" I yelled as I climbed out of the way. The robo-dog underneath all that padding had lasers and superior strength. Ensign Mowee might be a pain to live with, but he was *my* pain to live with.

Scruffy continued to dodge Mowee's murderous attacks, not allowing the cat to get close enough to scratch or bite, but also not running away. In two minutes, the cat was panting, his growls shorter and less virulent. Another five minutes passed and he was reduced to walking toward the giant pink cat. After ten minutes, he flopped down on his side, completely worn out. Scruffy flopped down next to him.

Ensign Mowee began grooming the pink fur on Scruffy's leg.

I stared at them. "Well, I guess we're ready to go then."

When our docking assignment came through, Scruffy piloted us in, lining us up so perfectly that it didn't even scrape the new paint job. If this all went wrong, the AI might have a glorious future as a cargo pilot.

I gave Ensign Mowee a quick head pat, collected my bag of tools, and went to the airlock hatch. Ho hum. Just another independent pilot looking for some extra credits by picking up a few shifts on the orbital. Nothing to see here.

When the hatch opened, orbital security was waiting for me, guns drawn.

THIRTY-SIX

MILDLY DAMAGED

Being arrested by orbital security was a new experience for me. When I thought about it, ever since I'd found Scruffy's AI back on Buatrier, I'd been having one new experience after another. *It's like you're the common denominator*, I told the AI.

The guards had extended an immobilizer field and now they towed me behind them as they walked through the corridors. See? New experience. The air carried a faint hint of onions and mold.

Perhaps you were living a very sheltered life. Scruffy tried to hide its worry, but I could feel it from the other side of the station.

With the way I was tilted, the ceiling filled my view. Over the sound of boots on bare metal, I listened to the guards complain about the new schedule and tried to ignore the tingling in the tip of my nose. Leave had been cancelled and nobody was happy.

The environmental techs really needed to include their ceilings in the station cleaning protocols, but it was probably too late. Once vent gnats got established on an orbital, they were nearly impossible to get rid of. *Remind me to never eat anything here. How are things going on the ship?*

A pause. *Ensign Mowee mildly damaged the search personnel and has been placed in quarantine.*

That didn't surprise me. My cat had been damaging people across the galaxy since I'd met him. But somehow he always found refuge with people willing to put up with him. If it turned out he was an intelligent alien lifeform that just *looked* like a cat, I wouldn't be shocked.

Scruffy picked up on my thoughts. *Any intelligent alien wouldn't require the medical unit as often as Ensign Mowee. But the technician brought in to establish quarantine showed evidence of amusement at his behavior. Evidently she does not like station officials — she has been sending images of the altercation to friends around the station.*

So Scruffy had already tapped into the station comms. Good. And it was a relief to know Mowee was in safe hands. If there had been somewhere else to leave him, I'd never have brought him along. *Are you out of the ship yet?*

On my way. Beginning second phase.

Everything was going to plan so far. Not that I expected it to last, but I could always hope. The guards stopped walking and from the corner of my eye, I could see them facing a closed hatch. My nose itched.

With a beep, the hatch opened, and it was like moving into a completely different station. Granted, all I could see was the ceiling, but *it* was polished clean, and the air smelled fresher. No mold spores for the Micklage family.

On the heels of that thought came a familiar voice. "Well, if it isn't the perfect present, all wrapped up for me."

Rance Micklage was here. Excellent. I'd been worried about that.

With a beep, the immobilizer field vanished and I dropped to the ground, grunting as the air went out of my lungs. Ignoring the burning that meant my nerves and muscles would soon be under my control, I concentrated on regulating my breathing.

Rance loomed over me — short black hair, brown eyes, and the pale shiny skin that comes from a prolonged stay in the med unit after, say, standing too close to a Lynx 3 lifting from the surface of Buatrier. That amused me enough to distract me from the pain.

He booted my shoulder, a tap that would leave a bruise. "I heard you were on your way here, but I didn't think you'd be that stupid."

"Star slime," I said through gritted teeth as the last of the tingles wore off. Rance wanted to surprise me, but I'd known leaked information had preceded *Tiger Lily* when station security had been waiting on arrival. My ship's identity change wasn't deep, but it would have taken at least a standard day to break it down.

This was fine. Better than fine, really. I'd needed someone to flag the false identity, and having Bett give the info to a Micklage spy helped her mop up on her end and spared me the trouble of "accidentally" running into Rance on the station.

Rance was the key. No way could I fly down to Trition's surface when the Micklage family readied for war. Maybe under normal circumstances, but now? Not a chance. The orbital was as close as I could get on my own. And if Rance hadn't been here, I'd have been deported to a stasis prison without ever seeing the planet.

But Rance would never let go of his new toy, not until he'd finished gloating. Especially if I wound him up. "Your family should get a refund from whoever spliced your genes sideways." I needed Rance to take me with him when he went down to Trition.

Careful, Scruffy warned. It knew from my memories how sensitive this subject was. The Micklages had paid a geneticist to ensure they produced a pilot. They'd ended up with Rance, who couldn't access hyperspace while grasping all the cardinal crystals in the universe.

With a hiss of mold-tainted air, the hatch opened again to admit a guard carrying a bound robo-dog covered in pink fur. I struggled to my feet. "Why'd you bring my cat's toy here?" It sounded as fake as I'd thought it would. I'd *never* been good at acting.

Rance smiled. "We need the crystal, but the AI is a security risk."

Before I could react, Rance lifted an electromagnetic stunner, held it against the robo-dog's body, and fired.

THIRTY-SEVEN

INSULTED

Watching the robo-dog spasm and go limp made my breath catch, even though I knew — I *knew* — this was what we'd planned. Everything was fine. Even so, I couldn't help calling across our group mind link. *Scruffy? You're okay, right?*

In front of me, Rance smiled in triumph. "I wondered how you got away from me on Buatrier. But then I figured out you'd woken up the AI. Gutsy move. Those things are too dangerous to exist."

I'm insulted.

So was I — because why would I need an AI to get away from Rance? — but hearing Scruffy's voice in my head was a relief. *I'm glad you're alright.*

Don't relax too much. You're supposed to believe my atoms just got scrambled.

Crud. Scruffy was right. The biggest weakness in our imperfect plan was my poor acting skills. With Rance looking at me curiously, I bit the inside of my lip hard enough to make my eyes water. *Are you close to getting on his ship?*

Working on it. If it helps you look sad, you should know Rance just killed the processor from Tiger Lily's new galley.

What? Now I really did want to cry. I'd thought we'd swapped Scruffy's AI with the cleaning bot's processor. "You festering bucket of slime!" My voice broke as I struggled against the guards. "Do you know what you just did?" I hadn't even gone through the entire menu yet.

(I know, I know, going back to eating reconstituted food is insignificant compared to saving the Independent Federation from invasion. However, anyone who thinks this isn't important has never eaten rehydrated red-flavored algae for twenty meals in a row. Look at the packaging — they gave up trying to make it taste like anything natural and named it after a *color*.)

Scruffy sounded defensive. *The cleaning bot's processor glitched too often to pilot remotely. We couldn't trust it.*

Of *course* the cleaning bot's processor glitched. I'd pulled it from a ship that had impacted Buatrier's surface hard enough to leave a crater. Anything left unbroken had burned in the subsequent fire. When I'd asked her to name a price for the bot, Orabella had laughed so hard she'd almost choked. Then she gave it to me for nothing, saying she hadn't heard anything that funny in a long time. I'd been able to get it to mostly work, but I couldn't perform miracles.

And now that I thought about it, the extra processor had looked awfully new when I'd made the swap. *After all I've done for you, you betray me like this?* The robo-dog's paws were dextrous enough for it to dismantle the cleaning bot — and *apparently* the new galley as well — but Scruffy couldn't remove its own hardware from the robo-dog without help.

We'll steal a new galley controller from the Micklages before we leave Trition, Scruffy promised.

It was humoring me, but I sniffed and felt better. Save the Independent Federation *and* replace my galley controller — why not?

"Put her on my shuttle." Rance had turned to leave, which I hoped meant we were on our way to the planet soon. Ending up in Micklage custody was a key part of the plan, but the faster we got through that bit, the better.

Behind me, the guards kept my arms pinned and didn't move. "Sir, we haven't finished scanning her for weapons yet." The guard infused a note of respect into his voice, which meant he was either a far better actor than I was, or he hadn't spent much time around Rance.

Rance turned, obviously annoyed. "Fine. Do your job and hurry up."

I stared at the ceiling while they ran their wand over me more thoroughly. There was nothing to find. I knew just enough about weapons to be sure that I was better off without any. Then they couldn't be used against me.

A pinprick on my forearm caught me by surprise. "Hey, watch it with that thing! It's got sharp edges."

The guard ignored me and stepped a pace to the side as he looked at the readout. "She's got some sort of active nanobots."

Oh... We hadn't expected them to scan that closely. If they figured out Scruffy and I were a group mind, this could go sideways in an instant. "Bumped my head a while back. They used medical nanos to keep my brains from leaking out."

Rance raised his eyebrows at the guard. The guard frowned at his screen and then glanced up uncertainly. "Could be. They aren't in the database."

They weren't in the database because the Chrysalis modified its nanobots faster than the rest of the universe could keep track. Which was good for me, or Rance might have figured out the whole group mind thing. And *that* might make him realize he was holding the scrambled remains of my galley's controller and not the synthetic crystal he'd been chasing after. But it also made me a little uncomfortable, because exactly how much testing had Crania done on those nanobots before injecting them into me?

Focus, Scruffy ordered, as my thoughts threatened to spiral into fresh worries about the impact of our group mind. *I'm not on the shuttle yet. You may need to delay.*

With Scruffy, that could mean anything from it was waiting for a chance to sneak onto the shuttle to the bot motor had broken down and it was using the scrubbing arm to paddle itself along the deck. It was probably better that I didn't know the details.

Did I have the acting chops to convince everyone I had fainted? I had my doubts. *Hurry up.*

Rance walked back to stare at the readout. Then he handed the electromagnetic stunner to the guard. "Hit her with this a few times. That should kill off the nanobots."

"Sir?"

Scruffy's quick *Don't let them...* collided with my spoken, "Hey, you can't do that!"

But Rance was already walking away. The guards looked at each other and then the one holding the stunner shrugged and held it up in front of my heart. "Hold still."

"Wait —"

He pressed the trigger. My entire body stiffened and everything went dark.

THIRTY-EIGHT
IRONY

When I came back to my senses, I was facedown on luggage webbing. In a shuttle? Opening my eyes, I saw a scratched and dented surface a mere hand-span away, but I'd recognize that paint color anywhere. This was a Micklage private fleet shuttle. I tried to push myself up, but I moved too quickly, triggering the automatic immobilizer field. My chest still rose and fell, allowing me to breathe, but I couldn't otherwise move. From the vibration of the engines and the increasingly erratic gravity, I figured we were about to land on Trition — one part of the plan Scruffy and I had come up with had fallen into place.

Unfortunately, the rest of our plan had run aground. Our group mind was just a memory, my thoughts completely my own, and no hint of a sarcastic AI looming behind every idea. Rance's electromagnetic stunner had knocked out the nanobots Crania had introduced, and I couldn't tell if it was temporary or permanent. At any other time, it would have been a bittersweet relief — ending the group mind had been on my list of things to accomplish someday soon.

Just not right now.

As the immobilizer field faded, I pushed myself up again, more slowly this time. A nearby voice said, "I'd stay there, if I was you. Traffic's heavy and we're on our third circuit." The voice belonged to the guard who had told Rance about my nanobots.

The only reason a private Micklage shuttle would have to wait to land was airspace being used by other — more important — Micklage family members. I couldn't stop the little smile at this evidence of Rance's lowered status; when I'd still worked for the Micklage private fleet, Rance had been near the top of the heap. But I sobered when I realized what else this meant. Bett had been right — if they were calling the entire family home, the invasion of the Independent Federation was imminent.

Scruffy and I needed to communicate, both to coordinate my escape from custody and to trigger the cascade that would take down the Micklage systems. If the Micklage teams found the code before it was entered, they could search their hardware and defeat the sabotage. Bett had known this and known both Scruffy and I were vulnerable in different ways. So the code was buried somewhere in my memories — I couldn't access it until I ran across the triggering image. Only Scruffy knew what that image was. Even if I got away on my own, I *still* wouldn't know how to start the cascade.

Unless Bett had given me a clue?

The shuttle jolted. A warning light reflected off the surface of the floor, the only thing in my field of vision since the immobilizer field had flipped on again, this time to keep the contents of the shuttle from being thrown around. "What's going on?"

Nobody answered me, but I heard panicked shouting

coming from the cockpit before the blare of an audio alarm drowned out the voice. I struggled to free myself from the luggage rack, but the immobilizer field meant I could only slide a bit at a time.

If I had freed Bett from stasis prison, piloted a huge spindle, and jumped through hyperspace carrying a bomb, and *then* died while trussed up in the luggage webbing during a routine shuttle flight, the irony would force my ghost to haunt this planet until the heat death of the universe.

Another jolt, larger this time, accompanied by the sound of rending metal that seemed to go on forever. Smoke filled my nostrils, and my eyes watered.

Then there was silence.

The immobilizer field fizzled out, and I fell from the luggage rack. With the way we had landed, I couldn't reach the main hatch, but an enormous crack in the hull showed dirt below and gray skies above. The universe had been watching over me to survive *that*.

From the approaching sirens, help would be here soon, which meant I needed to run. Had Scruffy's cleaning bot made it onto the shuttle before we left? I didn't see anything in the passenger area. "Scruffy?"

No response.

Avoiding the edges of the hull, I slid out of the ship and staggered to my feet in the blackened mud. The metal wasn't as hot as I'd expected it to be, which made me wonder if I had passed out during the crash. A phalanx of emergency vehicles streamed toward the shuttle and I slipped past them in the chaos.

We'd landed in the clear zone next to the port, but tall buildings surrounded the area. Straightening my clothes, I oriented myself. Mountains to the east, the port directly north... so I needed to turn around and go to the high-rises in the southwest. That was the visitor center, the only place a non-resident could enter. Once inside, I would find a terminal and hope that Bett hadn't hidden the code in my brain as well as we'd thought. Then I'd find Scruffy, and we'd steal a ship and get out of here.

In just a few minutes, I was walking through the revolving doors of the visitor center, where people dressed in off-world clothing crowded at the windows, looking toward the field and the broken shuttle. None of them looked up as I passed. Across the spacious lobby was a bank of public terminals.

This was it. All I needed to do was enter the code and Micklage would be unable to launch their attack against the Independent Federation. I stared at the entry keys. What was the code? Bett must have used an image we both had in common. I thought about the bar where we'd first met, and the spindle, and *Hideous Beauty*.

Nothing.

When we'd come up with our plan, we'd assumed Scruffy and I would still be linked, and the AI would supply the image.

Everyone else in the lobby remained transfixed by the crash, murmuring in hushed voices. When I followed their gazes, I saw smoke billowing from the remains of the shuttle. Hopefully, the emergency responders had gotten everyone else out. If they had even survived the landing...

Forcing my attention back to the terminal, I tried to think of any other places Bett and I had shared. Memories flashed by, of bars and alleys and ports and spacecraft. I smiled as I remembered the ox-drawn cart we'd shared when her identification had been red-flagged and none of the licensed cabs would pick us up.

No codes occurred to me.

My gaze went back to the window. Now flames dwarfed the shuttle cabin, and I could picture what the wreck would look like when it cooled. I'd seen enough examples at Orabella's shipyard. Crashes that nobody had walked away from.

... that *nobody* had walked away from.

Wait.

Abandoning the public terminal, I walked across the lobby to join the crowd staring at the disaster. I'd *seen* the results of crashes like that. There was no way I'd have survived, even if I'd been properly strapped in. Even if I'd survived a landing that tore the ship apart, the smoke would have killed me. And I hadn't even coughed.

This wasn't real.

I was in a simulation.

(Or I was dead. But I refused to believe the afterlife was a visitor's center on a world owned by the Micklages. I hadn't done enough bad things in my lifetime to deserve *that*.)

"I'm in a simulation," I said to the woman next to me. "You're not real." She frowned and went back to looking at the distant shuttle.

Moving away from the window, I sat down on what looked like a comfortable chair, then leaned back and crossed my legs. "You might as well stop this thing. I don't have the codes."

Everything around me shimmered and went gray, leaving me floating in an endless mist.

Suspicion confirmed.

Now how did I get myself out of here?

THIRTY-NINE
EVERY FAMILY HAS ONE

The white mist of the simulation went on for so long, I was starting to wonder if I really had died in a shuttle crash. Except I was pretty sure my dying neurons would come up with something more exciting.

Tilting my head back to look at the non-existent sky, I called, "Hey, if I'm stuck in a simulation, can you at least give me a vid to watch?"

I wished Scruffy were here, if only because then I would know it was safe.

When we had rescued Bett from the simulation pod, we'd been in a hurry, so we'd done an emergency shutdown. Maybe this was the normal disconnect. That took three hours — surely the mist had been drifting around me longer than that?

The mist thinned, and then everything abruptly went dark. I fell.

I landed on my hands and knees in a bright room, cold tiles bruising my flesh. Behind me, a simulation pod loomed, its door open. In front of me... Rance Micklage, his uncle Tiber, and his cousin Vira. Tiber dealt with family security, and Vira was the family's strategist. All three had gray-flecked hair and the sculpted Micklage features. I'd met Tiber and Vira once before, back when they were vetting potential pilots for Rance's private ship.

(Look, it's not their fault it didn't work out. They had an impossible task. They needed someone with enough scruples not to sell Rance to the highest bidder, but not encumbered with so many morals that they would kill Rance as a favor to humanity. I'd be offended they chose *me*, but Tiber and Vira hadn't known the extent of Rance's putrefaction.)

Based on the light coming through the window, we were on Trition. Or else I was still stuck in the simulator. I climbed to my feet, only then noticing they were bare. "Nice simulation, but next time, pick a wreck that someone might survive."

Tiber's jaw tightened, but Vira's eyes were amused. "I always thought you were smarter than you looked." A compliment wrapped around an insult — that was Vira to the core.

"Thanks. I always thought so, too." I made a show of looking around. Two doors, high windows, a few technicians in lab coats, and at least one heavily armed guard. Now was probably not the best time to make a run for it. "Have you seen my boots anywhere?"

Tiber held up a familiar processor, the galley unit I'd swapped into the robo-dog for Scruffy to pilot remotely. Now the casing was singed and warped. "Where's the AI?"

Focussing on Vira, I said, "Did Rance figure it out? He didn't, did he?" From the deepening red of Rance's face, he'd proudly presented my galley's processor and proclaimed that he'd saved the day.

Vira shrugged. "Every family has one. You just have to deal with it."

With a growl, Rance lunged forward, grabbing my throat with his hands. Then he stiffened and fell to the floor, twitching.

Tiber re-holstered his stunner. "The AI and the synthetic crystal?" Both he and Vira ignored Rance, who was now drooling at their feet.

I shrugged. "It's probably somewhere around here, unless it got on a ship and left the system while I was stuck in the pod." Unable to resist making Rance's outlook even worse, I added, "If he hadn't knocked out my nanobots up on the station, I'd know for sure. But that's Rance for you. He's a kill the nanobots first and ask the important questions later sort of person."

From the looks on their faces, they knew I was telling the truth.

"It might come back for her," Vira said to Tiber. "The pattern analysis suggests there's a bond between them."

"Unless that bond died with the nanobots." Tiber's jaw was so tight, he was about to grind his molars to dust.

"It's the best lead we have." Vira turned to the guard. "Put her in the secure suite on level five."

I cut in before she and Tiber could walk away. "My boots?"

But now that they knew I didn't have any information, I was nothing to them and they walked away without acknowledging my question. Apparently, I was going to walk to level five in bare feet. Oh well. At least I'd have a good view from the fifth floor.

Level five turned out to be five stories *underground*, and the secure suite had basic amenities but nothing else. After the door locked behind me, I checked it out. Living area, sleeping cubby, and facilities. The ventilation system was too small to fit through, there weren't any windows, and I was pretty sure the whole place was monitored. Other than the lock on the door, it wasn't a bad place to stay, though I suspected planet-dwellers would have found it claustrophobic. I'd lived in far smaller places.

Besides, I didn't intend to stay there for long.

They planned to use me as bait to catch Scruffy, which meant I had to escape now. First up, disable the cameras. That took an hour, mostly because I didn't have any tools and I was standing on top of a chair. Nobody stopped me, which meant they either weren't monitoring the room yet, or they didn't care.

Next step, get through the door. My plan to grab whoever delivered the food and use them as a shield until I got out of the building died a quick death — dinner was served by a guard aiming a weapon at me. He shoved a tray of food inside with his foot and then pulled the door closed.

All that and they'd given me no utensils that I could use as weapons or tools. I drank soup and considered the bowl. With access to tools, I might make something helpful, but I had to admit its uselessness in its current form. If I could break up the tray, though...

Ten minutes into my fruitless attempt to tear the tray apart, the door lock clicked. Expecting a trap, I cautiously pulled on the handle. The door swung open.

There were only two reasons for the door to unlock. Either they were letting me escape so I could lead them to Scruffy, or Scruffy had infiltrated the system and was trying to get me out. Either way, running seemed like a great idea.

The power went out, leaving the corridor lit by dim emergency lamps.

I ran.

FORTY
PRECIOUS TIME

In the orange glow of the emergency lamps, I sprinted down the corridor, my bare feet slapping against the tiles. Five stories underground — somehow I had to get upstairs and out of the building. After that, I'd get in contact with Scruffy, find out how to pull the hidden codes from my memories, and then shut down the Micklage corporation.

With the power out, I'd have to take the stairs. Unfortunately, if anyone was looking for me, that would be the first place they would go. So... A disguise would be nice. Or even just shoes. I wanted my boots back, but that could wait.

The rooms I passed were all lit with the same orange glow, letting me see if anyone was inside. The first two were occupied by multiple people. Protocol must have required them to stay put when the power went out, because otherwise everyone would have flooded the corridor. I'd seen enough situations like this on ships to know how people normally reacted: mill around uselessly and get in everyone's way.

The third room was unoccupied, but the door was locked. Same with the fourth and fifth. I was already getting worried that I hadn't seen any sign of the stairwell yet when I came to a cross corridor. Stars! This place was a maze and I had no idea how to get out.

Pulling on doors as I ran, I found one that hadn't fully latched. Inside were cleaning bots and other supplies. I had a brief moment of elation, thinking I'd found Scruffy in its current form, but no, these bots were a different brand. Still... It wouldn't hurt to check. "Scruffy, are you in here?"

Yes. This was now my life. Talking to random cleaning bots to find out if they were an illegal AI.

The entire row of bots powered up from their resting state. That had to be the cleaning bots reacting to a human voice, right? Or had Scruffy somehow infiltrated the cleaning bot network? There was no way to tell. The bots couldn't speak, and I couldn't transmit any data to them.

The tiny room held no uniforms or other clothing. Any janitorial staff would be expected to change before coming down to this level. There were some caustic chemicals, but I didn't see how that would help me. After all, *I* was the one in bare feet.

"If you *are* Scruffy, give me a sign to show me how to get out of here."

The cleaning bots remained in their waiting state. So, probably not Scruffy then. I was wasting precious time talking to a bunch of bots with a ten word vocabulary. Great.

I left a jug of cleaner holding open the door, just in case I needed to get back in. If nothing else, it might set off alarms when the power came back on, and the response team would have to waste resources checking that room.

Running down the corridor again, I passed the bot lift, a miniature elevator used only to transfer bots and supplies between the floors. Large buildings tended to have them because important people didn't want to be in the same space as cleaning bots. Bot lifts ran faster and were cheaper to build and maintain because they didn't have to worry about safety — if the cab got stuck for a few days or fell twenty stories, it didn't matter. At most, the company would be out the cost of the cargo, and probably not even that — those cleaning bots would roll away without a scratch.

The flap over the bot lift was open, showing the empty cab. I would fit inside, but that didn't help. With the power off, it wasn't going anywhere. And with the power on, I wouldn't be able to tell it where to take me. Plus, a human getting into the bot lift would definitely trigger an alarm. See prior note about not being safe for humans.

Another door hadn't latched properly, this one to some sort of office space. Who did you have to irritate to get stuck with a secretarial job five stories underground? And seriously, they were doing a terrible job of building mainte-nance if this many doors weren't closing. Or maybe it was related to the ventilation system being shut down. If nega-tive pressure inside the room normally caused the door to fully close, that meant someone had left this room since the power had gone out. My guess was the occupant going for a bathroom break, so they might be back at any second.

Two coats hung by the door, both about the same size. I grabbed one and looked around to see if the owner of the coat had left a second pair of shoes. Under the desk, I found... fuzzy slippers.

"You have *got* to be kidding me." I looked at my bare feet. Then I looked at the slippers. They were white, padded, with huge eyes and bunny ears sprouting from the sides. The sort of thing someone might wear at home as a joke. And this woman — based on the size I was betting it was a woman — wore hers at work.

The slippers might make me memorable. But probably not in the same way that bare feet would. I put them on and shuffled out the door as quickly as I could. At least they were comfortable.

In the distance, booted feet trotted on tiles. Not the occupant of that office — anyone who wore bunny slippers at work wouldn't be running around in military boots, and it sounded like at least two people. That had to be security, and I still hadn't found the stairwell.

I could hide in the office... if I hadn't let the door close already. Could I make it back to the room with the cleaning bots? The sound was hard to localize, but I was pretty sure I'd be running straight toward the guards. I needed somewhere to hide *right now*.

The bot lift! If I could get inside and hold the flap shut, they would assume the cab was on a different floor.

Sprinting in bulky bunny slippers wasn't easy, but I dove inside the bot lift and pulled the flap down just in time to hear a man open a nearby door and call, "Clear."

My breath was loud in the pitch black cab. A few seconds later, someone tugged on the lift flap, but I had a death grip on the edge and it didn't budge.

This was perfect. All I had to do was wait until the guards moved farther away. Then I could get out and go in the opposite direction, which probably led to the stairwell.

I was still congratulating myself on my cunning plan to get out of the maze when the whole building shuddered to life. Light leaked around the edges of the flap, and the cab vibrated.

Before I could move, the cab dropped.

FORTY-ONE
BY DESIGN

The bot lift dropped, and only my hand clapped over my mouth kept me from shrieking. Luckily, the noise from the building being powered up covered my muffled swearing until I had myself under control.

And that was when the lift halted.

Let me just say that if I had *ever* landed a passenger ship with that many gees, I would have been fired so fast I wouldn't have had time to pack my things. Sure, I'd had a few rough flights lately, but none of that was my fault, no matter how many complaints Scruffy made. The bot lift was that way by *design*.

When I'd recovered, I reached for the flap. Then I reconsidered. True, I was farther away from the guards. But I'd still have to get past them on the stairwell — assuming I could find it — and though I had no idea how many levels this building had below ground, we had dropped at least another five. If I had to run after climbing ten flights of stairs, I'd hurt myself.

On the flip side, if I *didn't* get out now, there was every chance this thing would drop further.

Before I could make up my mind, the lift slammed back into action, the acceleration pushing me down to the floor. "Scruffy," I gritted out, "if you're controlling this, remember that I still need my brain."

After another few seconds, it occurred to me to worry about how abruptly the lift would stop on the other end and what I might slam into at the top of the cab. But apparently they'd considered that, as my weight dropped for the last thirty seconds of the journey. The instant the lift halted, I rolled out, taking my chances in the hallway rather than risk the lift plummeting back down.

Luck was with me — nobody was in sight. From the view through the windows, I was near the top of the building. Walking down this many stairs would be better than climbing them, but maybe I could find an unwatched freight elevator.

I shuffled along in my stolen bunny slippers, checking the doors as I went. Up here, each door had a nameplate. One name made me pause, then clomp faster.

Vira Micklage.

Scruffy *had* to have been controlling that lift bot. I refused to believe I'd arrived where the Micklage strategist had her offices by accident. Unfortunately, I still didn't know what Scruffy's plan was. But maybe I could work it out.

Fact: Scruffy knew where I was and had directed the lift bot to get me up here. That meant the AI had access to the security feed and, since nobody was chasing after me right now, it was erasing me from the footage. There had to be something up here that Scruffy needed, or it would have sent me to a floor closer to the exit.

My boots? As much as I wished for my regular footwear, Scruffy had other priorities.

I heard people talking somewhere nearby and tried to look like I belonged (which, for the record, was not easy when wearing bunny slippers). The lock clicked on a door ahead of me, and I dove for the handle before it could latch again. Whatever Scruffy wanted had to be in here. I slipped into the room and pulled the door closed.

Automated lights came on when I entered the room, and my first impression was that this was the place they shoved everything they didn't need right away but didn't want to throw out. Or maybe it was being staged for later disposal. Chairs, old bots, hats... Was that a dinosaur costume? Rows and rows of shelves stuffed with crap.

If I had to find something without even knowing what I was looking for, I was in trouble.

Then I saw it: a long fuzzy pink tail dangling from the top shelf. Climbing atop a rolling chair — after riding in the bot lift, I was inured to safety hazards — I dug around until I found the robo-dog the tail was connected to. This *had* to be what Scruffy had sent me to retrieve. It made sense. The AI was no longer connected, but if I could restore the link, Scruffy could help clear a path to get me out of here. And we could talk.

The chair wobbled as I yanked at the fluffy outfit, but I finally got both of us safely to the floor. I flipped the robo-dog's power. Nothing.

Right. Whatever Rance had done with the electromagnetic stunner might have permanently scrambled the controller.

While the robo-dog rested on a charging plate, I looked around the room, ostensibly searching for something with a compatible controller, but mostly looking for my boots. Where else would they have put them? There couldn't possibly be *two* junk rooms.

But if my boots were in the mess, I couldn't find them. I was stuck with the bunny slippers. At least I'd found a simple toolkit and a massage chair with a controller to swap into the robo-dog. Why a massage chair would need a limited AI, I didn't know, but I'd pulled enough parts from them at Orabella's salvage yard to know what was under all the padding.

Fifteen minutes later, I had the chair opened up. Time to swap the controller and hope Scruffy could connect. Honestly, the hardest part of the whole business was finding the opening under all that pink fluff. I nearly gave up and cut the costume off. Then it was just a few screws and a self-seating connection. Voila! Scorch marks ran across the old controller, the one that had run my galley. I patted it sadly and settled it into the massage chair. "I wish I'd had a chance to know you better."

When I hit the robo-dog's power button, this time its eyes flashed red. Success. Now how long would it take Scruffy to establish a connection?

I'd just finished closing up the costume and brushing out the fur when the robo-dog flipped to its feet. "Captain de Mure," it started, and I flung my arms around its neck.

The relief I felt at no longer being alone was so strong, I missed the rest of its sentence. "Scruffy, I've never been so glad to talk to anybody!"

"Captain de Mure," it repeated, "hide!"

Someone was walking in the hallway outside.

FORTY-TWO
ARE YOU HAPPY NOW?

As the footsteps stopped right outside the door, I wiggled into the only space available — an open slot in the rack, between a heap of ancient cables and a large refrigeration unit. Even seated, my head hit the shelf above me. Scruffy's robo-dog sat down on top of me, effectively hiding my face, and leaving me with a mouthful of pink synthetic fur. My toes stuck out over the edge. Hopefully, nobody would notice the bunny slippers amidst all the other junk in the room.

The air pressure changed when the door opened, and I heard a familiar voice. Rance Micklage sounded aggrieved, his usual tone when he couldn't get his own way. "Yes, yes, fine, I'm looking. Are you happy now?"

Nobody answered. Whoever he was talking to wasn't here. Good. Scruffy had tranquilizer darts, if they hadn't been disabled before the robo-dog had been shoved in this room, but I didn't want to leave a trail of sleeping bodies showing everyone where we'd been. Synthetic fur went up my nostrils when I breathed in.

I didn't mind leaving *one* drugged body behind. Rance

deserved everything bad that might happen to him. It had almost been worth getting taken into custody just to see his uncle stun him. If Scruffy darted him, I might forgive the AI for that trip in the bot lift.

Of course, if I got caught again, it would be a whole lot less fun.

"Yes, I'm in the holding area. She's not here." His voice came closer as he walked the length of the room so he could look down each aisle. "You've been watching the security feed. She's gone to ground somewhere, or she made it out of the building while the power was out."

Now he was standing right in front of me. "It's still here. I'm looking right at it."

My nose tickled, and I could feel a sneeze building. Stupid synthetic fur. I could hold off until the door closed if Rance left now. But Rance seemed to have parked himself in the worst possible place until he could finish his conversation.

"You always treat me like this, and I'm sick of it. Just remember who grabbed her in the first place." He waited while the other person spoke. My need to sneeze grew. "Yes, but —. No, that —. Listen to me!" He stomped one foot, just like a small child would. "Forget it! I'm leaving. You can do whatever you want. Argh!" His yell of frustration was followed by the sound of his handheld impacting the floor, then hitting the wall after he kicked it. "You useless waste of space!"

I sneezed.

It was the loudest sneeze in the history of the universe, a sneeze so percussive I thought my brains would leak from my ears.

Silence greeted me. Mid-tantrum Rance might have

missed a delicate cough, but he would have had to be deaf to miss that sneeze.

"Is that...?" The robo-dog was pulled from my grasp, and suddenly I could see Rance's face right in front of me. He smiled slowly, cruelty twisting his lips. "I've been looking for you."

"Funny. Like most people, I've been trying to *avoid* you." Being crammed in the shelf wasn't how I wanted to have any conversation with Rance, so I threw myself forward, nearly butting his nose with my forehead before he yanked his head back. I scrambled to my feet, though I was still trapped in the aisle.

Only when Rance let the pink-clad robo-dog slide down to the floor did I realize he hadn't figured out Scruffy was remotely piloting it. All I had to do was keep his attention off the robo-dog, and Scruffy could knock him out. No problem. I'd just witnessed Rance's inability to keep calm under pressure. And he couldn't signal anyone that he'd found me, since he'd just destroyed his handheld. "Looks like your plan to take over the family empire ran into a few snags. Tiber certainly didn't mind using a stunner on you."

His cheeks flushed. "Where's the AI with the synthetic crystal?"

"That's a really great question." My attempt to look casual and confident was undercut by the bunny slippers. "Not here. But you already knew that."

His eyes narrowed. "I don't think you actually know. But I bet it will show up on its own if I threaten to throw you off the roof." He grabbed the back of my collar with one hand and shoved a stunner against my spine with the other, pushing me ahead of him. Looking at the ceiling, he said, "Did you hear that, AI? I'll throw her off the roof if you don't turn yourself in by the time we get there."

Our positioning was perfect for Scruffy to spring to life and shoot him full of tranquilizers. I waited, letting myself be pushed toward the hall.

Nothing happened.

Sweat broke out at my hairline. "Uh, Scruffy? Now would be good."

Still nothing. That was bad.

We reached the door. Maybe the power pack in the robo-dog had gone bad? Or something had happened to Scruffy, making it unable to remotely control the robo-dog. Either way, I had to lose Rance before we made it up to the roof. I didn't trust him not to throw me off in a fit of pique, even if Scruffy gave in to his demands.

The faintest whiff of burning plastic wafted through the air as I grabbed the door handle. Then Rance grunted in surprise. I flinched, expecting to feel the stunner shock my spine, but instead, Rance let go and slumped to the floor.

Spinning around, I kicked the stunner away from Rance's hand as he blinked up at me in confusion. "Muh..." His eyes unfocussed and fluttered closed.

I let out a long breath. "Cutting it close there, Scruffy."

Smoke rose from the robo-dog's covering, the pink fur charred and smoldering near the shoulders. "I apologize, Captain de Mure," it said as it walked forward. A scrap of fabric dropped to the floor. "This disguise covers the security features. I needed to cut the ports free before I could assist."

The fluffy pink fur had been chosen to make the robo-dog look harmless, back when we wanted Micklage to believe we were smuggling Scruffy down to the surface inside. Now, it looked weirdly battle-hardened and dangerous. Nobody would mistake it for a toy.

I opened the door. "After you."

Find a terminal, remember the codes, shut down Micklage Industries. Wait. No. I needed to find Scruffy first — its physical location. If this code caused as much chaos as Bett expected, our connection would get cut. Our plans had assumed the group mind link would be active. Yes, Scruffy could tell me where it was first, but if I was caught... No. "Scruffy, I need to be free of this building before we do anything else."

"Yes, Captain de Mure."

An entire building of Micklage security looking for us. No problem. What could possibly go wrong?

FORTY-THREE
BRUISES

Getting out of the building proved a challenge.

"I can take control of the elevator," Scruffy told me, "but once you reach the ground floor, you would be trapped. The exits are well guarded."

By *well guarded*, I assumed the AI meant there were more people than it could reasonably expect to combat with the robo-dog's tranquilizer darts. We were currently hiding on the top floor of the Micklage Industries headquarters, me in my stolen bunny slippers and Scruffy remotely piloting a robotic dog encased in scorched pink fur. It had tapped into building surveillance, but we weren't going to *sneak* past anyone.

Somehow, I *had* to get out of this building.

Scruffy raised its head. "The hallway is clear. Go right and enter the stairwell, then go up to the roof."

The roof? Even as I considered, I shuffled down the hall. "Are you picking me up in an air taxi?"

"Not quite." The robo-dog stopped in front of the stairwell door. "Be quiet inside. There are guards on the tenth floor landing."

The silence in the stairwell was deafening, making me glad for the first time that I was wearing padded slippers. The robo-dog's fuzzy mittens muffled the sound of it climbing. Halfway up the flight of stairs, it occurred to me that it might be so quiet because there were no guards to hear me, and Scruffy had just wanted to make me stop asking questions.

(Call me cynical, but sharing a group mind with Scruffy had made me aware of when it thought lying was appropriate. It was weirdly similar to my own criteria. Possibly Scruffy had picked it up from me.)

Because I wasn't completely sure it had lied, I waited until I'd closed the door behind us on the roof. "There weren't really any guards on the tenth floor, were there?" Wind whistled past us, and I realized how *high* we were. An incoming ship from the nearby spaceport banked harder than it should have needed — the Puma IVs were famous for wallowing, but *that* approach said the pilot wasn't paying attention — drowning out any reply Scruffy might have made.

We were far enough from the low wall around the edge of the roof that I should have felt secure, but I didn't. I *hated* heights. Still, it wasn't as if I'd be up here long. The entrance to one of the ventilation shafts was just a few steps away. I'd never thought they were big enough to hold a person, but Scruffy had the building plans, so it would know for sure.

"Never mind. Which ventilation shaft are we using and how do I get the cover off?"

"Captain de Mure, the ventilation shafts are not large enough, and the roof has the only outlets."

So no air taxi and no ventilation shafts... "Scruffy, you *do* have a plan, right? Am I just supposed to hide up here until the Micklages get bored and quit looking? Because you should have told me that before we left Rance drooling in that storage room." Rance had tracked me for months after he'd spent a few hours being handled with kid gloves at a port security station. This time he'd have *bruises*.

"Captain, there's another option. Are you aware of how the windows of the building are cleaned?"

I hadn't spent much time in buildings like this, but I'd occasionally seen cleaning bots hovering in the air, spraying cleaning solution and wiping it off. Small cleaning bots. *Very* small cleaning bots. I backed up to the door. "No. They can't possibly lift someone my size."

"You don't need to go up. You just need to fall slowly enough not to get injured."

I stared at the robo-dog. "You're joking, right?"

"Captain de Mure, I've examined the specifications on the window cleaning bots. From this height, you should be able to hold the bot and be going a safe speed when you land on the ground. If you start from the southwest corner and descend at an angle, you won't be visible from inside the building. I estimate we will have three minutes after you reach the ground before an armed response arrives."

It was serious about this.

Two cleaning bots whirred above the surface of the roof, heading for the corner Scruffy had specified. "I *never* should have let Bett talk me into this." Forget saving the Independent Federation. After *Tiger Lily* had been repaired, I should have changed course and headed for unclaimed territory. No Micklages *and* I'd still have my new galley unit.

Now I either had to jump off the top of the building or go back inside and fight my way out. On top of that, Rance would be waking up sometime soon. I wasn't sticking around for that.

I pushed my palms together, trying to psych myself up for the challenge. "Fine. Let's do this. But there'd better be a really big reward when we get you back to the Independent Federation."

"Yes, Captain de Mure."

I followed the robo-dog over to the corner where the bots waited. They were small orbs with a diameter equal to the length of my forearm. "How do I ride this thing?"

"I suggest you drape yourself over it so your weight is evenly distributed. Keeping yourself stable will be key, as the bots can only provide lift in one direction. If it flips over and stays, it can only accelerate toward the ground."

This was getting better and better. Sitting on the low wall, I swung one leg over and then made the mistake of looking down. "This is a terrible idea." With time and basic supplies, I could harness a few of these bots together. Then it would be a slightly better terrible idea.

"Captain, three guards are in the stairwell, approaching the roof." The robo-dog climbed onto the ledge directly over the second bot. "We need to go *now*."

What were the chances it was lying to me again? There hadn't been guards in the stairwell the last time. Scruffy could just be pressuring me, so I didn't think about this too hard and realize no sane person would grab a hovering bot and jump off the roof.

The door to the stairwell swung open.

"Ah, stars!" Wrapping myself around the other bot, I pitched over the edge, heading straight toward the ground.

FORTY-FOUR

THE BALLAD OF SPARKY BUTTONS

Scruffy's idea of getting down from the roof by riding on the window washing bots had been a good one. Unfortunately, there was one minor problem — me.

If I'd been carefully balanced, the bot would have held me up and allowed me to fight gravity long enough to make a fairly graceful landing. From the glimpses I caught of it, the robo-dog was descending in a staid, controlled manner.

Meanwhile, I was somersaulting away from the building. When I was upright, the bot slowed my fall. But I had enough angular momentum that I kept flipping over, at which point the bot cut its engines so we weren't accelerating toward the ground.

I flipped upright, and my breath was knocked out as the bot turned on its engines, ramming into my chest. Our periods of inversion had caught up with us — we were heading toward the ground at a fast clip. If I'd had thrusters, I would have deployed them. Instead, I continued the roll and now I was free falling again.

Throughout all this, I was trying to keep from screaming because the whole point was a stealthy getaway, and me doing my best air horn imitation was the opposite of stealth.

When Trition was built, the developers had the advantage of not needing to tear anything down first. It had been a big rock without an atmosphere when they started, which gave them the ability to arrange the biological components however they wanted. Luckily for me, they'd added a row of trees and shrubs along the monorail line going to the port, probably a scenic noise barrier.

I pitched into a tree hard enough to break the first branch and fell onto another one, which slowly collapsed, allowing me to make an almost dignified descent to the ground. A group of pedestrians did their best to ignore the person who had just appeared from the open sky.

When I dropped the last few inches, I realized the bunny slippers had fallen off at some point during my acrobatics. I was back to bare feet. The pavement was smooth enough to walk on without injury, but it made me stand out, which wasn't good. With my boots almost certainly back in the building I'd just fled from, I'd have to accept their loss and find new footwear. I took a moment to mourn my boots — we'd been through a lot together.

Movement in the sky caught my eye — Scruffy's robo-dog gliding along. Suddenly, there was a laser burst that hit a nearby building, and another. The window washing bot with the robo-dog dropped to the ground half a kilometer away.

I sprinted in that direction.

If I lost track of the robo-dog, I'd never find Scruffy's processor on my own. Our takedown of Micklage would have to wait until the AI found me again, and I'd be stuck trying to blend in despite looking like I'd gone five rounds with a tree.

The robo-dog met me in the middle, pink fur on its head still smoking. We were lucky whoever had been shooting had aimed for the head instead of the body, where the remote connection to Scruffy resided. Or maybe they'd just been a bad shot. There's really no excuse for missing your target with a laser.

"This way, Captain de Mure," it said as it cut sideways into a gap between buildings. "I was afraid you had been gravely injured at the speed at which you fell. Perhaps next time you should avoid rolling the bot."

Unbelievable. The AI wasn't apologizing for making me jump off the roof. It was blaming *me* for not being able to keep my balance atop a machine never meant to carry my weight.

I made a face as I ran after it. "Remember when I found you back in the salvage yard? My life would be a lot simpler if I'd just left you behind that panel."

"And I would certainly be housed in something more dignified than *this*," it replied and slowed. We walked through the automatic doors of a workshare building, the sort of place office drones went when they needed a more secure location than a corner of their bedroom and their business didn't have a local office.

As a place to hide, it was a smart choice. Everyone was used to seeing strange faces, and there was no standard dress code. Granted, most people would at least wear shoes, and the robo-dog's charred appearance might raise eyebrows, but we got to the elevator and pressed the button for the third floor without encountering anyone.

The doors closed. Scruffy said, "Remember the time you and Bett went to bail one of your passengers out of jail and he wouldn't stop singing in the cab on the way back to the hotel?"

A laugh escaped me. The passenger in question —
drunk enough to lose all sense — had been a famous singer,
and he'd insisted on "repaying" our deed by warbling his
way through forty-seven verses of *The Ballad of Sparky
Buttons*, a song about a depressed ship circling a black hole,
trying to decide whether to fly closer and remembering one
last task during every verse. It was a song usually reserved
for children and the very, very intoxicated.

Emerging from the elevator, the robo-dog went left,
leading me through a warren of fully enclosed cubicles. We
had to be getting close to Scruffy's processor. There was no
other reason to be up here.

"I know why *I* remember that, but where did you hear
about it?" Even as I asked, the answer was obvious. Bett had
told the AI. That was weird, because I didn't realize they'd
talked much to each other when I wasn't there.

With one charred paw, the robo-dog tapped a code into
a cubicle and the door slid open. "Can you sing it for me?"

Inside the cubicle was a standard terminal, an uncom-
fortable-looking chair... and the cleaning bot I'd put the AI
into before I'd left *Tiger Lily*. But even as I felt the sense of
relief about being reunited, the song Scruffy had asked for
welled up.

It wasn't the drunk musician's voice I heard in my mind,
but Bett's raspy contralto. And she wasn't singing about a
suicidal ship and its endless tasks, but a string of nonsense
words.

This was the code to bring down Micklage, waiting in
my head for Scruffy to bring it forward.

Sitting on the metal chair, I sang along to the words in
my head, the nonsense appearing on the terminal as Scruffy
transcribed it. The verses seemed to go on and on, perhaps

not Sparky Buttons's never-ending ballad in length, but long enough that my throat hurt by the time I sang the last word.

I closed my mouth and looked at the terminal. "That's it."

The screen flickered as the message was sent, but nothing else happened. I guess I'd been expecting, I don't know, explosions maybe? *Something* anyhow. But instead, I was still barefoot in a tiny cubicle with a cleaning bot and a robo-dog on a planet controlled by the Micklages.

Then the lights went out and somebody screamed.

FORTY-FIVE

DIGNITY

With the power off, the cubicle was pitch black. Windows were a luxury Scruffy hadn't bothered with. Before my eyes could adjust, a low glow from the robo-dog's eyes lit up the area enough for me to see shapes. "I guess it worked." My voice was unsteady.

In my imagination, unleashing the code on the Micklage equipment would happen comfortably far from me — not leave me in a dark building with air growing increasingly more stale by the minute. The person screaming had stopped, but I could hear other querying voices from nearby cubicles. Mostly, they seemed to be wondering if anyone knew how long this outage was supposed to last, and if not, was anyone else calling it quits for the day. All the other regular sounds of the building had stopped, leaving an eerie silence.

"Captain de Mure," the robo-dog said in a low voice, "this should delay pursuit, but I can no longer monitor alerts. We should leave soon."

Right. We needed to get to the port and find a way up to the orbital station where *Tiger Lily* and my cat waited.

But first... "Let's get you back in a form that can move quickly."

A search of the cubicle's drawers yielded a cheap set of tools, the sort of thing given to a non-technical employee to make them feel empowered without letting them cause trouble. Both wrenches were bent, the penlight didn't work, and the tiny display screen only lit up on the right side, but the kit had just enough usable items that I could remove Scruffy's processor from the cleaning bot and install it in the robo-dog again.

It drew back when I held up the pink fur outfit. "Captain, I believe it is time to restore some dignity to our travels."

I looked at the costume in my hands, and then at the gleaming metal of the robo-dog. "And this doesn't scream dignity to you?"

When I opened the cubicle door, a few people stood in the hallway talking. They didn't seem surprised to see a stranger, even one in bare feet. The robo-dog got a few odd looks, but Scruffy stayed at my side, and when I ignored it, everyone else did, too.

A woman wearing all white stood next to the dead elevator. "Are we just supposed to work through this?" she asked as I walked by.

It occurred to me that the more people there were on the street, the less I would stand out, so I shrugged. "I can't get my work done like this, so I'm going home."

And just like that, everyone else on the floor decided to leave. Sometimes, you really can lead from the middle of the pack.

The noise we all made going down the stairwell attracted people from other levels, causing a mass exodus. On the ground floor, a waist-high delivery cart had stopped in the middle of the lobby, its controller knocked out by the code Scruffy and I had entered. I moved to stand next to the wall, as if I were waiting for someone, and as soon as there was a lull in people going by, I pulled the cart into an empty room. Inside, some poor soul had been organizing a corporate retreat. Rolled banners with inspirational slogans were stacked on the table. *Do it right the first time; Learn the Micklage way.*

"We need a way to hide you," I said, pushing the cart onto its side so I could see how the controller was attached. With the aid of Scruffy's lasers, ten minutes later we had a cart I could push. It was a waste of resources to create cloth banners when nearly every meeting room had wall displays that could show the same thing, but it worked out for me. I took a few extra minutes to cut fabric strips, wind them around my feet, and tie them at the ankles. As a fashion statement, it was questionable, but it hid my feet and provided a little protection. Scruffy climbed into the cart, and I piled the extra posters on top, hiding the robo-dog and leaving no evidence behind.

Then I joined the next group of people walking outside. A man in a building security uniform even held the door open for me as he tried to get his handheld communicator working.

The monorail wasn't running, and the roads were completely blocked since all the automated systems had stopped working. By my estimate, traffic wouldn't move for at least the next twelve hours. So even though the Micklage family knew Scruffy and I would try to escape, if we could get to the port soon, there might not be enough people there to stop us.

HIDING in the shadows near the port, I recognized a ship waiting on the tarmac. "Surely Rance wouldn't mind if we borrowed his shuttle for a quick trip."

"Captain, I suspect he might mind," Scruffy said.

"Just another reason to choose it." While hyperspace ships with their precious cardinal crystals had extended security, a shuttle that could only make it to the space station in orbit around Trition wouldn't be as closely guarded. Even if Rance had removed me from the access list — and that was already a big if, since Rance was a little lazy about things like that — I was betting Scruffy could break through any code lock on the ship.

The trouble was the large open space between us and the shuttle, and the number of guards patrolling. Though the rest of the city was shut down, my optimism about getting away had been misplaced.

While Scruffy's robo-dog could cover that distance before anyone noticed, I'd be lucky to get halfway. The guards would probably have time for tea and a quick nap while waiting for me to hobble by. "Scruffy, maybe you should take the shuttle up and fly *Tiger Lily* back to the Independent Federation. I'll find someplace to hide down here until you can send someone."

"Captain, I'm not leaving you behind."

Maybe we could steal a vehicle? Or get the motor in our cart to work? I looked at the cart. Then I looked at Scruffy. It wasn't the *worst* idea I'd ever had... And Scruffy owed me for making me jump off the roof. "Remember when you said it was time to restore dignity to our travels?"

There was just the slightest pause before Scruffy answered. "Yes."

I drew in a slow breath. "We might have to hold off on that for just a bit."

FORTY-SIX
TALLYHO!

"Captain de Mure, this is a terrible idea." Scruffy's robo-dog body crouched in the shadows next to the cart as we watched the latest patrol go by.

With their high-tech monitoring knocked out by Bett's codes, the port guards had settled into a comfortable routine. They traveled around the perimeter in pairs, then through the avenues where the ships waited for ground control to recover, and finally returned to the security building to down a bracing cup of tea before starting all over again. The part about the tea was an assumption, since I couldn't see inside the building, but the guards looked warm and contented as they patrolled. Meanwhile, the wind whipped through my thin clothing and I was freezing.

"This is a *great* idea," I replied, rubbing my arms. "You just don't like it because you're worried your AI friends will laugh at you if they find out." The last pair rounded the corner of the first avenue. In another twenty seconds, they would be out of sight.

"Captain, after sharing a group mind with you, my self-respect setting has been recalibrated. But I still think this plan is unnecessarily risky."

"Do you have a better one?"

Only the sound of wind blowing between the buildings answered.

I climbed into the cart and put the loop of the makeshift rope — formed from inspirational banners — around the robo-dog's neck. The attachments to the cart left the Micklage logo flapping in the breeze, as if this were some odd prototype. While the placement hadn't been intentional, I hoped it might buy us an extra few seconds before the guards started shooting. Weirder things had been dreamed up by the dregs of the family, and *nobody* wanted to deal with an angry Micklage whose latest toy had been destroyed.

The guards made the final turn toward the security building and passed out of sight. "Tallyho!" I whispered.

Then I almost fell out the back of the cart when it jerked forward. "Keep going," I said, struggling to right myself. By the time I was right-side up, the robo-dog had hit its top speed, metal feet clattering on the pavement. This was faster than I could run, even with shoes.

It was also faster than the cart was meant to go. Designed for leisurely trips between cubicles in an office building, it had no shock absorption. And I was now realizing that by removing the motor so I could push it by hand, we'd raised the center of gravity. The tiny wheels rattled and screeched over unforgiving pavement. When a bump sent us into the air, the frame shuddered.

No problem. The cart just had to stay together until we reached Rance's shuttle.

We were halfway across the open space when the alert

sounded. I popped my head up to look around. "Those vacuum sucking meteorites! How'd they notice us so — oof." The last word came out with a rush of air when the front wheels caught and I flew forward into the rail. Only Scruffy's quick yank on the axle rope got the cart moving forward again. When I fell back, the frame creaked ominously. I dragged myself up to look over the edge. Six guards ran toward us. If we kept on our direct path to the shuttle, they would cut us off. "Scruffy!"

"I see them."

Scruffy cut sideways down an avenue parallel to the one we wanted. It was a good choice — we could get close to the shuttle, then scramble over the docking equipment between the spacecraft until we reached our destination.

But the hard turn was too much for the poor, abused cart.

As the cart swung wide, the frame completed its separation. The front right wheel popped off, and the right panel tumbled off with it. The rest of the cart skidded sideways. For a moment, I thought we might keep going on the other three wheels. Then the entire frame crumpled, and I tumbled, wrapped in the remains of a banner that exhorted *Careful choices make pleasant journeys. Follow the Micklage strategy.*

I slammed to a stop against the cargo entrance of a Lynx 9. It was a sturdy ramp, as befitted a cargo ship, though my collision probably bent the hinge pin. As I lay wheezing on the ground, staring up at the night sky, I thought about how mad their mechanic was going to be. Not my problem. I gave myself two shuddering breaths before I decided I hadn't broken anything important.

"Captain?" The robo-dog appeared in front of my face, blocking the stars. "Are you injured?"

"I don't think so." I rolled over and staggered to my feet. "Which direction?"

Without the cart, we didn't need to stick to the avenues. I trailed behind the robo-dog, letting it pull me forward through the dark with the remains of the harness. Behind us, I could hear guards shouting to each other as they came across the remains of the cart. Beams of light flashed around us, but Scruffy and I stayed ahead of them, ducking under launch platforms and a quiet resupply truck.

When we reached the shuttle, I glanced around. To unlock the door, I'd need to stand in the open for five seconds. And if my codes no longer worked, Scruffy would have to finesse the system — that might take a while.

Five seconds. I could do this. Trotting up the ramp, I punched in the unlock code and let it scan my palm.

Waiting.

"Hey!" a gruff voice yelled from the other side of the Jaguar IV two avenues over. "You there! Put your hands up and turn around!"

Waiting.

"Hands in the air!" Another guard yelled from the other side.

If I took my hand off the scanner, the shuttle wouldn't complete the opening sequence. But if I didn't put my hands up, some overeager Micklage goon might shoot me.

Beep.

The hatch slid open. I pitched inside, Scruffy scrambling in behind me. A blast of energy from a hand weapon blackened the hull as I hit the emergency close-and-lock button.

In the quiet shuttle, I blew out a long breath. We were safe. Nothing the guards carried would be strong enough to break into the ship. "See? It was a *great* plan."

"Captain." Scruffy's voice was flat, with no hint at the relief it should be feeling.

Turning slowly, I followed its gaze. On the other side of the cargo bay, stunner in one hand, stood a smiling Rance Micklage.

FORTY-SEVEN
EXPENDABLE

Inside the shuttle, it was quiet, the insulated hull muting the shouting and sirens outside. Ignoring the stunner, I stared at Rance. "What are *you* doing here?"

So... not my finest moment. Technically, it was *his* shuttle. Scruffy and I had merely broken in. But Rance wasn't a pilot. With luxury hotels and resorts available nearby, why would he sit in the unpowered shuttle, one that didn't even have a dedicated sleeping area? Rance Micklage's family literally owned the planet.

Leaning one shoulder against the bulkhead, he acted nonchalant. "I asked myself where you would go next, and the answer was obvious."

"Only to people who know how lax your security is." Glancing around the otherwise empty shuttle, I raised one eyebrow. "That's why you're the only one here, isn't it? You don't want to admit that someone you fired still has valid access codes."

From the thinning of his lips, I'd hit my mark, but he replied, "And allow my uncle to get the credit for capturing you? Not likely."

And that, in two sentences, summed up Rance's character. Instead of working with a team and ensuring he captured his quarry, he was willing to take a chance on me getting away, as long as it meant he wouldn't have to share the credit if he succeeded. His family *really* deserved a refund from whomever they paid to tweak his embryonic genes.

Coming after us on his own proved Rance was an idiot — the robo-dog had knocked him out with tranquilizer darts once before. There was nothing stopping us from doing it again. "Scruffy? Would you please...?"

A hiss of air accompanied two darts. Rance flinched as they hit his chest and thigh, but then his smile widened. "The antidote to that drug lasts two days."

Well, crud. Maybe I was the idiot, not Rance. That thought hurt. Deeply.

Next to me, the robo-dog folded down to the deck, lowered its head, and stopped moving.

Rance frowned. "What is it doing?"

Honestly, I had no idea, but since it was something I'd never seen the robo-dog do, I assumed Scruffy had a plan. "It needs to charge. The thing has been giving warnings all day." Nothing said "harmless" like a low power indicator.

Gesturing with the stunner, Rance said, "Turn around, hands up, and open the hatch."

I raised my hands above my head, and then dropped them. "Which is it? Raise my hands or open the hatch?"

"What?"

"I can't very well open the hatch if my hands are over my head. This is your problem, Rance. You never think ahead."

The vein at his temple throbbed, and I knew I had him. Once he got angry, Rance stopped thinking straight. He'd forget about the robo-dog, leaving Scruffy free to do what-ever it planned. Of course, he'd also do his best to beat me to a pulp, so I was hoping Scruffy's plans included rescuing me.

Rance strode forward, stunner extended. He could have subdued me from where he stood, but he wanted to jam the weapon into my back when he set it off, so he could feel my muscles spasm.

Just as I'd predicted, he'd forgotten about the robo-dog, stepping over it with no more thought than if it had been a piece of furniture. And that was when Scruffy shot up, slamming into Rance's groin with a force that lifted the man off his feet.

Rance collapsed to the deck, keening as he sucked in air. Then he curled into a fetal position.

I picked up the stunner from where it had fallen. "Nice job, Scruffy. There's probably not an antidote for *that*, is there?"

"That maneuver seemed less likely to cause permanent damage than using my lasers."

Given my feelings about Rance, I wasn't particularly worried about damaging him permanently. When I finished tying him up, he was still having trouble catching his breath.

"There we go." As much as I wanted a Rance-free ship, having a Micklage as a hostage might make some things easier. "Scruffy, see if you can contact the control tower and let them know we have Rance aboard. We'll leave him at the station as soon as we're back on our own ship." That might keep some overeager gunner from shooting us down.

"Yes, captain."

DESPITE WHAT BETT'S codes had done on the planet, the orbital station hadn't been visibly affected. Maybe they hadn't received as much tainted equipment, or maybe whoever was in charge of security had done a better job. Either way, it took a live feed of a trussed-up Rance begging them to let us dock so he could have medical care before they allowed the shuttle to approach.

As a bonus, during my search for better weapons, I found my boots. "Scruffy, the universe loves us!" Just putting them on gave me a boost of confidence. My feet were still bruised and sore, but at least I could walk without wondering about what I might step in.

Once we'd docked, I pulled on an EVA suit before opening the hatch. If I'd been in charge of the station, I'd have waited until we were out of the shuttle and then laced the air with sedative gas. A good station security chief was sneaky — I'd have to be sneakier. Pushing a moaning Rance in front of me as a shield, I inched forward onto the station. Scruffy trotted out to the side for a better look.

The corridor was empty aside from one woman in a security jumpsuit. Three pips on her collar made her the chief. "We've done what you asked," she said, arms to the side, palms forward. "Let him go so he can get medical help."

"I'll send him out in the EVA suit right before we go into hyperspace. Do you have my cat?" An angry snarl answered my words, followed by a yelp and panicked yells. "Never mind. Let us all onto *Tiger Lily*, and nobody will get hurt."

Nobody would get hurt other than whoever Ensign Mowee had just assaulted, I meant, but that wasn't *my* fault. Morally, at least. Legally and financially, I was probably still responsible, but I wouldn't be coming back to this station again, so that didn't matter.

The security chief let her hands drop. "How do I know you'll let him go once you're on your ship?"

I risked making eye contact over Rance's shoulder. "If you've ever met this guy, you'd know I don't want him polluting the air of my ship any longer than necessary. And I didn't kill him before, so I'm probably not likely to do so now."

Rance snarled, "She's not going to kill me. Just shoot her now."

Ducking back behind Rance, I whispered, "Scruffy could finish the job it started, you know, and the universe would be a better place for it."

Rance subsided.

Keeping Rance between me and the security chief, with Scruffy scouting ahead to search for anyone hidden in our path, I slowly walked to *Tiger Lily*.

As I punched in the code to open the hatch, the security chief cocked her head, as if someone was speaking to her over the comms.

I swore silently. This was all about to fall apart. "Scruffy, get the ship warmed up and ready to go." If I was right, the Micklage family had just decided Rance was expendable. Raising my voice, I called, "Mowee! Time to go!" The hatch opened behind me with a rush of recycled air.

A howl from two corridors away greeted my words, and then a gray and white blur streaked by, clawing my boots along the way. If I'd been in bare feet, I'd have lost a toe.

The security chief reached for her sidearm. Pushing Rance in her direction, I scrambled through the hatch and hit the emergency close. "Scruffy, I'm aboard. We have to go! Now!"

FORTY-EIGHT

SHOWING LOVE

The hatch closed with a thunk, and *Tiger Lily's* engines hummed. Against all odds, we'd completed our mission on Trition and escaped. The Micklage family was well and truly hobbled. Now all we had to do was get Scruffy back to the Independent Federation — I'd get my reward, and I could *buy* a new controller for the galley. No more freeze-dried rations ever again.

Plus, I had a nice new EVA suit that had probably been pressure tested within my lifetime. Things really were looking up. I unfastened the suit, wiggling out by clamping the soles to the deck and pulling myself up the ladder to the control deck.

Then the ship jolted, making me nearly lose my grip. Scrambling up the rungs, I yelled, "Scruffy, what's going on?" But I already knew.

"Captain, the station overrode our command to release the docking clamps," Scruffy confirmed.

"Fire up the hyperspace engines." Skipping the last rung, I heaved myself onto the deck. We had to get away from the station before they got other ships in place to stop us.

It was *Tiger Lily* who spoke. "Using hyperspace engines within the traffic zone of an inhabited station is punishable by —"

"Relax. We're not going to use them."

Probably.

If we opened a path into hyperspace this close to the station, we ran the risk of pulling part of it with us. That risk increased exponentially if we were still connected to the station by docking clamps. Of course, dragging part of the station into the hyperspace path would likely tear *Tiger Lily* apart as well.

As I settled into the pilot's chair, I felt the thrum of the hyperspace engines. Ensign Mowee catapulted onto my shoulder, digging his claws into my skin to keep from falling. I raised a hand to scratch his cheek. "I missed you, too, friend." He bit my ear.

Bloodletting was Mowee's way of showing love.

A panicked voice came over the comms. "*Tiger Lily*, this is Flight Safety. We're showing power to your hyperspace drives." Sirens nearly drowned out the speaker's voice. "Check your console, please, and power down."

From the sound of it, Flight Safety — which was responsible for keeping the station intact despite the screw-ups of inexperienced pilots — thought I'd powered up by mistake. That meant security hadn't informed them of the drama down here. Maybe I could use that. "Flight safety, this is *Tiger Lily*. We are treating your override of our docking clamp release as piracy. Following standard anti-boarding protocol, we will be entering hyperspace in ten seconds unless the clamps are released."

The beauty of blaming something on protocol was that nobody could ever accuse you of lying. I owned the ship. Anything was possible.

"What?" The voice from Flight Safety sounded even more panicked. "We don't..."

"Check with your security. Eight seconds." Muting the comms, I increased power to our normal space engines. "See, Scruffy, the thing about docking clamps is they're usually engineered to break away before the station is damaged."

"Usually."

I shrugged. "The real question is if they will break away before we tear off a piece of *Tiger Lily*." The smart thing would be to get back into that EVA suit with the cat. There were three components on the ship that might fail. Damage to two of them would be bad, but not catastrophic. That third, though...

The engines throttled down — by Scruffy's command, since I hadn't touched the console. "Captain, perhaps we could negotiate for my surrender. You could leave, and I will find a way to escape later."

"What?" Mowee dug his claws harder as I swiveled to look at the robo-dog. "Absolutely not. I'm not leaving you behind."

"Captain, if the ship is torn apart, you will die, Ensign Mowee will die, and I will *still* be here."

"No." I tried to swallow, but my throat wouldn't cooperate. "I am *not* leaving you here." Slamming the comms button, I grated out, "Flight safety, I'm about to head into hyperspace with part of your station if you don't unlock those clamps *right now*."

My original plan had been a bluff, but now I was serious. I put a hand on Scruffy's body so I could access the synthetic crystal.

Scruffy moved away from me. "Captain, I cannot allow you to do this."

"Really? You choose *now* to bail?" I stood up, one hand holding Mowee in place, and followed Scruffy around the room. If I could grab the robo-dog, I'd be able to send us into hyperspace as soon as I got back to the controls.

"Captain, this is the optimal solution." It backed through the door.

The ship jolted again, and the rumble of the engines smoothed. "*Tiger Lily*, this is Flight Safety. You should be clear to depart. I repeat, you should be clear to depart."

I looked at Scruffy and then back at the helm. The ship was moving and nobody was piloting. Scruffy and I scrambled back to the pilot's chair. Urging the normal space engines to their maximum power, I maneuvered around a tug that had drifted into our lane. "Thank you, Flight Safety. Safe orbit."

Cutting the comms, I reached out for Scruffy again. "We need to be ready to go. There's a good chance security is going to start firing at us."

"Agreed."

I closed my eyes and searched the available hyperspace paths. Something short would do, as long as it took us away from this system. Then we could regroup and plan a better route — right after I kicked Scruffy's metallic rear for attempting a noble sacrifice back there.

There. *That* would do. And it was even outside the traffic zone. I would have patted myself on the back for following space regulations, but Mowee was in the way. "Everybody ready? Hang on."

In a perfect universe, I would have lined up *Tiger Lily* a little better, but we weren't too far off the correct angle. The hyperspace drive kicked us onto the path with only a tiny course correction that left me with scratches along my shoulder. In my cabin, something clattered onto the deck.

And then a child's voice said, "Oops!"

FORTY-NINE

POPPY

It was one of those moments when I was convinced my brain had glitched. *Tiger Lily's* view screen showed the moire of hyperspace, Mowee's claws were still digging into my shoulders, and the robo-dog holding Scruffy stood next to my left hand. We were all on the flight control deck.

So who had just spoken in my cabin?

"Ship?" I stood, setting Ensign Mowee on the chair. This hyperspace path was stable enough that I wouldn't need to make course corrections. "Did you take on passengers while I was away?"

"No, Captain de Mure." *Tiger Lily's* voice was as calm as it always was.

"So..." I glanced at Scruffy, hoping for some alternate explanation, but the robo-dog was looking at me, head tilted. "Who is in my cabin?"

"Ensign Micklage," *Tiger Lily* replied.

That, right there, was the reason nobody should ever trust a ship's computer. Sure, I'd worked with some people who couldn't remember their own name, but even the most unreliable sort would never be convinced to take on a child as crew, especially a Micklage.

Closing my eyes, I took a deep breath and let it out slowly. Now that it was too late to do anything about it, I saw how it had happened. "Mowee got a promotion, didn't he?"

"Lieutenant Mowee received a bravery commendation. Combined with his time in service, his promotion was automatic."

Mowee's rank had been part joke, part workaround to avoid pet quarantine, requiring only a bit of paperwork and tricky accounting. But it put the cat in the ship's command hierarchy. That hadn't seemed a drawback at the time, since I was the only other member of the crew — if I died, it wouldn't really matter that the cat was acting captain. Eventually, someone would figure out what to do with the ship.

Since I didn't allow ensigns hiring decisions, everything had been fine. But *someone* had exploited the system by giving Mowee a medal, and then convincing *Tiger Lily* that the newly minted Lieutenant Mowee had hired a replacement ensign.

And I knew exactly who that was.

"Why does the universe hate me?" I opened my eyes. "Poppy! Get out here!"

A girl with light brown skin and a shock of purple hair poked her head out of the cabin. She smiled uncertainly. "Hi, Rose! Don't be angry."

Poppy was one of Rance's distant cousins. I'd seen her a few times when I'd been working for the Micklages — she was a bright kid who hadn't yet been warped to fit the family's needs. Since I didn't mind spending the evening talking to an eight-year-old, she'd attached herself to me when I'd attended events on Trition. Giving the ship's cat a rank to get around quarantine had been *her* suggestion, long before I'd dumped Rance at Dancig City and bought my own ship.

I liked the kid, but having a Micklage stowaway was the last thing I needed.

"Poppy, I can't have a ten-year-old onboard. They're going to think I *kidnapped* you."

"Ten?" She looked at me in offended disbelief. "I'll be thirteen soon."

I gave her my best skeptical look. "Standard years?"

"Yes!"

"Sorry." Had it really been that long? Maybe it had. "But I still can't have you on this ship." Scruffy shifted next to me, and even without our group mind, I knew what it wanted. "Poppy, this is Scruffy Note of Disrespect. Be nice." I wasn't sure which one needed the admonition. Maybe both.

Poppy's face lit up, her black eyes flashing. "That's the AI everyone's been looking for." She bowed deeply. "It's an honor to meet you."

Scruffy replicated the bow as much as it could, though the robo-dog looked like it was adjusting its neck joints. "The pleasure is mine, Ensign Micklage."

"No, no, no." I shook one finger at both of them. "Absolutely not. Mowee's demoted back to ensign, Poppy has no rank, and the first thing we're going to do is find a safe place to drop her off."

That last part would be a challenge. Anyplace safe for Poppy to stay would likely blast *Tiger Lily* out of the sky as soon as we emerged from hyperspace, especially if news got out about the shutdown on Trition. Even though I hadn't known Poppy was on the ship, now she was my responsibility. If she got kidnapped before she made it back home, I'd have to rescue her or die trying.

Scruffy looked up at me. "She may be safer with us."

Poppy nodded. "I want to stay with you! I can take care of Mowee. And I'll be really quiet. You won't even know I'm here."

"No." Could I leave her with one of Bett One-arm's clones? I trusted Bett with my life, but she would see Poppy as a weapon to be wielded in the war to save the Independent Federation. Maybe that was the logical approach, but... I liked Poppy. The thought of her coming to harm made my muscles tense.

With her arms crossed over her chest, Poppy lifted her chin. "If you leave me somewhere, I'll just run away again."

Mowee wandered over to twine himself around Poppy's legs.

Great. Everyone on my ship was against me. I sighed. "Fine. You'll stay until we can figure out a better plan. But you have to follow my commands without complaining, or so help me, I'll turn this ship around and dump you on Trition myself."

"Thank you, Rose! You won't regret this!"

Ignoring her excited exclamation, I pointed to the pilot's chair. "Get over here. We're going to record a message for your family so they know you're safe. And then I'm going to show you how to do maintenance on the air filters." It was a dirty, exacting task, and Poppy would probably be delighted to be entrusted with it.

My argument with Rance Micklage hadn't interested the rest of his family, and they were smart enough to realize I hadn't orchestrated the code that had taken down most of Trition's infrastructure. But they would come after me with everything they had if they thought I had kidnapped a child of the family.

We'd have to take on supplies before the bounty hunters caught our trail — if it wasn't already too late.

FIFTY

OUTLAW

Poppy's delight with her new life as an outlaw lasted until I handed her a packet of freeze-dried ocean steak with clam sauce. Confusion furrowed her brow. "What's this?"

"That's dinner." Hooking the galley's nozzle to my meal, I snapped the seal, which let the water inside. The packaging was designed to work in zero gravity. At least we didn't have to worry about that. Not that I would have eaten something with reconstituted clam sauce if there was a possibility the globules could drift off. There was a reason these meals were cheap — they smelled fine right after being hydrated, but later... Our newly changed air filters would handle it, but only if we didn't spill anything and immediately put the packaging in the recycler.

Poppy looked from the package to me. "But that galley unit is new."

"Rance destroyed the controller." Even now, it hurt to remember.

Looking dubious, Poppy followed my example, adding water and shaking the contents before pulling the heating tab. In five minutes, the food would be as good as it was ever going to be. Which, to be clear, wasn't very good. There was a reason the manufacturer had used a name that didn't promise a specific type of fish, or even that it actually *contained* fish.

We'd dropped out of hyperspace to hijack a message buoy, and now Poppy's vid explaining that she *hadn't* been kidnapped was on its way to her people on Trition. Presumably, she'd sprinkled in enough codewords to let them know she wasn't being coerced, but I doubted that would make the Micklage family happy. We needed a plan.

Through the view port, a sterile moon reflected the amber light of the nearest star. "Why are you here, Poppy?" Even if the prominent nose and cheekbones hadn't marked her as one of the Micklage family, her mind made it obvious. Rance was reasonably smart and he had the family ambition, but he lacked the discipline to work with others.

Poppy, though... Poppy could sooth wounded egos or trigger an argument, all without anyone suspecting she'd done it intentionally. I'd seen her do so more than once. She'd tripped in front of one cousin, sending him crashing into a rival's shoulder. In the resulting confusion, her tutor had been dispatched to help one combatant to the medical unit, and Poppy had slipped away from her chaperone.

Eyes wide, Poppy opened her mouth to speak. Then she caught my look and grinned. "I should have picked a dumber captain if I wanted to lie, hm?"

"Answer the question."

"Fine." The stubborn look came back. "I was supposed to start interning for Gerd on the *Lucky Cow* after my next birthday. I don't trust him."

The Micklage family often fostered out promising teens to pass down important skills. I knew nothing about Gerd Micklage, other than that Rance had also interned with him. Apparently, the younger Rance had been considered worthy of special interest. Had Gerd not noticed Rance's proclivities or just not thought them worth correcting? Either way, I trusted Poppy's instincts.

"Your..." Both parents had died in an accident when she'd been a baby, and two family members had been tasked with raising her. I didn't think I'd ever heard their names. "Your guardians can't do anything about that?"

"No." She shifted, so she was looking out the view port and no longer facing me. "They think it's an honor. They were never considered for anything other than low-level administration."

With that background, Poppy's guardians had probably been awed and excited by the opportunity. Which left Poppy with nobody to protect her. Still, life on *Tiger Lily* wasn't safe enough for a child, no matter how smart she was. We were heading into an area that would probably be a war zone soon. "Maybe we can work something out with Vira or Tiber." Except, now that I thought about it, they'd been willing to leave me in a simulation without my consent. Not great role models. "Or..."

"I'm not going back. Dump me on the next station we come to if you're worried about me being a spy. Just don't send me back."

Poppy, a spy? I hadn't even considered that, though I should have. The Micklage family would have no qualms about sending a child to retrieve Scruffy and the synthetic crystal embedded in its processor.

Poppy would have considered it if she'd been in my position.

Our conversation was interrupted by the pop of the timer telling me my meal was ready. When I opened the seal, Poppy involuntarily drew back.

"That smells *awful*."

"You get used to it." Maybe this would convince her that *Tiger Lily* wasn't the place for her.

The appalled look she gave me nearly made the smell of not-quite-clam sauce worth it. She patted the useless galley unit. "If I can get it working again, can I stay?"

Even I wasn't stupid enough to agree to that. "Nice try." Then I remembered the few meals I'd had before we got to Trition and wavered. "Is that even possible? The processor isn't there."

Before Poppy could reply, Scruffy's voice called from the control deck. "Captain de Mure, you should probably see this."

Leaving the "ocean steak" to cool on the table, I hurried to the control deck, where recently demoted Ensign Mowee sprawled on the pilot's chair next to Scruffy. On the console, a wanted notice scrolled, showing a picture of Poppy, looking three years younger and impossibly innocent.

In contrast, the picture they'd chosen for me was taken from security footage of our wild ride from Rance's shuttle. My hair stuck out in all directions, my clothes were dirty and torn, and there was engine oil smeared across one cheek. My expression really made it all come together — I looked insane and dangerous. Nobody would trust me with a rock, much less a child.

Poppy clapped a hand over her mouth. "You look *amazing* there."

"I look unhinged." Then I saw the amount they were offering for Poppy's safe return. It was enough to terraform an entire planet. Taking a deep breath, I let it out slowly. I certainly hadn't expected the amount to be so high. Even *I* would have considered turning us in. We'd have half the universe searching for us. "This complicates things."

FIFTY-ONE
AN IDEA

Our emergence into the Micandero system was heralded by thirty seconds of comm silence, and then a welcome sequence from station control so obfuscated by encrypted traffic that I could just barely make out the greeting. A Lynx 14 broke off its approach to the station and turned toward us.

"Wandering stars," I muttered. This was the third station we'd attempted to dock at, and by now I was prepared.

At the first, we'd nearly been caught — *Tiger Lily* had notified me of stray chatter about us on an unencrypted channel just before a ship had tried to grapple us.

With the second station, we hadn't broadcast our identification, a minor infraction that should have gone unnoticed by everyone other than station control. We'd nearly managed to hire a courier ship to bring supplies to our orbit, but then some bright pilot figured out *why* we hadn't announced ourselves, and that was the end of that.

This time, I hadn't bothered to spin down the hyperspace drive. Two seconds later, we were traveling outbound again, safe from everyone hoping to get the reward for returning Poppy to the Micklage family. But we were running out of fuel.

"Captain," Scruffy said next to my knee, "perhaps we should temporarily abandon this ship and arrange other transportation."

"I have an idea," Poppy said from her crash seat. Since we were expecting resistance, I'd forced her to strap in before we dropped out of hyperspace.

Ignoring Poppy, I responded to Scruffy's suggestion of leaving the ship. "How? What little credit I have is worthless, and even if we left *Tiger Lily*, our group would be easy to spot." Sure, we could make an effort to disguise me and Poppy, and I could hide Scruffy's processor in something other than the robo-dog, but Ensign Mowee was always going to look like a cat and everyone chasing us knew about him. "We may have to chance a message to Bett."

Bett One-arm would help us. But the very nature of her not-quite-legal businesses meant she was surrounded by people willing to ignore the rules in order to get rich.

A small part of me wished I'd stuffed Poppy into the EVA suit and dropped her off outside the Trition station. And yet, I still couldn't regret bringing her along. Not that it mattered now — she was here, on the ship, and everyone in the universe was looking for us.

"Perhaps we could send a message to Bett through the Chrysalis," Scruffy suggested. "We parted with Crania on good terms."

I wasn't sure *good terms* had any meaning when talking about a decentralized being. "How do you think Crania will react when they find out our group mind is gone?"

"I have an idea," Poppy repeated, more forcefully this time. She'd unlatched the harness, but stayed in the seat.

"How would Crania know our group mind is gone?" Scruffy asked. "I don't believe it would be obvious in a short message."

My reluctance to use Crania as an intermediary wasn't entirely because of our defunct group mind. As much as I'd missed my connection to Scruffy when Rance destroyed the nanobots in my system, I didn't want to run the risk of having replacements forced on me. Staying far away from the Chrysalis seemed like a good idea. "Maybe we could disguise a message to Bett. Make it look like it was coming from another of her clones."

Poppy was practically jumping up and down now. "I have an *idea!*"

I acknowledged her, mostly so she would quiet down and let me figure out how to get out of this mess. "What?"

"We could get what we need from my family's emergency supplies." Her face practically glowed with excitement. "Nobody would think to look for us *there.*"

Poppy was right. The Micklage family had boltholes and emergency caches littered in places where they might be useful — fifteen that I knew of and likely more by now. Most were sites that had seen clandestine construction, followed by apparent abandonment so as not to draw attention. Found on desolate planets, sterile moons, and lifeless ship husks, they were meant to be used once, held in reserve for true emergencies. Only the Micklage family members knew where they were — and me, because I'd been Rance's pilot and Rance couldn't be bothered to memorize the list.

"It's the first place they'll look," I said, though my tone made it clear I wasn't rejecting the idea outright. Surely Rance would have told them I knew where all the caches were, wouldn't he?

"Some were moved after you quit." Poppy's eyes flicked

to me, as if trying to gauge how I would react. "I overheard Tibor talking about it. But I know where they were moved to." She winced. "I *think* I know where they are now. Everything might have been changed again. I was reading over my guardian's shoulder — they didn't send it to me."

Leaning back in the pilot's chair, I regarded Poppy. This could be a trap. Probably not a deliberate one by Poppy, but her presence here could have been orchestrated by her family. Then again, why bother? It was a lot of extra work when they could have just planted a bomb on *Tiger Lily* and waited for us to be far enough from the station that an explosion wouldn't cause too much damage.

(Even though thoughts like those were supposed to make me feel better, I made a note to check all the storage spaces on the ship the next time we were in normal space. Just in case.)

We would likely only get one chance. If we arrived to find nothing there, we could be stuck. Ocean steak with clam sauce was bad, but sitting on a dead ship with no rations at all would be worse.

Did we have a choice?

With the flick of one finger, I activated the console in front of the crash couch. "Give me the list of the ones you remember."

As she worked, I entered the list I'd memorized back when I'd been working for Rance. When we'd both finished, I compared our information.

Three sites on Poppy's list were close enough for us to reach. Two of those were on my list as well. I highlighted the third. That would be the one Micklage wouldn't expect us to go to. "Scruffy, if you have any better ideas, now's the time to speak up."

The robo-dog stayed silent.

"Excellent. We have a plan." Closing my eyes, I slid *Tiger Lily* onto a second hyperspace path, then another and another, until we were heading in the right direction.

When we finally emerged from hyperspace, the console warnings had turned into alarms, letting me know the hyperspace drive would power down soon. We weren't going anywhere until we refueled.

Around us, empty space loomed. There was no emergency cache.

FIFTY-TWO
COMFORTING THOUGHTS

Stuck in the middle of nowhere with no fuel and no way to signal for help was a test scenario I hadn't trained for in pilot school — because there was no solution. Now I was living it and I still didn't have a good way out.

"This is all my fault." Poppy looked stricken, as only a child who took on adult responsibility and failed could. "I must have remembered it wrong."

It was just as likely she'd seen a list of potential sites, or even a list meant to mislead outsiders. None of that mattered now. "You gave me the information you had. *I* made the decision. The captain is responsible for the passengers, not the other way around." That held true, even if the passenger in question had stowed away without my knowledge. "We'll figure something out."

Poppy didn't look convinced, but she kept quiet.

Luckily, we had time to examine our options. We had enough freeze-dried rations to last for a while, Ensign Mowee had his own supplies, and if we could get the galley unit working again, food wouldn't be a problem for months. It was far more likely some part of *Tiger Lily's* environmental control would fail and kill us before we ran out of things to eat.

That actually wasn't the comforting thought I'd meant it to be.

"Ship, start scanning anything large enough to be a refueling station." Maybe the Micklages had *hidden* their emergency supplies. "In fact, tag anything anomalous." Standing up, I said, "Poppy, you had an idea for how to fix the galley unit, right? You and Scruffy work on that. I'm going to double check our inventory. Ensign Mowee's with me."

I wasn't sure there was a way for Poppy to bypass the missing galley controller, but we all needed something to do.

TWO HOURS LATER, we met in the cargo bay to go over what we'd learned. "Good news, bad news," I said, starting us off. "The good news is that nobody's shooting at us and the air scrubbing system should be good for longer than we need it."

Both the robo-dog and Poppy turned to look at me.

Apparently, I'd forgotten how to give comforting speeches. Clearing my throat, I continued. "Which brings us to the bad news. We're missing backups for the water reclamation and recycling module. We can stretch things out a bit with some modifications, but it would be good if we found someplace to go in the next ten days or so. Ship, what are our options?"

"Captain, I believe I have identified fragments of what was originally a Micklage-brand crash pod." A crash pod was the ultimate bolthole — small, portable, filled with all the supplies and entertainment necessary for an extended period, and stasis chambers if a longer stay was needed. But crash pods weren't supposed to be in fragments. "Some pieces show evidence of recent high velocity impacts."

"How recent?"

"From shortly before we arrived in the system."

Scruffy turned its head to look at the ceiling. Lately, it had been mimicking my gestures to compensate for a lack of facial movement. "A more superstitious person might blame you for pointing out nobody was shooting at us."

"A more superstitious person might have called you a bad luck token and dropped you into the nearest star," I replied.

Scruffy stopped staring at the ceiling and looked my way. I ignored it.

The timing was just too perfect. Someone had figured out we were likely to need supplies, which they would know because *Tiger Lily* had been sitting unguarded at Trition Station, and they knew we would have access to multiple supply caches. With insufficient resources to wait at each one, they did the next best thing — destroy the supplies so we couldn't refuel and leave. We were lucky we hadn't run into our pursuers. Yet.

We needed to get out of here.

"Ship, does it look like there are any usable supplies in the wreckage?"

Tiger Lily put up a holo display showing each piece. Mowee leaped into the air, clawing at a small piece that rotated just out of his reach. Only one part of the wreckage was big enough to maintain any structural integrity. I pointed. "Head for this one, as fast as we can go."

"Yes, captain. Estimated time of arrival: three hours." The holo display disappeared. Mowee checked under one paw to ensure he hadn't grabbed it after all. Then he stalked off in disgust.

That just left the galley unit. I gave Poppy an inquiring look. "Is our last meal going to be rehydrated ocean steak, or do you have some good news?"

"Uh..." She gaped at me.

Oops. Apparently, my gallows humor had been taken literally. "Don't mind me. Did you have any luck?"

"Yes."

The hesitant way she'd replied made me think this wasn't an unqualified success. "Now tell me the bad news."

"We can hook Scruffy up to the galley, but Scruffy doesn't have any information about how the nutrients should be combined or prepared."

"I am an unrestricted artificial intelligence," Scruffy said. "I can learn."

Great. The AI that half the universe was hunting would be working as a line cook, and it was probably going to be terrible at it. "Fine. Run some experiments, but try not to poison anyone." I resigned myself to eating rehydrated meals.

If what was left of this crash pod didn't have fuel for our hyperspace drives, we'd be sitting here waiting until someone showed up to apprehend us or the water reclamation system failed.

I couldn't decide which option was worse.

Stars sparkled in the distance, providing just enough contrast that I could make out the light-eating void in front of me that was the camouflaged fragment of the crash pod. What had looked like one piece from far away had turned out to be two.

My death grip on *Tiger Lily's* hand-hold tightened.

The first debris section had once held packs of water, now frozen glitter in the vacuum. If we were still stuck here when *Tiger Lily's* filters gave out, I'd have all kinds of time to figure out how to recover the ice crystals. Preferably some way that didn't involve me leaving the artificial gravity of the ship. My stomach lurched.

I would *not* throw up in this EVA suit.

My link back to *Tiger Lily* chimed. *"Captain de Mure, you seem to be experiencing physical distress. Can I offer any assistance?"*

Over the comms, Poppy sniffed. "What kind of pilot can't handle zero-g?" She was angry at me because *she* wanted to be the one risking her life out here. As if I'd let a kid do a space walk near jagged debris that could tear a hole in the suit.

After ten minutes of arguing, I'd told her to put on the suit just to shut her up. All the ship's EVA suits were meant for adults — in an emergency, I could stuff Poppy inside one to provide her with atmosphere, but there was no way she could accomplish manual tasks when the neck seal of the helmet was directly in front of her eyes.

Now she was frustrated that she couldn't do more to help, mad at herself, mad at me, and mad at the universe in general. Ah, adolescence.

Concentrating on keeping my breathing steady, I aimed my light at the second pod fragment slowly rotating in front of me. The side I was looking at had originally been part of the exterior. In another minute, the debris would rotate enough that I could jump over and access anything left inside. It wasn't even a dangerous leap — if I missed completely, my ship could pick me up. Plus, I had maneuvering jets, in case I was headed toward something too jagged to safely grab. This was completely safe. Without the constant falling sensation, I wouldn't have hesitated.

The comm came to life again. Scruffy, this time. "Captain de Mure, perhaps I should join you."

The robo-dog's appendages weren't suitable for this task. If Scruffy came outside the ship, it would only be for moral support. "No. I'm fine." The interior of the pod rotated into view. Before I could think too much, I jumped.

My angle was off a bit, but a quick burst with the hand jet fixed it, and I grabbed an interior bar to anchor myself. Once I'd clipped my harness to the bar, I looked at what was left. The missile or bomb or whatever had torn the pod apart had left this section relatively intact. I relaxed.

"Poppy, you need to send a thank-you message to whoever stocked this thing." We now had hyperspace fuel packs in an armored crate, filters, oxygen canisters, and everything else that might be needed to restock a ship. "I'll slot in the fuel packs first. If we have time, we can grab everything else." One hour, maybe two, and we'd be ready to go straight to the Independent Federation without having to find a resupply station that didn't have bounty hunters lining up to grab us.

The crate of fuel packs was a pain to muscle through the jagged opening, but at least I didn't have to take it through an airlock with gravity. Holding the crate in front of me, I jumped across the void.

Poppy's voice came over the comms. "How many times are you going to correct your course? You look like you're drunk out there."

"Hey, next time you stow away on a ship, bring a suit that fits you and you can see how much fun it is to—"

Scruffy's voice cut off my rant. "Captain, another ship just appeared in the system."

Swallowing my curse, I said, "Acknowledged. I'll install these as quickly as I can." One second later, my boots clicked onto *Tiger Lily's* hull. The fuel packs were meant to be installed by a robotic arm attached to a station. Pulling the crate with me, I carefully stepped across the hull to the first fuel port. "Ship, unlock and open port one."

The hatch popped open, and I crouched to remove all twelve empty fuel packs, automatically clipping them onto my belt so they didn't become navigation hazards. Sweat droplets hovered around my eyes. When the latch on the crate stuck, I had to lever it open with the pry bar on my utility belt.

I had three of the new fuel packs slotted in place when Scruffy spoke. "Captain, we are being ordered to surrender."

"Can they see me out here?" Reminding myself that rushing wouldn't help, I continued slotting new fuel packs into place. *Tiger Lily* could fly with just one of the four ports fueled, but all twelve slots within the port had to be filled. Four... Five...

"Unlikely. The bulk of *Tiger Lily* is between you and the enemy ship."

"Good. Keep it that way." Six. "Poppy, I want you to talk to them. Stall. Do whatever you can to keep them from rushing over here." The seventh fuel pack didn't seat properly. I pulled it out and tried again. Success. "Scruffy, I need a private channel with you while she's doing that."

Two seconds later, Scruffy's voice was in my ear, all the background noise gone. "Captain?"

"Be ready to pilot the ship into hyperspace." Eight.

"Captain, it will take the other ship over an hour to dock with us, even if we don't move." Scruffy understood my point without guessing why I thought it might be needed. Nine.

"That ship won't be bounty hunters." No hired help would have these coordinates. "Depending on which Micklage is on board, they may not bother docking." Publicly, every member of the Micklage family would swear to do anything to get Poppy back safely. But without witnesses, half of them would see this as the perfect opportunity to get rid of an inconvenient rival. Ten.

After a moment of silence, Scruffy said, "Understood."

With any luck, I'd be back inside the ship before this became an issue, but it was better to be prepared. Eleven. One more. The twelfth pack slid in with a thunk I felt through the gloves. Closing the hatch, I switched to my link with the ship. "Quick-check the first fuel port."

Diagnostic lights blinked as each of the fuel packs was tested and brought online. *"Fuel port filled and verified."*

Blowing out a breath, I began the trek toward the airlock, tugging the crate behind me. In five minutes, I'd be out of this suit and standing in gravity. We could flee, loading the rest of the fuel packs in a spot where no ships loomed.

Scruffy's voice cut into my thoughts. "Captain, the approaching ship has fired on us. Evasive maneuvers required."

Tiger Lily couldn't perform evasive maneuvers without knocking me off the hull. I didn't have time to make it to the airlock.

If I stopped to think about what I was doing, I'd freeze. Holding the crate tight against my chest, I jumped toward the pod wreckage, watching *Tiger Lily* get smaller under my feet. "Keep Poppy safe."

"Captain..."

"Go!" I reached the pod wreckage and attached my tether. If I lost contact and floated away, nobody would pick me up. My only chance was waiting right here for *Tiger Lily* to return.

From the remains of the crash pod, I watched as *Tiger Lily* accelerated away in normal space. Then, between one instant and the next, the ship winked into hyperspace.

I was alone.

FIFTY-FOUR

BANGING ON MY FACEPLATE

They say that if you stare into the void too long, eventually it stares back at you. After *Tiger Lily* disappeared into hyperspace, leaving me hiding in the wreckage of a crash pod in an EVA suit, the void wasn't so much staring as banging on my faceplate.

"Stars, I hate this sort of thing." My voice buzzed in my helmet.

Tiger Lily would be back. I just needed to stay hidden and alive long enough for whatever Micklage ship had just fired on us to get bored and go away. The void would have to wait. It wasn't going anywhere.

First, though, I needed to make sure my EVA suit wasn't broadcasting a signal that would alert the other ship to my presence. The suits that came with *Tiger Lily*, the ones that I didn't fully trust to keep the void away, had their emergency beacons disabled. As I said, it was entirely possible Fast Rami had sold me a stolen ship. His usual clientele didn't want anything betraying their locations, and I hadn't complained.

But I wasn't out here in one of my own suits. I was using

the suit I'd taken from Rance Micklage's shuttle. If a Micklage ship sent out a ping, this suit would respond, making my attempt to hide like sneaking around in the shadows while wearing a strobe light.

Luckily, this was the same model of EVA suit I'd used when I'd worked for Micklage as a pilot. The only way to turn off the beacon was to disable the comms system. With the bulky gloves, it took me seven tense minutes to turn the dials and undock the comms module. It beeped once and then the background hum disappeared, leaving me with just the sound of my own breathing.

I looked over the jagged edge of the crash pod. Yep. The void was still there. "Just checking."

My air supply readout claimed I had just over three hours. That was probably a conservative estimate — it was calibrated for a larger person who was doing physical labor. So if I didn't move around much, I'd have... say, four hours at a minimum. That wasn't especially soothing.

Though the crash pod hadn't been designed to take a missile hit, it *had* been set up to handle hard use. Most of the contents were still secured in closed cupboards. Pulling myself deeper into the pod, I decided to inventory everything that was left. After all, I had to do *something* until *Tiger Lily* returned.

Or until I ran out of air.

The contents of the first cabinet had green and yellow biological-warning tags. I closed that one without examining it further. The last thing I needed was to accidentally bring some nanobot back to *Tiger Lily*. Nothing stored in a crash pod should be harmful, but I didn't trust the Micklage family not to keep some last ditch body modification process in case of extended stay. One nanobot-induced group mind was enough for this lifetime.

Cabinet number two held games, art supplies, and puzzles, none of which I could use in a zero gravity vacuum with bulky gloves. The third cabinet was locked, which worried me a bit. If the biologics weren't worth locking up, what could possibly be in there? Weapons, at a guess. From the entertainment choices, the pod had been stocked with children in mind.

Which made the biologics even more interesting. They had to have been added as an afterthought.

I kept searching through the supplies as I thought about that. Clothing, hygiene items, a pack of freeze-dried food — that had to be a backup in case the galley unit failed. If only the galley unit had been in this part of the pod, I could have spent my time extracting the controller. Still, I added the food to my collection because even in an emergency, a Micklage would expect something more palatable than ocean steak in clam sauce.

"Hel-lo!" Spare oxygen tanks stood on racks along the wall. The crash pod had its own filtration and oxygen extraction system, so the tanks were only intended to be used in an emergency. If this didn't qualify, I didn't know what did. Though I still had plenty of air left, I went through the exercise of hooking a new tank to my auxiliary intake, figuring I didn't want to be doing it for the first time when I was about to run out of air.

With my biggest problem solved, I relaxed a little. I had over one hundred hours of air, more than enough time for *Tiger Lily* to return for me. Now, I just had to wait.

"SIXTY-TWO!" Seven hours later, I'd set yet another record in crash pod counter toss, a game I'd made up, which consisted of me floating behind an imaginary line, flipping a counter toward any surface, and catching it on the rebound. A long series of rules kept it from being too easy.

In my quest to become the reigning champion, I'd nearly forgotten the reason I was out here.

"Sixty-three — aaah!" The counter flipped past my head when something tapped me on my shoulder. Since I'd thought I was the only being within one light-year, I hurled myself away. At some point in my confused tumble, I realized the robo-dog had bumped me. "Scruffy, you almost scared me into hyperspace! Why didn't you *say* something?"

And yes, that was the point I remembered: my comm module was still unplugged. After a few minutes of fumbling, I got the module reseated. "I'm glad to see you again."

"Captain, the entire crew is delighted to find you in good health. Perhaps we should return to the ship so we can leave this system now."

"Excellent idea." I couldn't wait to get back on my ship and out of the EVA suit. We could stop somewhere else and slot in the remaining hyperspace fuel packs. "And then I need to get word to Bett One-arm about the biologics I found here. The Independent Federation needs to be prepared."

FIFTY-FIVE
TETHER

I'd never been so happy to be in the middle of nowhere, with no other ships in sight. There was a splendid view of the surrounding nothingness through the helmet of my EVA suit. "Just let me get these fuel packs slotted and I swear I'll never complain about anything ever again." At least I'd taken some pills to combat nausea before I'd left the airlock.

Through my comms, Scruffy said, "Captain, I have been watching you for some time, and that promise may not be in your skill set."

Poppy giggled.

Pushing the crate we'd stolen from the crash pod debris ahead of me, I clomped across the hull. I should have been pulling myself along, but my arms were full. "Ship, unlock and open port two." As I crouched down to pull out the spent fuel packs, I opened a private comm channel to Scruffy. "Were you able to figure out anything about the biologics?"

"Captain, I don't have the specialized knowledge to decode nanobot behavior. If we could connect to a scientific library, I would have a much better foundation."

There was zero chance of that happening now. With the bounty hunters looking for us because of Poppy, we couldn't go anywhere near a station big enough to have a decent library. If we knew exactly what we were looking for, we could hijack a message buoy and get the data remotely, but that would only work for tiny chunks of information. Anything bigger and we might as well put up a big sign saying, *We're right over here and we have no weapons!*

The eleventh fuel pack was wedged in against the twelfth. "How did this pass the installation tests?" Using all my strength, I jerked and it suddenly released. That gave me enough upward momentum that my boots lost contact with the hull. Suddenly, I was tumbling away from *Tiger Lily*.

Poppy cut in. "Do you need us to grab you?"

"No. I'm fine." By the time I'd clipped the spent fuel pack to my belt and pulled up the thruster controls, the ship was growing smaller. Two brief bursts halted my spin, and another sent me sailing back toward *Tiger Lily*. "I just wanted to get a better look at the ship. Make sure it didn't have any other damage." When I finished this job, I was never going out on the hull again.

"If we get a suit that fits me, I can do all the space walks." Poppy hadn't given up on the idea that she would be crewing the ship with me.

As if I'd let a child do all the dangerous work.

It only took one more burst from the thruster to get my feet on the hull. This time, I clipped my tether properly. "We'll talk about it when you're old enough to sign on."

Scruffy spoke on our private channel. "We may need to take this to Bett."

"Yeah." I slotted in the replacement packs, closed the hatch, and switched to my link with the ship. "Quick-check the second fuel port, please." Lights flickered while I waited. From what I could tell, the biologics I'd stolen were some sort of nanobot antidote, but I didn't know to *what*.

That worried me. The crash pod would have had the best medical unit available, but this extra package had been recently shoved in a cupboard. It was as if they'd been planning to unleash a disaster and wanted to make sure the family wouldn't be affected.

I'd originally planned to take what I'd found to one of Bett's clones, but we had the same problem there that we had trying to get near a library — Bett wouldn't turn us in for the bounty, but at least half the people around her would.

"Fuel port filled and verified."

Great. Two down, eight to go. At this rate, the Micklage family would have invaded the Independent Federation before I finished refueling my ship. I unclipped my tether and clomped to the next location. "Ship, unlock and open port three." On my private channel to Scruffy, I said, "Maybe we could dump it somewhere and notify Bett."

"It's a risk."

Scruffy was right. Everyone looking for us would know to monitor Bett's communications, though I wasn't sure how many people knew there was more than one Bett. That seemed like something I could use to our advantage, but I only knew where one clone currently was. If we sent a message, there was a good chance Bett wouldn't be the one to pick up the biologics. "I don't have any better ideas."

Levering myself into position so I could deal with more fuel packs, I remembered I'd forgotten to clip my tether again. If I took another solo trip away from the ship, Poppy would never let me hear the end of it. I sighed, the sound loud in my helmet.

The group comm channel lit up and Poppy asked, "While we're waiting, do you want me to document this stuff you brought back, or are you hiding it for a reason?"

I'd locked the biologics case away because I didn't know what it did and I had a child on board. Scruffy must have pulled it out to examine. Now I had to make sure I didn't offend Poppy by treating her like a child, while still keeping us all safe. "Poppy, I don't know what it does or how dangerous it is. I think it's better if we just put it..."

"Oh, it's not that dangerous, unless the contents don't match the manifest, but they're pretty strict about that." Her tone was matter of fact, as if deciphering the specs was no big deal.

If I'd still been connected in a group mind with Scruffy, we would have had a *lot* to say to each other. As it was, there was a long moment of silence before I cleared my throat. "So... You can figure that stuff out?"

"It's easy." She paused, then added a bit sheepishly, "It's what they tweaked my genes for. That's probably why they want me back so much."

Right. This *child*, who could read biologic data manifests like I perused a menu, an ability that made her in high demand all over the universe, had stowed away on my ship because what she *really* wanted to do was carry small cargo on trips through hyperspace. Things were starting to make a little more sense. No wonder the Micklage family wanted her back so urgently.

I clipped my tether and started pulling out spent fuel packs. "Can you give me the ten second overview?"

Poppy paused for a moment. "It looks like these block the nanobots that form the group minds. Sort of like the Chrysalis. Do you know what that is?"

"Yes." I'd learned more about the Chrysalis than I'd ever wanted to know.

"But it's odd. You wouldn't need blockers like this unless the nanobots were contagious. But that's not the way the group minds add people."

Adrenaline made my fingertips tingle. If I was right, we needed to get to the Independent Federation. And we needed to get there *now*.

FIFTY-SIX
PROTO-ENSIGN

We were finally — *finally!* — on our way to the Independent Federation, the destination I'd been trying to reach ever since I first found Scruffy in Orabella Fink's salvage yard. But instead of being excited to collect a reward for ferrying the AI home, I was desperate to stop a plague of group-mind nanobots from being unleashed on the unsuspecting population of Cuitrec, the swarm of ships orbiting a low-atmosphere planet.

That plague possibility was an extrapolation on my part, and, as much as I hoped I was wrong, I would have bet every last credit on it.

"Captain," Scruffy said from where it sat near the piloting console, "pacing around the bridge will not influence our speed in hyperspace." Scruffy and I were taking turns piloting so we could minimize downtime.

"I know. But if I pace down in the cargo hold, I'll break Poppy's concentration, and I need her to finish analyzing the biologics." If Scruffy hadn't accidentally left out the package I'd taken from the destroyed crash pod, I'd never have known Poppy could make sense of it all.

Bett One-arm had identified the technology collective of Cuitrec as the Micklage family's goal. Nearly all the advanced or illegal tech in the oligarchy had started out in Cuitrec. Scruffy, an unbound AI with a synthetic cardinal crystal, was the perfect example. If Micklage could take control of Cuitrec, they'd have completed their stranglehold on piloting in all inhabited space.

According to Bett, the Micklage family had slowly taken over Cuitrec's allies in the Independent Federation, preparing for an invasion. To slow them down, Bett had sent me and Scruffy to Trition to set off the code bomb she'd been planting in Micklage hardware for years. When it went off, the Micklage family hadn't been nearly as upset as I'd expected...

...*until* I'd left the station with Poppy, the Micklage child whose genes had been tweaked specifically to make her a genius at nanobot design. Suddenly, half the galaxy was chasing us.

"It all makes sense," I said aloud. Infect everyone in the Cuitrec fleet with mind control nanobots and the invasion would be finished with no shots fired.

"So do a variety of other scenarios," Scruffy cautioned. "It is senseless to make plans before Poppy gives her opinion."

From down in the hold, a child's voice piped up. "Scruffy! Are you free? I want to experiment in the galley!"

Gesturing to Scruffy to stay where it was, I walked over to the ladder that led to the hold. "How's it going down there?"

"I'm hungry. I thought maybe we'd try for something savory with more acid and a lot more texture."

So far, Poppy and Scruffy had created a thin liquid with a sweet and fishy taste, a salty slab of protein I nearly broke a tooth on, and some sort of "noodles" that dissolved on the tongue like spun sugar. Luckily, we had enough freeze-dried meals to last until we could hit up a library for the actual galley unit instructions.

"Great." Rubbing my forehead, I called back down. "I meant, how is it going with the analysis?"

"Oh. That." Small boots clanged on ladder rungs, and her head popped up. "It was pretty much what I thought. The stuff in that kit stays dormant, mostly in your spleen, unless a specific nanobot shows up. Then it destroys it and goes back to sleep." She rested her elbows on the deck. "It's careful about what nanobots it goes after — you wouldn't want it to destroy nanites that treat disease. So I can tell a fair amount about what it's meant to counteract."

I waited.

She licked her lips. "I want to have an official crew rank."

The little twit was *extorting* me. "You're not old enough to be a crew member."

"You told me you make your own rules on your ship."

I stared at her. Part of me wanted to grab her by the nape of the neck and shake the information out of her. This was the safety of an entire solar system we were talking about. Another part of me wanted to teach her everything I knew about negotiations and body language — asking for a promotion when her head was at the level of my boots was a terrible idea. Somehow, I found this child both exasperating and charming, all at the same time. "Fine. You can be Proto-ensign Poppy."

"That's not a rank."

"It's a rank if I say it is. When you're old enough, I'll upgrade you to ensign." She looked like she was going to argue, so I raised my eyebrows. "Take it or leave it."

"Fine." She boosted herself up to sit on the deck. "It's looking for inhaled nanobots coming through the lungs. As far as what they do... Something in the brain, and it looks like they have reception. So similar in some ways to a group mind. But different in that there's no way to transmit back. Mind control. Zombies without the eating of brains. Well, I can't swear they won't eat brains, but that seems unlikely." Her eyes tightened. "Someone in my family created this thing, didn't they?"

"I think so."

Poppy ran her hand along Ensign Mowee's back as he glided by on his way to shed fur all over the pilot's chair. "There's only ten doses of the antidote. We don't have the tech on *Tiger Lily* to mass produce more. If we could get to the right equipment..."

Not going to lie — I felt much better about having access to those ten doses. But maybe we wouldn't need to replicate them. "If we can stop the original nanobots from being released, we may not *need* more."

Poppy's nose wrinkled. "It's probably too late."

I hadn't checked the news feeds recently for anything about Cuitrec, but surely someone would have noticed if an entire system had gone silent. "We would have heard if everyone had been taken over."

"It wouldn't be active right away. Individual ships make perfect quarantine zones, if you cut them off in time. So you'd have to infect *everyone* before the first person showed symptoms." She bit her lower lip. "It's probably waiting for the control signal to activate."

I leaned against the wall, trying to decide the best course of action. "So, if we can get to the right facility, you can make more of the antidote, right?"

Poppy brightened. "Yes. I can probably even modify it to

be airborne, so it could replicate and infect everyone that way."

She was so happy it scared me, but I worked to keep that off my face. "Then we'll just have to get to Cuitrec and borrow some equipment."

FIFTY-SEVEN
CANCEL THE HAIL

We dropped out of hyperspace at the far edge of the Cuitrec fleet. From everything I'd heard, I'd expected a vibrant, chaotic hive of half a million ships, mostly working together for a common goal. The comms should have been filled with the chatter of people who were tired of being stuck on the same ship with the same people and looking for something new. Even the few larger hubs meant for entertainment got boring after a while.

But we were greeted with silence.

"Ship, cancel the hail." *Tiger Lily* would have automatically broadcast our ship name and registration, a sign we were here with good intentions, but I didn't want to alert any invaders to our presence — if they hadn't noticed us already. Besides, nobody from Cuitrec was listening. "We're too late."

Poppy pressed her thumbnail against her lower lip. "How long do you think it's been like this?" She dropped her hand and shoved it into the pocket of her flight suit. "I don't think people will eat or drink when they're affected."

Scruffy spoke up from its spot near the pilot's console.

"One hour. I'm communicating with several ships. They are distressed about the state of their crews."

"Can you use them to find out where the Micklage ships are?" If we did any but the most basic navigation scans, we'd light up our position like a beacon on a dark night.

On the holo display showing the location of all the ships in local space, a cluster of white dots blinked red. The Micklages hadn't bothered to bring more than a tiny fleet, but why would they? They'd already disabled the enemy. By pure luck, we'd exited the hyperspace path in an area away from the bulk of the Micklage forces.

One hour. We had time to fix this before it turned into genocide. "We need to find a ship capable of replicating the antidote, get Poppy inside, create enough doses to inoculate everyone in the system, and then fight off the invading fleet." Staring at the display with hundreds of thousands of dots, each representing a ship with at least one person, the enormity of the task hit me. We would never get this done in time. "Right."

Scruffy must have heard something in my voice. "Captain, when the inoculations start, we'll have help."

"Good point." As soon as we released the antidote, exponential growth would be in our favor.

If the antidote nanobots *worked*. Poppy and I had injected ourselves with two of the ten doses in the kit. It hadn't killed us — yes, I was a pessimist — but we didn't know how effective it was, either. If we turned into zombies while trying to save Cuitrec, I'd never get my reward for saving Scruffy. Also, I'd be a zombie.

Poppy was thinking more practically. "How are we going to get aboard? A ship's AI won't just let someone in, even in an emergency, unless they have an order from the port authority." She was a Micklage — she knew ships.

There was a way, even though I didn't like it. "I have an idea."

IT TOOK Scruffy just a few minutes to find a vessel that matched my criteria: *Dilly Dally* was one of a small group of ships that traveled together, there was a nanobot facility on another ship in the group, and — most importantly — a *Dilly Dally* crew member was outside the hull when the crew became zombies. With this many ships in the area, I'd figured somebody had to be on the hull repairing *something*. And nanobot facilities sprang up like weeds in this environment.

Scruffy took over piloting duties as I pulled on the EVA suit, which had lost its factory-fresh scent. Now it smelled like someone nervous about zero-g had been stuck inside it far too long. It also had a layer of cat hair. "Ensign Mowee! The EVA suit is *not* an acceptable place to sleep!" When I fastened the collar, fur drifted through the air.

Poppy giggled while she ran a vacuum attachment over the inside of the helmet for me. "Ensign Mowee likes you."

"The cat is the scourge of the universe. But he's pretty good at defending the ship." I took a deep breath of mostly clean air before lifting the helmet over my head. "Scruffy's in charge while I'm out there. If anything happens to me, do what it tells you, right?"

Poppy narrowed her eyes. "Isn't Scruffy technically a passenger? It doesn't have a rank. I'd be in charge."

The helmet settled into the collar with a reassuring click. Switching over to comms, I said, "If you go with that logic, Ensign Mowee's in charge. Nobody wants that. Gather up everything you'll need for the replication — the sooner we get this done, the better." I closed the inner airlock door and started it cycling. "Scruffy, I'm ready. How close?"

"Fifteen seconds. You should have visual now."

Through the scratched and dirty hatch window, I could see a shiny object looming. That would be *Dilly Dally*, a Chicken class freighter. I just had to find the person outside the hull and hope they were still alive.

"Captain, we have arrived."

From the outer airlock, I climbed onto the hull, and leaped. No tethers this time — the other ship was too far away.

My comms crackled on, Poppy's voice ringing in the helmet. "Why are you so bad with the thrusters? It's not that hard. It's just simple vectors."

"Did it ever occur to you that maybe the thrusters are misaligned?" Another short burst corrected my aim and my feet hit the hull of *Dilly Dally*, a little faster than I'd planned, but I was able to soften the landing by bending my knees. I didn't see another EVA suit. "Scruffy, I'm on the hull. Where do I go from here?"

Nothing is ever compatible when you need it to be. My suit didn't recognize the other person's beacon, so *Dilly Dally* had to tell Scruffy the location and it would pass the information along.

"Continue around *Dilly Dally's* axis and look aft. You should be able to see her from there."

There were no handholds in the direction I needed to go, so walking it was. Clomping around on a ship's hull in a bulky suit was no fun. After we finished saving the Independent Federation and I got my reward, I was never going outside any ship again.

But there she was — *Dilly Dally's* wayward crew

member, in a personalized purple EVA suit covered with logos and graffiti, not moving. I didn't even have to use my thrusters to collect her, because she'd very sensibly tethered herself to her ship. "I see her. I'll grab her and head back over."

A garbled whisper was the only response on the comms. This close to *Dilly Dally*, its shielding prevented a connection to *Tiger Lily*. That problem would correct itself when I went back around to the other side and we had a line of sight.

I unclipped the other woman. "I've got you. Don't worry." She couldn't hear me talking, but my words made *me* feel better. There was no point in checking for signs of life yet — I couldn't do anything to help out here. Instead, I walked around the hull of a strange ship, towing an inert passenger, and speaking encouraging words she couldn't possibly hear. I flipped back to comms. "Scruffy, can you hear me yet? I'm on my way back to *Tiger Lily*."

But as I traveled around the arc of the ship, silence greeted me, along with empty space where there should have been a ship.

Tiger Lily was gone.

FIFTY-EIGHT
SAPPHIRE

"You know," I told the uncaring universe as I looked at the distant ships glittering around me, "the way my ship keeps disappearing while I'm outside, it's starting to feel a little personal." Scruffy wouldn't have taken *Tiger Lily* away unless there had been an immediate threat, but *still*. Now I was stuck in this suit towing a zombified stranger, and I didn't even know where the danger was. This was the sort of experience that gave rescue missions a bad name.

"Change of plans," I told the unresponsive woman at the other end of the tether. "Let's hope your ship will open the airlock."

My original idea had been to take this person back to *Tiger Lily*, pressurize the airlock, and remove enough of her suit so I could administer the antidote nanobots. Assuming everything worked, she could then get us onto the ship with the nanite replicator so Poppy could begin producing more of the antidote. And if it *didn't* work, nobody else would have been exposed.

Luckily, I had five doses of the antidote with me, tucked into an outside flap of my EVA suit. We just had to convince *Dilly Dally* to let us inside. If I'd been on my own, I would have had no chance. But *Dilly Dally's* AI had been worried enough about the crew member outside the ship that it had responded to Scruffy's query.

First step: get to the airlock. Chicken class freighters hadn't been too common at Orabella's salvage yard, because most people used them for long hauls and then transferred cargo into a smaller ship for the last stage of delivery. Why waste fuel taking extra weight down to the planet and back up again? But they *could* handle atmosphere, and enough pilots had miscalculated their loads that Orabella had two of them.

My passenger's custom suit had a nameplate. "Come on, Sapphire." I tugged her along behind me as I hiked across the ship. In a few minutes, we reached the airlock. "Here goes nothing," I said as I slapped the panel.

Nothing.

Fine. I hated when I was right. Pulling Sapphire closer, I maneuvered her suit so *her* glove was on the panel.

The airlock hatch opened.

Good. *Dilly Dally* had decided to help me skirt regulations as much as possible. It probably had strict rules about opening that hatch to anyone but registered crew members, and it would have been well within its rights to keep us out.

Though the airlock could technically hold two people, that assumed they were both cooperating. After the third time the hatch failed to close because a sensor was triggering on Sapphire's hand or foot, I trussed her up in her tether rope, then contorted myself to fit beside her. The hatch closed, air hissed, and the gravity slowly increased. Sure, I was squished under a stranger, but when the inner airlock door opened, I'd have more room to maneuver.

The inner airlock door stayed shut.

"Come on, *Dilly Dally*." I called, hoping it could hear me when I yelled. "I need some space to work."

The door stayed shut.

"Thanks for nothing." According to my readouts, the atmosphere was good. With a concerted heave, I rolled Sapphire off my arm and unfastened her helmet, getting a good look at her face for the first time. Her skin was an unnatural red, but I thought that was either a dye job or a gene mod because it fit with her hair, a shock of gray-white with red tips. She was still breathing, anyway, and that was what counted. Her slack face and open eyes were beyond creepy; I jumped in my suit the first time she blinked.

After more uncomfortable maneuvering and a lot of swearing, I got my hand to the flap on my suit and pulled out a hypospray with the antidote. There. Now all I had to do was get the tip over a vein and we'd be on our way to saving the entire Independent Federation.

But I couldn't work the hypo with my outer gloves on. We hadn't taken that into account in our original plan. I'd have to take my gloves off, ruining the integrity of my suit, thereby exposing myself to the nanobots that had turned Sapphire into a zombie. If the antidote didn't work, that would be the end of me.

Then again, if the antidote didn't work, this was the end anyway. I unsealed my gloves and took them off. Actually deploying the hypospray was anticlimactic. Sapphire didn't react at all. When I thought about it, that made sense — it would take a while for the antidote nanobots to find and destroy the zombie nanites. I hoped that length of time was less than an hour, because my right foot had already fallen asleep.

After a moment, I turned off my suit environmentals and removed my helmet. Might as well save my suit's air.

(There was another reason I hadn't wanted to do this while sitting in the airlock — if things went disastrously wrong, there was nothing stopping *Dilly Dally* from overriding the safety on the outer airlock door and jettisoning me into space. So... no pressure or anything.)

"*Dilly Dally*, I'm Captain Rose de Mure of *Tiger Lily*." I waited. No response. The ship had to have audio sensors in here, but either it still considered me a suspicious person or it just wasn't very chatty. "I've given your crew member the antidote, but I don't know how long it will take to work. Can you give me *Tiger Lily's* status?"

Dilly Dally didn't respond.

I sighed and tried to find a comfortable position. It took less than three minutes to go from a worried "I may turn into a zombie and die" to "This is really boring" and only a few more before I reached the state of "If I *do* turn into a zombie and die, I hope it happens soon."

Patience has never been my strong suit.

With the way I was crammed against the wall, sleep was impossible, but I'd managed a light doze when I felt Sapphire take a deep, shuddering breath. My eyes flew open. "Sapphire?" I really hoped she was okay, and not taking her dying breath.

Sapphire screamed.

FIFTY-NINE
CAPTAIN PORTHOS

Being crammed in an airlock with a stranger who was either dying or recovering from zombie nanobots had never been high on my list of fears, but I decided I would have to make a spot for it. It belonged somewhere between falling and having a swarm of Lubetan mites attack my eyeballs.

After Sapphire's initial scream, she'd gone quiet, but she was restless and sweating. *Probably* that was a good thing — before I'd injected the antidote nanobots, she hadn't moved on her own at all — but I needed her to wake up and tell *Dilly Dally* to let us through the inner airlock door. The longer it took to manufacture more of the antidote, the more people were going to die.

"Hey, Sapphire, wake up." I tapped her forehead, not entirely gently. "This is an emergency."

"Mmh?" She moved her arm to bat me away, and even though she completely missed her target, it was the most encouraging sign I'd seen yet. "Leave... alone."

Dilly Dally obviously agreed with my assessment, because the inner airlock hatch clicked open, letting in a gust of fresh air. I crawled out from under the other woman and took the time to get out of my EVA suit before dragging Sapphire into the ship and closing the airlock. Excellent. Phase one of the rescue plan was complete.

I still had four doses of the antidote with me. Time to plan for the worst: assuming *Tiger Lily* didn't or couldn't return, that left three doses to cure people and one to be used for study so it could be replicated. We would need a technician on the ship that had the replicator, since I knew exactly as much about replicators as I knew about Aramis farming in the hills of D'artagnan. As much as I wanted to cure everyone on this ship, that only left two doses for people on *Dilly Dally*. I needed to maximize the impact. "Ship, please direct me to the captain. And the medical officer, if you have one."

A strip of blue lights extending down the corridor blinked. Leaving Sapphire lying on her side next to the airlock, I grabbed two hyposprays from my suit and followed the lights.

Dilly Dally was... weird. People who live on orbitals are already strange, but people who spend all their time on a small stationary ship take it to a whole new level. From the hull, I'd known this was a Chicken-class freighter, but inside, the inhabitants played with the light, temperature, gravity, and atmosphere such that every time we turned a corner, it was like walking onto a different tiny planet. Presumably, once people had been there for a while, they learned to brace themselves when walking from the cool, low-light room to the hot, dry hallway with twice normal gravity. Or maybe there was some way to walk around the ship without going down this hallway. Each step was an adventure.

After nearly face planting into a hideous pink gel floor, I

was ready for a little less adventure and a little more speed. "Is there really not a faster way to get where we're going?"

Dilly Dally didn't respond.

The worst part was the crew. They stood singly and in groups, still holding cups of long-cold tea or whatever else had been in their hands when the zombie nanites had been activated. With their total lack of expression, it was like walking past statues that might wake up at any moment. Plus, if the Micklage fleet knew I was here, they could probably send all these people after me. My neck prickled.

The ship's AI didn't speak to me at all. Maybe it couldn't? Scruffy had talked to it, but Scruffy was another AI. In some ships, the AI wasn't allowed to speak with the crew. If there was an emergency, the appropriate people would be alerted via their handhelds or implants, but otherwise, the AI stayed silent, so the crew could forget they were under surveillance every minute. Still, I talked to it as I went, hoping it would respond with news of *Tiger Lily*.

I found the captain in a large meeting room. Not that I would have known her rank if the ship hadn't led me there — like the rest of the crew, she wore no uniform. She looked like an older version of Sapphire, without the skin and hair mods — hers were a more standard brown and black instead of red and gray. Possibly a clone, but my money was on a close relative. After I used the hypospray on her, I took her unresisting hand and led her in the direction the ship indicated the medical officer might be found.

An hour later, all three of the crew I'd treated had recovered enough to ask questions about who I was and what I was doing on board their ship. For one tense moment, I thought the captain — Porthos — might use her stunner on me, but *Dilly Dally* must have sent her some signal, and she relaxed.

I quickly relayed the plan for rescuing the citizens of Cuitrec as we sat in the corridor. "Ideally, we would use the design my crew mate produced, but even if she doesn't return, a tech should be able to replicate the existing bots." Stars, where was *Tiger Lily*? It was starting to worry me. Scruffy might have taken the ship into hyperspace to throw off pursuit, but I'd expected the ship to be back by now.

Captain Porthos rubbed her face. "*Athos Returns* will allow me access to its docking bay. I'll take you over in the shuttle. My cousin is a replicator technician there. She'll know what to do." Turning to the medic, she added. "Do what you can to keep everyone alive until we have the cure."

Since the medic had been the last to be treated, she was still groggy, but her training kicked in. "I'll try plasma transfusions. It will be slower, but if it works, it gives us another treatment."

"Good." Porthos put a hand on Sapphire's shoulder. "I need you to create a connection diagram so we can get everyone treated. Find out who the ships have trusted relationships with and the fastest way we can distribute this cure once we have it. Prioritize ships with replicators and the emergency response fleet." When Sapphire indicated understanding, the captain struggled to her feet and looked at me. "Let's go."

SIXTY

COMFORTING

Athos Returns was another Chicken-class freighter just a few minutes away from *Dilly Dally*. I spent the travel time looking out the view port, hoping in vain for a glimpse of *Tiger Lily*.

"There's no debris," Porthos commented. It was meant to be comforting, but it was obvious she'd never been a commercial pilot. When I'd been in school, we'd had to take a social interaction class so we knew how to speak to the passengers. Porthos was an example of why the class was required.

She was right, though — there was no debris, so at least we knew my ship hadn't been blown apart nearby.

But Scruffy would never have kept *Tiger Lily* away this long unless the ship was either being chased, or there was some technical reason it couldn't return. Maybe it didn't matter — I still had a job to do here — but I needed to find out what was going on. "How can I query the wider fleet to get information about my ship?" When Porthos didn't respond, I added, "It could be important. Poppy has a newer design for the antidote that wouldn't require direct contact. It could save millions of lives."

She glanced my way before concentrating on docking with *Athos Returns*. "I'll talk to the ships while we're waiting for my cousin to wake up."

Six hours later, I'd lost track of Porthos and I still hadn't heard from *Tiger Lily*. The nanobot replicator on *Athos Returns* had created enough doses to rescue a third ship and wake up a Cuitrec emergency coordinator. With that person's help, we woke the emergency fleet — a group of ships tasked with mutual aid. Sapphire's connection diagram of trusted relationships was paying off, though the process was slow. Too slow.

I was ferrying fresh doses of the antidote between ships using a borrowed shuttle, first from *Athos Returns*, and then from *Autumn Moon*, a larger factory ship. With each trip I made, more pilots took to their shuttles to deliver the antidote.

If the Micklage fleet hadn't noticed the extra activity, it was only because they weren't looking.

My current flight was ferrying the antidote along with one passenger to a cruise liner. *Raven's Pride* hadn't been on Sapphire's original diagram — it wasn't even part of the Cuitrec fleet, merely a ship that happened to be there long enough for the zombie nanobots to infect everyone on board. But it was hosting a convention for medical facility employees, and we desperately needed medics. So the previously vacationing Steward Darby and I were on our way to wake them up.

Darby was everything I expected from a steward of his fleet — ornamental, polite, and utterly incapable of focussing on anything important. So far he had shrieked theatrically at the state of the shuttle's passenger seats, asked if we could take a "quick detour" to his friend's ship on the way, and sullenly muttered, "Leave it to shuttle drivers to think they're starship captains," when I declined to alter our destination. I was almost too tired to laugh.

But I'd known enough stewards when I'd flown passenger ships to understand how valuable he was. The Darbys of the universe could handle any emergency if motivated properly. All I needed was the right key.

"Has anyone ever told you," I said as I lined up the shuttle with the docking bay of *Raven's Pride*, "that you look like that holovid actor? You know the one I mean." In fact, I didn't have any idea who he was trying to emulate, but the black-and-white striped hair, excessively sculpted cheekbones, and glow-tattooed skin had to be a look he'd pilfered from someone he admired.

"Gen Dream," he said, sitting up straight. "Do you really think so? I've been trying different mods to get his *vibe* without trying to be his *clone*. So tacky, replicating someone's features, right? I think I *finally* hit the right combination." All his animosity was gone, and he turned in his seat to face me. "The medic from his new series, *Detective Crow*, is one of our passengers, you know." His eyes widened, and he clutched his hands as he stared at me.

I knew my cue. "Maybe you should be the one to give him the antidote. Who knows? He might be so grateful you could get invited to see them make *Detective Crow*." For all I knew, Gen Dream was an AI-generated hologram and not a biological person, but I needed Darby on my side. Besides, I'd be long gone by the time he got around to asking this medic for his reward.

"Thank you, thank you, thank you!" Only years of safety training kept him from launching himself across the cabin to hug me.

"Just remember, we also have to track down and treat the rest of the medics, too."

"Oh, that will be simple." He waved that problem away. "*Raven's Pride* keeps track of that group separately. They wanted special water and air filtration, so they're in a different part of the ship. We won't have any trouble finding them." He clapped his hands together. "I can't believe I may get to meet Gen Dream!"

We were coasting into the docking bay, waiting for the ship's artificial gravity to pull us to a halt, when Darby made a puzzled face. "What's that?"

Through the port view screen, a white cloud expanded, frozen vapor glittering in the light of the sun. A ship's hull had been breached. The wreck was no danger to us at that distance, but I expanded my navigation screens as wide as they would go. The shuttle helpfully tagged the new navigation hazard using information pulled from other ships. "Well, this might make things more difficult."

The Micklage invaders had noticed our resistance.

SIXTY-ONE
NOT JUST A ROBODOG

Raven's Pride was everything a luxury liner cruising around the galaxy should be: sleek, expensive, and comfortable. Even the mandatory emergency warnings had a touch of class I'd never replicate on *Tiger Lily*.

The zombified humans standing on every deck ruined the look. And Steward Darby wasn't handling it well.

"Ew!" He shrank back from two elderly men in bathrobes who had been waiting in front of the elevator. "They're so... creepy!" Their eyes were sunken, a result of dehydration after standing in place for eight hours. The ship had two medical bots roving among the passengers, but they had been designed for individual emergencies, not to stabilize every passenger and crew member.

With one hand between Darby's shoulder blades, I pushed him around the living obstacle. "Just keep going. The sooner we get to the medics, the sooner we can fix everyone."

Darby turned sideways so he could slide past a group of women without touching any of them, muttering something under his breath.

I couldn't quite make the words out. "What?"

He drew himself up. "I said 'Meet Gen Dream' because this will all be worth it when I meet Gen Dream."

We finally reached the "Treasure Nest," the section of the ship holding the medics. They'd been gathered in a banquet hall with lower gravity, the walls and ceiling showing underwater scenes from some planet I didn't recognize. Bottles and glasses littered every table. In my experience, pilot conventions had lower budgets and more violence, but about the same amount of alcohol.

Darby drew out one hypospray from the bag I carried. "Stay right here for a minute while I find the medic for *Detective Crow*. I want to be sure I'm the person who saves him." He moved off, searching each table for his target in the dim underwater light of a distant ocean.

Instead of arguing, I took a moment to open a channel to Captain Porthos. "It looked like there was a hull breach near the Micklage ships. Do you have any information?"

"One of theirs," she said, but her voice didn't hold the triumph I might have expected. "The *Crazy Ivan* jumped to their position and took out one of their ships before being destroyed. Idiots."

I agreed with her assessment. "If the *Crazy Ivan* had held off another hour, we could have attacked with enough force to destroy *all* the ships."

"It's worse than that," Porthos replied. "They sent out a pulse that destroyed all the cardinal crystals. At least all the ones we've checked. Now we can't get into hyperspace. They can pick us off one by one because we can't even run."

Scruffy and its synthetic crystal could still guide a ship into hyperspace — as long as it hadn't been destroyed. And if I was right, somewhere nearby was the vessel that had created the unfettered AI. *That* would be the Micklage's primary target, and keeping it away from them was our only hope for survival.

Pulling a handful of hyposprays from my bag, I worked my way around the first table, injecting each person as I went. From across the room, I heard Darby give a cry of success as he found his special medic.

Scruffy might know what ship had created it, but the AI had disappeared with *Tiger Lily*. Which meant there was no way around it — I'd just have to stop trying to be subtle and ask. "Do the AIs on your ships gossip like they do everywhere else?"

Porthos snorted. "Have you ever met any that didn't?"

I hadn't. "We need to find out who created an AI called Scruffy Note of Disrespect. They've created at least one synthetic crystal in the past — if we're lucky, they have more."

Captain Porthos was silent for a moment. "You're sure? I've always assumed those rumors were space dust."

"Positive. If we could find *Tiger Lily*, I'd prove it to you."

"Didn't...?" The connection went silent for three long seconds, as if Porthos had switched to another channel to check on something. Then she was back. "I apologize. I thought you'd been notified. We have *Tiger Lily* here, tethered to *Dilly Dally*. Limped in about an hour ago — scratch that, it's been longer than that. We pulled the kid, some monstrous feline, and a robo-dog onboard *Dilly Dally*, but *Tiger Lily* itself is probably a total loss. The kid said someone sabotaged the fuel packs. She and the robo-dog went to *Athos Returns* to improve the bots. Somehow, we got stuck with the cat."

I sagged in relief, nearly missing the next medic's neck with the hypospray. Poppy and Scruffy were safe. "Sorry about Ensign Mowee. I'll come get him as soon as I can."

Then her words about *Tiger Lily* sank in. "As soon as I have someplace to take him," I amended.

"We owe you," she said. "Take as long as you need."

I couldn't help my laugh. "You say that now, but..." Forcing myself to keep working since we needed these medics helping us, I thought about our next steps. The push to get the antidote nanobots distributed would continue without me. But Scruffy held our only hope of long-term survival. "Can you get me in touch with the robo-dog?" Because of the current state of emergency, all communications channels had been locked down. I'd only been given access because I was helping with the rescue effort. "It may know where the crystals would be."

"The robo-dog?"

"It's not just a robo-dog."

"Of course it's not." She sighed. "Give me a minute. They're pretty busy over there."

I moved on to the fourth table, thinking about the best way to proceed. Assuming Scruffy or the rumor mill could tell us where the AI had been constructed, we needed to hop over there, liberate any other synthetic crystals they had, and distribute them to ships willing to fight the invaders. To do that, I needed a hyperspace ship, preferably something small and maneuverable.

Something like a flyer a rich person might dock on a luxury liner.

Turning to look across the room where the steward still hovered over his only patient, I smiled.

"Hey, Darby! I need to borrow a ship."

SIXTY-TWO
INSPECT YOUR ELDERS

Back on *Raven's Pride*, the medics at the conference were in the first stages of waking up, and I was in a borrowed flitter on my way to pick up Scruffy. Darby hadn't wanted me to leave, and *especially* hadn't wanted to authorize my commandeering the flitter, but as the only member of the ship's crew not under control of the zombie nanobots, he was the acting captain. "If you don't do this," I told him when he balked, "none of the Cuitrec ships will be able to leave and you'll never get your chance to meet Gen Dream."

"Meet Gen Dream," he echoed, though his mantra sounded increasingly hollow. But he'd overridden the security locks and only looked a little ill as he watched me climb into the most expensive flitter in the bay. "Please bring it back unharmed!"

I waved assent and closed the hatch. The chances of this toy returning at all were pretty slim — the Micklage fleet would be looking for vessels still able to enter hyperspace and they had the advantage of numbers — but there was no point in ruining his day. Once inside, I did a quick systems check and blasted toward *Athos Returns*. It was a nice little flitter, with artificial gravity, room for four people, and a decent galley unit. If the cardinal crystal hadn't been shattered, I could have been there in minutes. As it was, I had time for a nice meal and a few minutes to nap before I reached my destination.

In that time, Scruffy and Sapphire had worked out the fastest way to get us onboard the *Inspect Your Elders*, the unfettered AI's origin having — we hoped — a cache of artificial crystals. Which was why, when I opened the hatch at *Athos Returns*, I found Scruffy, Poppy, and seven fully suited strangers waiting.

Poppy ran forward, her flying hug sending me crashing into the bulkhead. "I'm so glad you're not dead!"

"You, too." I set her back on her feet. "How is it going with the antidote?"

"We're sending you out with the new aerosolized version. It works faster, too." She shoved her hands into her pockets. "I want to go with you, but..."

"But there's no room," I agreed, thankful I hadn't borrowed a larger ship. I wanted to keep her as far away from the action as possible. "I'll be back as soon as I can."

Inspect Your Elders held a position near the edge of the Cuitrec fleet, but that spot was much closer to the Micklage ships than *Athos Returns*. So far, our rescue efforts hadn't reached that section. Four of my passengers had connections to ships in the area and would start the long process of waking people and replicating the antidote. But we didn't have any direct path onto *Inspect Your Elders*.

"They're either paranoid or security conscious," said a tiny woman with purple and gold braids. "We're not entirely sure who is off ship and still has access, so we're trying the most likely places." She clung to the back of one seat, hunched over to fit in a space that wasn't meant to hold passengers as we worked out how to fit eight people and a robo-dog inside a space meant to hold four.

Scruffy was sitting between my legs, its head on one thigh where I could easily reach it. "Captain, it is possible *Inspect Your Elders* will recognize me and allow us to board, but I have been unable to contact it."

A clunk and swearing from behind me told me another attempt to wedge two people into that seat hadn't worked. We were denting the interior pretty badly, which would undoubtedly distress Steward Darby if I lived long enough to return the flitter. "Make sure you have something to hold on to."

Scruffy made a noise that might have been its version of a laugh.

Finally, we had everyone on board or, in one case, in the airlock. It violated every safety standard I'd been taught, but we were in the Independent Federation and I hadn't been licensed there anyhow. "Everyone ready?"

A chorus of assents greeted my words, so I aimed the ship toward the nearest patch of unoccupied space at an acceleration the artificial gravity could compensate for. "Hold tight!"

Accessing Scruffy's crystal, I found and discarded multiple hyperspace paths, ones that took us too far out of the way or let us out too near another ship. Crashing into a freighter would put an abrupt end to our rescue mission and destroy the one synthetic crystal available to the Cuitrec fleet. There! We had a path that was just big enough for the flitter to bring us near our first destination.

I maneuvered the flitter toward it, compensating for the

spin caused by our unbalanced cargo, and we entered the path almost completely straight, though there was a crash as one of my passengers slipped from his seat to land on the galley. The hum of the hyperspace engines vibrated through the cabin, and then we were back in normal space, the ungainly curves of a Hopper III visible through the view port. "Two minutes until we get to the *Start Stop*."

A man's voice came from the airlock. "Nice flying, captain. I hope we never have to do this again." Laughter from the other passengers drowned out the sound of the inner airlock hatch closing.

We stayed in normal space to drop off the rest of the passengers outside their target ships, and then finally it was just me and Scruffy on our way to *Inspect Your Elders*. It was an ancient Rat class freighter, a model old enough that it might have been one of the first ships in the Cuitrec fleet. Welded patches broke the lines of the pitted hull in multiple places, and there looked to be no power to the aft section. I would have taken *Tiger Lily* over this wreck any day of the week — even considering *Tiger Lily's* current condition.

"Are you *sure* we have the right ship?" It was hard to believe this was the birthplace of the most advanced AI in the galaxy *and* the synthetic crystals. "Maybe this was just someplace you stopped along the way." If we couldn't find someone with the connections to let us in, perhaps we could just drill a hole in the side.

"No." Scruffy had moved to the seat next to mine when space had freed up. Now, it turned its head to look at *Inspect Your Elders* as we drifted. "Commencing short range communication."

"For all the good that's going to do," I muttered,

wondering how long we would end up waiting. Surely, *somebody* on one of the nearby ships would have access.

A flicker of light caught my eye, and I turned to see all the metal "patches" on *Inspect Your Elders'* hull rotate to the side. Suddenly, we were targeted by dozens of weapons.

SIXTY-THREE
UNTRUSTWORTHY

So there we were in yet another situation.

The good news: Now I believed that this derelict-looking Rat-class freighter, *Inspect Your Elders*, really was Scruffy's home.

The bad news: They were about to blow us out of the sky.

"Uh, Scruffy? What exactly did you say to them?" With all the extra people we'd been transporting in this flitter, there hadn't been room for an extra EVA suit. One little hole in the hull and I'd be sucking vacuum.

At least Poppy and Ensign Mowee were safe.

"Captain, I apologize. It appears I was removed from this ship without authorization and have been tagged 'untrustworthy.'" Scruffy sounded... Surprised? Hurt? The robo-dog's vocal box didn't have much range, so it was hard to tell.

This was supposed to be our moment of triumph. From the instant I'd found the AI at Orabella Fink's salvage yard, this had been our goal. Scruffy would be back home, and I would have enough reward money to buy the best galley unit in existence. Then I would fly off in *Tiger Lily,* and Scruffy would do whatever it was built to do.

Instead, *Tiger Lily* was too damaged to fly, I'd brought a kid into a war zone, and now it looked like Scruffy couldn't go home after all. Worse, if we couldn't get onto *Inspect Your Elders* and find more synthetic crystals, the Micklage fleet would take over all of Cuitrec.

"They haven't fired on us yet," I pointed out. "We'll just have to wait until we find another way on board. Once the crew is awake, I'm sure we'll be able to clear up the misunderstanding."

Scruffy didn't reply.

We drifted, waiting for a signal from the ships where we'd dropped our passengers. Though I was tempted to go back to *Athos Returns* for another run, I stayed put. The more hyperspace jumps we made, the more likely the invaders were to notice us. The success of the entire system's defense rested on getting more synthetic crystals.

Inspect Your Elders kept its weapons trained on us.

My mind wandered. "I'm a little surprised Bett hasn't shown up yet. At least one of her." Had the zombie nanobots been released everywhere? If the signal to activate them had propagated across the galaxy, entire systems would be doomed. We would never get to them with the antidote in time, even if we knew where to go.

Scruffy pushed its head against my shoulder. "It's likely Bett is taking advantage of the invasion here to strike against the Micklage bases elsewhere."

I patted its metal head absently. Scruffy was right. Just because Bett hadn't appeared, lasers blasting, didn't mean everything had gone wrong. "So what *did* happen when I was retrieving Sapphire outside *Dilly Dally*? One minute I was talking to you, and the next *Tiger Lily* had disappeared."

"One of the fuel packs you took from the crash pod suddenly showed signs of catastrophic instability. There was no time to remove it, so I took *Tiger Lily* through hyperspace to a clear area in order to protect other ships from debris."

"Quick thinking."

"Unfortunately, the blast compromised structural integrity. The ship is no longer hyperspace-capable. Also, the communications array was destroyed."

"Ah." I knew my ship. The communications array was nowhere near the fuel ports. Half of *Tiger Lily* must have been severely injured. There had been ships abandoned at Orabella's yard with less damage than that. "You saved the fleet, and you saved your passengers."

"By the time we made it through normal space to *Dilly Dally*, you had already moved on." It curled up in the co-pilot's seat. "Captain, I must apologize. As a direct result of your assistance, you have been repeatedly endangered and your ship has been damaged. Now, it appears I may not be able to give you the promised reward."

"I haven't given up on that reward," I said firmly. "But about the rest... Ensign Mowee and I would still be stuck on Buatrier if you hadn't come along." I shifted so I could look at the robo-dog directly. "You just had your third solo hyperspace jump, right? That's a big achievement. Normally, the senior pilots would take you to a bar..." I trailed off, wondering how an AI could celebrate. "We'll have to work on that."

"Assuming we live long enough."

"Yeah, yeah, whatever." I levered myself out of my seat and went back to the galley unit. Might as well enjoy it as long as it was available. A dent marred the gleaming surface, making half the controls inaccessible. "Remind me to have someone else bring this boat back to *Raven's Pride*. I don't think I'm getting my deposit back."

"Captain, we are being hailed by the *Sabrett*. They have a staff scientist from *Inspect Your Elders* on board and request that we transport her to her ship."

That was what we'd been waiting for. "Let them know we're on our way."

Despite a detour to keep us from going any nearer to the freighter's guns, it still only took fifteen minutes to slide into *Sabrett's* docking bay, where a woman with the wrinkled face of great age waited. Since wrinkles could be erased by any med unit, it was an interesting choice. Whoever this woman was, she wanted people to know her as an elder. I opened the hatch. "Are you the scientist from *Inspect Your Elders?* I'm Captain Rose de Mure. Welcome aboard."

Her movements were effortless, with no sign of stiffness or weakness. Like I'd thought, the wrinkles were a choice. "I'm Dr. Mayer, chief intelligence engineer."

Chief intelligence engineer... This was almost certainly someone who had helped create Scruffy. I waved her into a free seat, not even looking at the robo-dog.

But her eyes narrowed as she caught sight of the metallic form in the co-pilot's chair. "And who is this?"

If I hadn't needed to take a breath to speak, I would have lied and told her the robo-dog was a bodyguard that any sane captain would take on hazardous journeys.

But the robo-dog didn't need to breathe and it beat me to it. "Hello again, Dr. Mayer. I'm Scruffy Note of Disrespect. I've returned."

Dr. Mayer's face drooped, as if sadness had overtaken her. Then her lips firmed. She pulled a stunner from her pocket and aimed at the robo-dog.

"Wait!" I waved my hands, trying to distract her. "Wait!"

Dr. Mayer fired.

SIXTY-FOUR
TERRIBLE AIM

Luckily, Dr. Mayer had terrible aim. A good thing, too, because judging by the char on the docking bay wall, she had the stunner maxed out. If she'd hit me, I would have needed a few hours in a med unit, and med units were in short supply at the moment.

If she'd hit Scruffy in the right spot, she would have destroyed it.

Before she could get off a second shot, I dove, crashing into her knees. She went down hard on one elbow, losing the stunner, which skittered under the flitter. Her grunt of pain made me feel better about the bruises I'd be sporting soon.

I rolled away, but kept a wary eye on her. "What is *wrong* with you?" Was this a side-effect of the zombie nanobots? None of the other people who'd woken up had been homicidal.

Clutching her elbow, she glared at me. "That AI was stolen from my lab and sent to the Micklages. It's working for them. We have to destroy it before it can kill us."

It appeared Dr. Mayer wasn't fully aware of the current state of Cuitrec. "If it wanted to kill everyone, it wouldn't have helped bring the antidote nanobots."

Scruffy retrieved the stunner and dropped it by my side. "I was disconnected from my environment and reconnected in this robotic frame after Captain de Mure found me. If my abductor intended to send me to the Micklages, something interrupted their plan."

"The ship you were hidden in crashed," I told it. "And someone knew you were there and sent me to rescue you." Another possibility occurred to me. "Or Rance Micklage knew you would be found when anyone opened the panel, so he arranged to have the part removed."

That would be just like Rance. Not wanting to climb around an abandoned ship himself, he tricked someone else into retrieving the AI and inadvertently made it possible for Scruffy to escape. Of course, Rance hadn't known I was working for Orabella in her salvage yard, but his family still deserved their credits back — plus damages — from whomever had tweaked his embryonic genes.

But Dr. Mayer shook her head. "This AI returned in the middle of the Micklage invasion. Even the timing is suspicious."

"And I worked for the Micklages for years." My hip twinged as I stood. I'd banged into the side of the flitter when I'd jumped. "But if Scruffy and I hadn't come here when we did, every single person in Cuitrec would be dead or dying right now. What have *you* done to stop the invasion?" I waited a beat. "Oh, that's right, you tried to destroy the only working crystal in the system."

"What?" Dr. Mayer, who had been getting to her feet, froze and stared at me.

"All the cardinal crystals shattered." I waved a hand when it looked like she was going to interrupt for details. "They have some kind of pulse weapon. Now Scruffy is the only one who can make it into hyperspace. Unless other ships have synthetic crystals?" I waited, eyebrows raised. If they'd been outfitting other ships, we might already have our defense fleet.

"No." She stood, looking thoughtful. "After the theft, we lost time because of the investigation. It set us back. We've only just started to build new prototypes. But you said the crystal *worked?* You've used it?"

Scruffy and I looked at each other. "Yes," we said together.

Dr. Mayer frowned as she rubbed her elbow. "Our test pilot... He said it only partially worked. The paths were visible, but not open."

My first thought was *That would have been a good thing to know before I gambled with our lives getting away from Orabella's shipyard.* Though I might have lifted from Dancig City anyhow — with Rance on our heels, any chance was worth taking.

My second thought was more helpful for the present moment. "Did you ever find out who stole Scruffy from your lab?"

"A technician, but we think she had help." Dr. Mayer looked up, and I saw her make the same connections. "You think the test pilot..."

"I'm good, but there's no way I'm the only person who could use that crystal." Even Scruffy, who had never piloted before, had learned. Though I wasn't going to tell *her* that. "What better way to delay the project?"

The Micklages hadn't been able to risk attacking the

Independent Federation until they were ready. And for all her intelligence and training, Dr. Mayer wasn't a pilot. But the Micklages had a ready source of them. Sending in a Micklage pilot to delay the development of a crystal that could make the Micklage holdings obsolete would have been easy.

Her nostrils flared. "I'll *kill* him."

Not without some practice at the firing range, she wouldn't. But that wasn't my problem. "Are there more crystals?" We'd been counting on extra synthetic crystals to equip a fleet to fight the invaders. If Dr. Mayer's lab had stopped producing them because the pilot had said they didn't work, we were in trouble. One ship did not a fleet make.

"No. Yes. I don't know." She threw up her hands. "I've been re-examining my equations and each step of the manufacturing process for months. There's an entire bin of rejects. But now you're telling me they may work after all." Drawing herself up to her full height, she said, "I need to get back to *Inspect Your Elders* without delay. And I need you to come with me to examine the crystals."

Crossing my arms, I leaned against the flitter. "Apologize to Scruffy first."

From its place near my knee, Scruffy said, "Captain de Mure, this is not necessary."

"Yes, it is."

For a moment, I thought Dr. Mayer would refuse. Then she took a deep breath, and the rebelliousness faded from her features. "Scruffy Note of Disrespect, I apologize for trying to harm you. I ask your forgiveness."

"Granted," said the robo-dog.

I sighed. Scruffy didn't hold a grudge very well. We

would have to work on that. And no matter how prettily Dr. Mayer apologized, I was keeping the stunner.

Pushing myself onto my feet, I swept my hand toward the flitter's hatch. "Excellent. Let's get going, shall we?"

We had a cranky ship to visit.

SIXTY-FIVE
STOLEN PROPERTY

Inspect Your Elders responded more politely when we showed up with Dr. Mayer, and it didn't take long before the flitter was safely in the docking bay. Though *safe* was a relative term — given the extent of the weaponry pointed toward the outside universe, I had no doubt *Inspect Your Elders* could cut us down inside the freighter as well.

Holding up the antidote canister as we went through the hatch, I said, "We need to add this to the ventilation system. Post-filtration," I added. Most of the Cuitrec fleet didn't filter their air for nanobots or else they wouldn't have been in this situation. But if any ship did, it would be this one.

Dr. Mayer looked like she might argue, then straightened her shoulders. "This way." She'd been focused on getting back to her bin of rejected synthetic crystals, muttering threats against the test pilot under her breath.

In the corridor, we were greeted by a faint whiff of decay. It might have been from an unwatched experiment, but odds were that someone in the crew hadn't survived the zombie nanobot takeover. We passed two crew members collapsed on the deck; both were breathing and showed signs of having been attended by a portable med-bot. Dr. Mayer didn't slow to look at their faces.

(People obsessed with their professions are funny that way. I'd rescued a research orbital crew after they'd been stuck on their platform for over two years. Nine of them were so grateful they nearly cried. The tenth had to be coaxed from his workbench, disgruntled because he would be missing the next stage of the star's evolution, which would have killed everyone on board.)

"Here," Dr. Mayer said, pulling a panel from the wall to expose something that looked nothing like an air circulation system. We were in the wrong place. My fault — I should have asked to see schematics. What were the chances that the scientist responsible for creating synthetic crystals and integrating them with an AI would have ever done ship maintenance?

My doubts must have shown, because she took the canister from me. "The ship says this is where it needs to go." A small hatch opened. She twisted the canister to activate it and then dropped it inside. The hatch closed. "Trust the ship."

This ship had threatened to destroy us while Scruffy and I were trying to save Cuitrec, but now was not the time to talk about the basis for trust. Either the antidote was flowing around the ship already, or the crew would have to wait until someone else came with another dose and a more humble guide. "The crystals?"

"This way." She strode back in the direction we'd come, speaking without checking to see if Scruffy and I were following. "After the initial partial success — or what we *thought* was partial success — my team integrated a crystal with an AI on the chance that stabilization was the limiting component..."

She quickly lost me in technical jargon, and I stopped paying attention. It felt like a rehearsed speech that she'd given before, probably while updating whoever funded this enterprise. Instead, I looked around as we walked. Though the hull may have been ancient, the interior felt new, with none of the dings and scuff marks that void the warranty the instant a ship leaves the manufacturer.

It was a mystery until we passed a closed door with a hazard sign. *Caution: Nanobot-assisted laboratory remodeling in process. Do not enter.* That explained it. Like Crania, this ship used nanobots to tear down and build new spaces, though at least they seemed to confine the construction to the interior of the ship. I tried to imagine letting something like that loose on *Tiger Lily*. A custom cabin would be nice, but given everything else that had gone wrong with my ship, I assumed that process would just be a novel way to die.

We passed another man lying on the floor. He blinked and tracked us as we went by, which was encouraging. Dr. Mayer had put the canister in the correct spot, after all. I nearly ran into her as she stopped to open a hatch.

"This is it." She stepped over a woman making confused noises on the floor and yanked a half-filled bin the size of the robo-dog from under a bench, hefting it onto a clean space. "I'm sure some of them truly don't work, but we've been testing the process for months, trying to find the flaw..."

I goggled. I'd been expecting maybe a dozen crystals, which would give us a fighting chance, but there had to be *thousands* here, each mounted on a cassette. If even a tenth of them worked, Cuitrec could field a fleet to rout the invaders.

But first, I needed to check them. There was no point distributing the bad ones. Grabbing a handful, I spread them out on the bench. Dr. Mayer watched as I picked up the first, closed my eyes, and concentrated on the pilot's sphere. Hyperspace paths blossomed in my vision. "This one's good," I said.

Dr. Mayer's eyes glistened with unshed tears. "We *did* it," she whispered. Then she turned her attention toward helping the people in the lab.

That was fine with me; Scruffy could test crystals, too, but I didn't want Dr. Mayer to know it had that ability. I pushed a handful toward the robo-dog. "Let's find at least ten good ones and get the distribution process rolling."

Scruffy and I were both concentrating on the crystals, ignoring everything else in the room so we could get as many Cuitrec ships hyperspace-capable as fast as possible. Even if we hadn't needed to fight the Micklage fleet, there were swathes of the system the antidote hadn't reached. The sooner we could get there, the more people would survive.

So that was why the first I knew of the nearby conflict was Dr. Mayer screaming, "How *could* you?" followed by the crash of glass breaking. Scruffy and I looked up to see a man dressed in a trendy jacket, trousers, and pilot's boots shield his face with one forearm as a handheld flew through the air. "This was my life's work!"

The man, I surmised, was Dr. Mayer's lying test pilot. "Huh." I grabbed another handful of crystals out of the bin. "I assumed he would have left before the nanobots were activated."

Dr. Mayer launched herself at him, her hands locking

around his throat. He broke her hold and darted away, keeping a bench between them.

"Or would have at least been given the antidote by the Micklages," Scruffy agreed. It nudged a cassette with a bare metal paw. "We have fifty working synthetic crystals. That should get things started."

"Time to go," I agreed. With Scruffy carrying the vetted crystals in a bag and myself balancing the bin of untested cassettes on my head, we skirted the room to avoid the combatants. The test pilot had youth on his side, but Dr. Mayer had a lifetime of rage. My money was on her, though I suspected the ship would intervene before anyone was seriously hurt.

Scruffy led the way to the docking bay, moving as quickly as it could without leaving me behind. Only then did I realize what I should have considered before — Dr. Mayer considered the AI to be stolen property. *Her* stolen property. Taking Scruffy with me might be considered a second theft. We needed to leave while she was occupied.

Holding the bin with both hands, I sprinted after the robo-dog.

SIXTY-SIX
BRACE FOR IMPACT

Since *Athos Returns* was already a hub for antidote distribution, Scruffy and I returned there with the synthetic crystals and continued sorting through the bin in a tiny conference room. Through the open door, we could hear the busy ad hoc command center working to get the antidote nanites distributed.

Captain Porthos's weariness bled into her voice. "Has anyone found a way into the London fleet? Surely somebody from a hundred ships must be traveling." There was an unintelligible response from one of the remote screens. Porthos cut them off. "We're not settling any scores now. Sapphire, you concentrate on them, right? Who's next?"

After the first of the synthetic crystals restored hyperspace travel, antidote distribution was swift, and the command center estimated 98% dispersal within two hours. That still left a huge death toll, but nothing like what it would have been if *Tiger Lily* hadn't arrived.

Porthos cleared her throat, cutting into a speech that had been droning on. "Let's concentrate on the first tier, please. Do we have confirmation on *Howdy Howdy?*"

Nearly all the crystals Scruffy and I tested were good. Cuitrec would have hundreds of working crystals — minus the one I'd shoved inside my flight suit before we'd left the flitter. I'd lived through enough large-scale emergencies to know how it would go: when things got back to normal, only a few people would remember what my crew had done and every ship would require a new crystal, even if they didn't *need* it right away. After I got *Tiger Lily* repaired, I'd be stuck without a crystal until the demand slacked.

(Given the way my life went, I'd probably also end up with a bill for all the dings I'd put into the flitter I'd borrowed from *Raven's Pride*. And another bill from whomever had been taking care of Ensign Mowee, but that was legitimate.)

Scruffy had a crystal in its brain, but the Independent Federation was its home. It wouldn't want to travel back to the Oligarchy, where it would be destroyed if anyone realized just how unfettered the AI was. I needed a crystal of my own.

If there were more combat pilots than crystals, I'd surrender the one I'd purloined so we'd get rid of the invaders, but Cuitrec didn't really have a defense fleet. Why would it? In the event of an invasion, the ships could just leave. That had been the theory, anyway. They hadn't taken zombie nanobots and cardinal-crystal-destroying weapons into account.

The Independent Federation's navy hadn't arrived yet, which was maybe a good thing since the Micklages might have suborned it. The real wild card was Bett — I'd expected her to arrive before now. The invading fleet seemed to be waiting for something to happen, which made me nervous.

Poppy swung around the doorway, her purple hair

hidden under a tight cap with "Athos Returns" printed in multiple scripts. "You're back!" Her exuberant hug scattered the cassettes on the table. "And Scruffy, too! I thought you might stay on *Inspect Your Elders*."

The kid had clearly been keeping tabs on us. "Aren't you supposed to be doing your girl genius thing with the nanobots?"

Poppy sighed dramatically. "The design's done and the techs are better at replication than I am. They keep trying to find me jobs just to keep me busy. I'm taking a rest break so they can stop worrying about me." She slouched in a chair, looking her age for the first time. "I'm glad you're back. Can I go with you on the next delivery?"

"If it's safe," I replied.

She took a breath, maybe to argue about safety or just to change the subject, but an angry exclamation from Porthos made all of us look at the corridor.

"That's a Micklage tug. Where did they—?" The screech and flashing lights of a proximity alert cut her off. "Ship, evade and alert the crew to brace for impact."

Gravity flickered as the ship's acceleration briefly outstripped its ability to compensate. All along the corridor, hatches clanged shut. The crew members had implants to pass along the captain's message. In our conference room, a pleasant automated voice crooned, "Warning! A collision is imminent. Secure all loose items and prepare for impact. Warning! A collision —"

The table was sensibly locked in place, so I grabbed on, wishing I was in the pilot's seat and could see what was happening.

The impact, when it came, was both gentler than I'd feared and lasted longer. Having seen a lot of bad piloting during my career, I could picture the other ship scraping along the hull. That sort of thing was bound to tear up both ships. It wasn't any sort of military maneuver.

(Seriously, back when I flew a regular route that I couldn't change, I saw some *spectacular* collisions at Runa, when it was still a major orbital. At the time, anybody could call themself a pilot and the worst thing that would happen — assuming they didn't die through their incompetence — was a fine that even *I* could have paid. Bett set up a competing orbital in the same system, banned anyone who couldn't mind their piloting manners, and took over in less than two years. Last I heard, Runa's orbit had destabilized after one of the remaining pilots had misjudged their approach, and they weren't sure if it was going to fall to the planet's surface or not.)

After what felt like forever, the groan of the hull stopped and we still had atmosphere. "Scruffy, can you tell what's happening?"

"A Micklage ship, *Gremlin Host*, came out of hyper-space on a collision course with *Athos Returns*. There are no reports of casualties yet."

My training would have had me coordinating the emergency response, but I wasn't in charge and I didn't know this ship. The best thing I could do was wait until the crew needed my help.

Poppy released her death grip on the table and rubbed her arms. "*Gremlin Host* is a private ship."

She didn't elaborate, but I knew what that meant. That ship wasn't part of the contract-based Micklage fleet; there was a good chance a Micklage was in command. And there weren't many reasons a Micklage would leave the safety of their fleet.

Poppy and I looked at each other. She finally broke the silence. "Do you think they're here for you? Or me?"

SIXTY-SEVEN
GREMLIN HOST

We heard the distinctive sound of the hull being cut open as we raced toward the emergency lockers. Glancing toward the noise, I said, "That's one way to avoid the booby trapped airlock."

The question of whether *Gremlin Host* was looking for Poppy or me only really mattered if we planned to hide. But I wasn't willing to huddle in safety while the Micklage soldiers destroyed *Athos Returns,* and neither was Poppy. Even Scruffy — who actually *could* have successfully hidden if removed from the robo-dog — refused to leave, though I did convince it to stay with the rest of the crew. We would need a hyperspace pilot with a synthetic crystal when we escaped.

The monitor near the emergency lockers showed an airlock umbilicus had been sealed to the hull first. "That might be a good thing," I told Porthos.

"A good thing," she repeated, deadpan.

We were all hurrying into clunky emergency evacuation suits, which would provide basic life support until another ship could pick us up, just in case *Gremlin Host* decided the easiest way to deal with resistance was letting the atmosphere escape.

(Or in case somebody screwed up. They *were* cutting into the hull of a pressurized ship. Accidents happen.)

I sealed the evac suit everywhere but my hands and head. To make the suit functional, you sealed the hood down and pulled your hands in, but then you were stuck in a giant bag. That made it hard to do anything other than sit around and wait to be rescued. Besides, the suits only held about two hours of air, so you wanted to wait as long as possible. "This ship's not armed. They might ignore your crew after they grab Poppy."

"And you?"

Depending on which Micklage was on the ship, they might ignore, detain, or shoot me on sight. Those sorts of options made life exciting. "It's probably better if they don't have to take the ship apart to find me."

Our eyes met. Neither of us wanted to talk about how *Gremlin Host* had known which ship to target. While I thought it unlikely there was a Micklage spy on *Athos Returns*, there was a real possibility the ship had been compromised.

Even here, in the Independent Federation, many of the ship's parts — including the hobbled AI that ran everything — would have come from Micklage factories. The invaders had taken out the people with zombie nanobots. A disabling AI-virus might be impossible to embed, but something that sent information would be harder to notice and nearly as effective. "Might be a good idea to look for a leak when you have a chance."

Porthos nodded. Next to me, Poppy kept silent. The crew all knew she was a Micklage now. Most had responded with shrugs, but a few had drawn away. Smart people were wary of the Micklages even when they *weren't* invading the system. On the other hand, everyone knew Poppy's antidote modifications had saved people, so the crew were unlikely to shove her out the airlock.

Scruffy settled in next to the crew. "Be careful, Captain de Mure."

After we suited up, Poppy and I waited with Porthos at the hatch near *Gremlin Host's* new door into the ship. A monitor showed us the smoky room as the last section of hull plating melted. Tiny arachnoid bots surged inside.

"Sniffers," Porthos told Poppy. "Programmed to search a small area looking for specific DNA."

It made me glad I hadn't gone to the trouble of finding us a good hiding spot. The sniffers would have reported that we'd been on the ship at some point, and then the invaders would have taken the entire thing apart.

Scruffy had no DNA. If they were looking for the AI, they'd have to find another way.

Once the ship's scrubbers had cleared away the smoke, we opened the hatch. The sniffers surged forward, hundreds of them climbing up Poppy and me until they reached our exposed heads, where they swarmed, climbing around each other. Porthos, they ignored.

"Well, that answers that question," I said through pursed lips. Though I didn't have any phobia about creepy crawlies, I didn't think I could handle them in my mouth without embarrassing myself. "They're after both of us."

Poppy squeaked something unintelligible, panic in her voice.

I wanted to kill whoever had sent these things after a child. "It's okay. They'll go away soon."

Through the mass of sniffers on my face, I glimpsed two armored people come out of the hole onto the ship. When one spoke, the mass of sniffers scrambled down our bodies and streamed back into *Gremlin Host*. Poppy reached out and clutched my hand.

A man spoke, his deep voice muffled by his helmet. "Rose de Mure. Paloma Sierra Viola Micklage. Step forward."

"Paloma?" I whispered from the side of my mouth, even as we complied. "Really?"

"Nobody ever calls me that." Her chin came up, and she dropped my hand. "Who's in charge here?"

It was a good effort. If she'd been ten years older, I'm pretty sure they would have automatically responded to her orders. But nobody takes kids seriously, even if they look and sound like your boss. They didn't answer, just spun me around to restrain my wrists behind my back. Poppy got a pair of cuffs, too, but they left her hands in front of her. That was a mistake — of the two of us, I was betting Poppy had more hand-to-hand training.

Captain Porthos spoke from where she stood by the hatch, carefully not presenting a threat. "The seizure of these people during armed conflict has been observed and recorded. Humanitarian rules of combat apply." That was why she'd come with us, despite my urging otherwise. Someday, there might be trials, and human memories held more weight than machine recordings.

Since that would only really matter if we died, I was hoping having a human witness wasn't necessary. Still, I appreciated the gesture. And maybe it would remind someone there were rules.

Our guards towed us across the umbilicus into their own airlock and then cycled us through to *Gremlin Host*. I was relieved they left the umbilicus in place. Porthos and her crew would already be slapping a temporary patch over the breach, but the invaders could have depressurized that section of the ship if they'd wanted to.

Deep padding muffled our footsteps as we walked. Poppy was still channeling her inner Micklage, back straight, chin up. But I was playing tourist, marveling at the custom scenes of a forest with mythical creatures on the metal walls. Nanobot created, I suspected, and had that confirmed by minute movements in the tableau when we paused. A dragon's jaws closed just a fraction on the person held in its claws. We stood still as the dragon slowly bit the head off. Obviously, we were waiting for something, but what?

Through an open hatch, I heard a man say in the carefully neutral tones of someone who knows his words won't be welcome, "Sir, our orders are clear. We were to remain in the staging area until the rest of the fleet arrived. The other ships are now reporting enemy engagement, and we cannot help them from here."

A familiar voice came down the corridor. "I don't *care* what the orders are. This is *my* ship and you will do what *I* say. We've picked up the traitors. Now, we make an example of them."

Poppy glanced back, and we shared a silent look. I sighed. Rance Micklage. Of course.

SIXTY-EIGHT

OLD SCORES

Now I knew why we were waiting in the corridor. Someone with a cooler head, probably the person talking to Rance right now, was afraid of what would happen if we arrived before Rance had finished throwing his tantrum.

"Maybe we should get a cup of tea and relax," I suggested to the guard next to me. "I used to work for this idiot. It's going to take at least fifteen minutes before he sees reason."

To his credit, the guard thought about it for a few seconds. Then I heard him say something in a low voice, the words muffled by his helmet. At the same time, the person talking to Rance said something, of which I only caught the words Paloma, family, and orders. Rance might think he had the right to punish Poppy for joining me, but the Micklages had put enormous resources into that child. He might actually face open revolt if he tried to kill her.

Unfortunately, threatening me wouldn't cause the same reaction.

The guard finished his conversation and turned around. "This way."

Gremlin Host had a full cafeteria with seating for twenty, far enough from the command room that we could no longer hear Rance yelling. Poppy and I eyed the galley unit speculatively.

"We have bigger issues," I reminded her. "And it sounds like *Tiger Lily* needs major repair work, anyway."

"We don't even need the controller," she protested. "Just the food library."

There was a good chance I would never need a galley unit or even a ship after we left this room. My thoughts must have shown on my face, because Poppy gave a tiny smile. "We just need to wait twenty minutes."

Obviously, she was up to something, but I had no idea what. Maybe she knew the ship's crew and they'd passed her a message. If we were lucky, Rance might "accidentally" fall out the airlock, leaving Poppy as the last Micklage on board.

While we waited, Poppy had tea and a series of rose-scented pastry bits. Since my hands were still bound behind me, getting food into my mouth would have been difficult. I opted for dignity over satiety, though I did catch the one Poppy arced toward me. It was sweet, floral, and not what I would have chosen if I'd ever planned my last meal.

Poppy had just finished the last of her tea when the guards jumped to their feet. We'd been summoned.

"Do whatever you need to do to stay safe," I told Poppy as we walked down the corridor. "The crew might help you if you let them."

Her chin came up in a stubborn tilt. "We're leaving this ship together."

"Poppy," I warned.

"Rose," she echoed in the same tone. "We're not on *Tiger Lily*. I don't have to listen to you."

Teenagers. It's a wonder any of them live long enough to keep the species alive.

Rance was waiting for us on the bridge — in the pilot's chair, I noticed. Since he wasn't a pilot, that was just theater, which was stupid in the middle of a war zone. So... typical Rance Micklage. He smiled when he saw us.

"Cousin Paloma. And Rose. So good of you to grace us with your presence. We've been looking for you." He leaned back and rested his elbow on the console. A warning light came on since he'd just started the sequence to eject the fuel packs while the engines were still spun up.

A nervous man who had been trying to fade into the background stepped forward to clear the error and lock the console, all while avoiding eye contact. That had to be the pilot. I wondered what he'd done to get stuck with this job.

Twenty minutes, Poppy had said. We had to be getting close to that and I knew how to derail Rance to buy us time. "Nearly killing everyone in the system seems extreme, even for your family." And then I saw it, the tightening of his jaw and the slight hunch of his shoulders, both signs that he'd screwed something up and was looking for some way to dump the responsibility on others. "Wait. That was a *mistake?*"

Rance sat up straighter. "They sent me here, with hardly any support, to activate the nanites. But the first signal was only going to incapacitate half the people. Do you know how many ships there are in this system? I had to change the signal. We would have been slaughtered."

Activating the zombie nanobots in half the people would have kept the other half too busy to effectively fight. But, of course, Rance didn't understand that, because he would never have bothered to take care of the injured. From the looks of shock on the other faces around the room, this was all news to them.

"That's a war crime, no matter who's in charge." Though my eyes were on Rance, my words were aimed at the pilot and any other members of the crew who might listen.

Rance stood up, restlessly pacing. "What are you talking about? It obviously didn't work anyway. Have you seen the number of ships flying around out there?"

"You can thank your cousin for that. She may have kept the death toll under a million." I nodded at the wall screen, where the Cuitrec fleet was a scatter of lights. "So they sent you here to initiate the first phase and then what? What's the big plan?"

He stared at me, his breathing audible.

"They didn't tell him the plan," Poppy said. "That way, he couldn't screw it up."

They hadn't told him the plan, and then something had happened to the rest of the Micklage fleet. Faced with that problem, anyone with a head for strategy would have worked to establish communication with the missing forces.

Rance had merely decided to settle old scores.

There was no coming back from what he'd done. Even Rance had to see that. Unfortunately, that meant there was nothing stopping him from killing me. He must have come to the same conclusion, because he smiled and unholstered his stunner. "I've waited a long time for this opportunity."

His back was to the wall screen, so he didn't see multiple clusters of ships suddenly shimmer into being around the edges of the Cuitrec fleet. The ships he had been waiting for, I thought, delayed but finally here. Which might be good for me and Poppy, but definitely bad for everyone else in the system.

Then alarms blared as the new forces attacked the Micklage fleet.

SIXTY-NINE
WORTHWHILE

"What's happening?" Rance yelled at the pilot over the sound of sirens. If the pilot had been in his chair, he could have muted the alarms so they could plan a strategy. But because Rance had wanted to play-act, the pilot was on the other side of the bridge. By the time the man made a wide berth around Rance and got to the console, the proximity alarms were going off as well.

The relief of the silence after the pilot killed the alarms almost overrode my consternation at what I was seeing. On the wall screen, an Armadillo-class warship hung off our bow, weapons engaged. If we'd had a view port, we could have waved. Obviously, they were here for Rance. Poppy and I might end up as collateral damage, which would be an extremely irritating way to die.

"Sir," the pilot started, "there's a —"

Rance cut him off. "I can see that, you fool! Get us out of here!"

If we tried to jump now, the other ship would have plenty of time to blast us into smithereens. But the pilot started keying in sequences without arguing. He was so rattled, he didn't even notice the console was still locked.

I took a step forward. "We can't get out of here in time. You'll have to surrender."

Rance looked at the screen and voiced a frustrated growl. Then he looked back at me and snarled, "Either way, you go first." Pulling the stunner from its holster, he dialed the power to the max. With a tight smile, he said, "Watching you die will make this all worthwhile."

He squeezed the trigger.

To be honest, I missed seeing it because I had my eyes closed. But when I heard the sizzle and didn't feel any pain, I cracked one eye open. There was a scorched deck plate in front of my toes. If it hadn't been Rance, I would have assumed it had been meant as a threat, but that seemed out of character. Surely he hadn't *missed* from that distance, had he?

Rance frowned at the stunner and raised it to aim at me again. A look of confusion passed over his face as the stunner drooped to point at the floor. "What is *happening*?" The last word was indistinct, as if he was intoxicated.

Then he slumped to the floor, eyes open. A few garbled sounds came from his slack mouth, but I couldn't understand anything.

With a pleased sniff, Poppy walked forward and kicked the stunner away from his hand. Then she ignored the figure at her feet and addressed the crew. "As the only fully functional Micklage on this ship, I am assuming control." She raised her bound wrists. "Get these off of me and open a channel to surrender."

Rance moaned angrily.

For a moment, I thought the crew would rebel against following a teenager. And maybe if there hadn't been a ship threatening to blow us out of the sky, they would have. But surrendering was the smart move and everyone knew it.

In ten seconds, both Poppy and I were free, and the pilot was hailing the warship on the now-unlocked console. Poppy pointed at Rance, who was still lying on the floor, and ordered a guard to put him in a med unit. "It took a little longer than I thought it would," she told me in a low voice. "Sorry about that."

"What did you do to him?" I whispered back.

"I added a little extra check in the antidote nanites. When they recognized his DNA, they blocked the release of acetylcholine." Poppy gave a little smile that would have been frightening if I hadn't known her. "It causes paralysis. The minute we came through the airlock, we started infecting everyone with our antidote." She cast a worried glance at the wall screen. "Why aren't they responding?"

A laser cannon flared, burning a hole in our hyperspace drive.

Something wasn't right. The other ship could have instantly destroyed us. That had been a warning shot, but you don't send a warning shot to a ship that is already trying to surrender.

"They aren't getting our signals," I said. "Long range comms are down."

"Our comms are up," the pilot argued. "See?" He pointed to the section of the board where any comms error alerts would show. "I'll restart." When he punched in the sequence, amber lights flashed. "Oh. That's bad."

The ship jolted as another shot ignited a fuel pack.

I pushed Poppy toward the bridge's hatch. "Get back to *Athos Returns* and have them send our surrender." She had just taken a breath to argue when I thought of a better idea. "Hold on." I was still wearing the emergency evacuation suit, which had a rudimentary comms system. Normally, I wouldn't expect anyone to be monitoring the frequency, but we'd left Scruffy back on *Athos Returns*.

When the power light on the suit blinked, I keyed the microphone. "Scruffy? Are you listening?"

The AI's words were rushed. "Captain de Mure, I'm waiting by the airlock. Do you need me to enter *Gremlin Host*? My weapons are charged."

"Negative. We're fine. Poppy's in charge of the ship. But I need you to contact the Armadillo off our bow and tell them we surrender. The comms here are down."

"One moment."

The cannons fired again, this time hitting a fuel pack on the other side of the ship. If this kept up, it would tear the hull apart.

I looked at Poppy. "You may have the universe's shortest command."

"Figures." She shrugged. "Good thing I never wanted to be in charge. I'll have the crew prepare to evacuate." Lights flashed and cabinets holding emergency evacuation suits opened all over the ship.

Scruffy's voice in my ear distracted me. "Captain de Mure, I have a direct channel open for you to verify your identity."

Suddenly, a familiar voice rang out. "Rosey? Is that really you over on that Micklage garbage scow?" Bett One-arm's laughter overwhelmed the speaker.

"Not for long if you don't stop shooting holes in us."

Bett laughed again. "Sorry about that. I thought that swamp muck Rance Micklage was in charge, and he sometimes needs extra reminders." She gave an inaudible order to someone, then returned. "The rest of their fleet tried to trap us near Rechees. Big mistake on their part, but it took a while to resolve."

"At least you got here, eventually."

"Looks like you had everything under control."

"Yes. Absolutely. Completely under control." I glanced at the console, which the hapless pilot had abandoned so he could get into his evacuation suit. The hull tolerances skewed into the danger range. That last blow had done something to the ship's frame, and it didn't seem to be stopping. Something didn't make sense. "Hey, Bett?" Throwing myself into the pilot's chair, I keyed in the sequence to close the interior hatches and increased the alarm level.

"Yes, Rosey?"

"Is your emergency recovery team ready to get some practice?" As I watched, the cargo bay reported a catastrophic failure of life support. What had they been storing inside?

Under my feet, the deck shuddered. Then the lights went out, the life support alarms blared, and I was suddenly weightless.

SEVENTY
BLAME IT ON ROSEY

By the time Poppy and I were evacuated from *Gremlin Host*, the answer to what had happened in the cargo bay had become very clear. Rance had stored samples of nanobots taken from the Chrysalis, the ones that reconfigured the ship as needed. Whether he planned to use them to rebuild parts of the Cuitrec fleet or he had some other purpose, nobody knew, but one of Bett's disabling shots had breached the containment. Without a group mind to direct them, the nanobots started reconfiguring the ship into something that was no longer a ship. The result was weirdly beautiful, but — understandably — none of the Cuitrec fleet wanted it anywhere near them.

Everyone on board had been safely evacuated and *thoroughly* decontaminated. Even the med unit with Rance's inert form had been brought over to Bett's ship, *Anne Bonny*. With enough time in the med unit, Rance would eventually recover from whatever Poppy had done to him. Or so she swore to me. In the meantime, he'd been transferred into the custody of the Independent Federation to face charges of attempted genocide.

Two days after *Gremlin Host* had begun its life as an art installation, Bett, Scruffy, Poppy, and I watched through a view port as the Cuitrec environmental hazard team began using lasers to push the remains toward the nearest sun. It was a sign of how great Cuitrec considered the threat that it was the first thing they worked on. After mopping up the invading forces and providing emergency relief to crews who were late in getting the zombie antidote, of course.

Poppy sighed. "Not a great start to my career."

I rested a hand on her shoulder. "Do you really want to captain starships for the rest of your life?"

"Well, no, but still. This looks really bad."

"Blame it on Rosey," Bett suggested. "She's hard on her ships."

I'd taken a breath to argue when Scruffy cut in with a credible imitation of my voice. "Hang on. This might be a little rough."

Bett and Poppy snickered. I thought about kicking the metal robo-dog, but I would have felt guilty if I dented it since everyone with any skill in metal working was already busy. Besides, Ensign Mowee was sprawled on the robo-dog's back, occasionally growling at Bett, and I didn't want to disturb him. So I just glared at the traitorous AI. "Got you out of the Oligarchy, though, didn't I?"

"You did. Thank you, Captain de Mure," it said with evident sincerity.

"And now?"

"I've communicated with Dr. Mayer. She would like me to return to *Inspect Your Elders* so her team can evaluate my performance."

To say that I didn't trust the scientist was an understatement. Dr. Mayer had been ready to destroy Scruffy without hesitation, and even now, I didn't think she saw it as a person. With the synthetic crystal I'd swiped, I no longer *needed* Scruffy whenever Tiger Lily was spaceworthy, but the thought of parting ways made my stomach lurch. "What do *you* want to do?"

"I would prefer to continue traveling."

Bett hitched her lower set up thumbs in her pockets. "I always need good pilots working for me."

Naturally, Bett had figured out Scruffy could pilot a ship into hyperspace. At least she knew how to keep a secret. She turned her head to look at Poppy. "The contract to fetch you back to your family has been canceled. You should be able to go on your merry way."

The contract had been canceled because the entire Micklage organization had imploded. Between the strike we'd made on Trition, the failed invasion of the Independent Federation, and the loss of their cardinal crystal monopoly, the family's power had disappeared overnight. They still had resources and I suspected they would rebuild quickly, but Poppy was safe from them, at least for now. And she'd already had job offers from thirty ships in the Cuitrec fleet that I knew of. She'd be alright.

So that left just me. I had a crystal and my cat, but my ship wasn't in any shape to fly or even live on, and I had no credit to fix it. There would be no reward for returning Scruffy to *Inspect Your Elders* unless I forced the AI to go back. And that wasn't going to happen.

I sighed and looked at Bett. "You have room on the roster for one more pilot?"

She smiled and rubbed her upper hands together. "It's funny you should say that. Why don't you all have a seat? I have some of those little fish made of sugared ginger and sweet bean curd that you like."

I couldn't help it. I started laughing. Poppy looked

concerned, but Scruffy and Bett carried on as if I wasn't there. "What sort of job is it?" the AI asked.

"Will we have a decent food galley?" Poppy put in.

Bett folded her legs under her as she sat. "Oh, it's just a little thing, but I think the three of you would be perfect for what I have in mind, and you can even bring that horrible cat. I'll have *Tiger Lily* in perfect shape by the time you're done." Then she looked at me. "How do you feel about heights?"

As Bett and Scruffy talked about the job, I stared out the view port into the black emptiness dotted with far away stars. There were worse ways to live my life. Running a hand along Ensign Mowee's soft fur, I listened to what the future would bring.

THIS BOOK WAS *a blast to write and I hope you enjoyed it was much as I did! Ready for more fun science fiction adventures? Check out* The Chaos Job (Jackpot Drift #1)*!*

ACKNOWLEDGMENTS

This book was originally written and published as a serial, which works perfectly for the space opera genre. Unfortunately, serial fiction is a hard sell these days and that platform no longer exists, but I'd like to thank everyone who gave it a try!

My critique group looked at the novel after it was finished and gave me a lot of helpful advice. They're a great bunch of writers, and I learn something every time we meet.

A big burst of gratitude goes to my tiny but mighty ARC team and to everyone else who reviews books by independent authors. You all help my books find an audience, which is the whole point of publishing!

Thanks also go to my brother Eric, who checked the manuscript for typos. Obviously, if you find any still in there, it's his fault. You can always blame your older siblings for anything, right? I'm pretty sure that's how it works.

ABOUT THE AUTHOR

T. M. Baumgartner is a speculative fiction writer who has difficulty following directions. This probably explains why the IRS recalculates her tax refund after she files it every year. At various times she has been a veterinarian, Unix system administrator, software developer, and after-hours book-shelver in a medical library.

Theresa currently lives in Northern California in a house with too many animals. She knits hats for garden gnomes and fails to grow tomatoes despite living in the perfect climate.

She also writes cozy mysteries under the pen name Tess Baytree.

Want updates about new releases? Silly dog anecdotes? Free stories? Join the newsletter mailing list! Go to https://tmbaumgartner.com/subscribe/ or point your phone's camera at the QR code above.

The marketing department here at Speculative Turtle Press is great at tail wagging, but a little challenged by tasks that require thumbs.

If you enjoyed this book and would like to help other readers find it, please tell your friends and consider leaving a review at your favorite site.

ALSO BY T.M. BAUMGARTNER

As T.M. Baumgartner:

Shift Happens

The Chaos Job (Jackpot Drift #1)

The Chaos Connection (Jackpot Drift #2)

The Chaos Nexus (Jackpot Drift #3)

Dragon Freehold

All Gremlins Great & Small (The Portal Storms #0)

All Rocs Wise & Wonderful (The Portal Storms #1)

All Basilisks Wild & Sparking (The Portal Storms #2)

Theoretical Magic (The Floodmouth Files #1)

As Tess Baytree:

Death Walks a Dog (Penelope Standing #1)

Death Tracks the Scent (Penelope Standing #2)

Death Smells a Rose (Penelope Standing #3)

Death Trims the Tree (holiday novella)

Death Crashes a Wedding (Penelope Standing #4)

Death Paints a Picture (Penelope Standing #5)